# Choice of the Elect

# Choice of the Elect

## Jean Giraudoux

Translated from the French by Henry Russell

Northwestern University Press
Evanston, Illinois

*Ouvrage publié avec le concours du Ministère français chargé de la culture — Centre national du livre.* [This work is published with the assistance of the French Ministry of Culture — National Center for the Book.]

Northwestern University Press
Evanston, Illinois 60208-4210

ISBN 0-8101-1924-2

Library of Congress Cataloging-in-Publication Data

Giraudoux, Jean, 1882–1944.
    [Choix des élues. English]
    Choice of the elect / Jean Giraudoux ; translated from the French
by Henry Russell.
        p. cm.
    ISBN 0-8101-1924-2 (alk. paper)
    I. Russell, Henry Bosworth, 1932– II. Title.
    PQ2613.I74 C513 2002
    843'.912 — dc21
                                                    2002002020

# CONTENTS

# TRANSLATOR'S FOREWORD

*Choix des Elues: Choice of the Elect.* What a pity that for more than sixty years a novel of such poetic charm has never been available in English. Published in 1939 and the last of Jean Giraudoux's novels, it is as if this lovely work had been simply lying about, forgotten for a while. Perhaps it was mainly a combination of two things—there was Giraudoux's increasing prestige as a playwright, and much more important, there was the onslaught of a war that was to totally disrupt all life in Europe and abroad. The poetic flights of fancy were soon forgotten amid the horrors of World War II. But the world is now full of readers who knew little or nothing of those horrors, and the curtain has, to some degree, been brought down on that era. Who knows? Now that the late century has come to a close, perhaps the time is ripe to bring a translation out at last, and this story of a French engineer and his wife living in California in the 1930s may take on the added nostalgia of a world now vanished.

The story of Pierre and Edmée, or rather Edmée and Pierre, for the story is really hers, is what we might call a sort of metaphysical comedy, a novel of spiritual quest, but with a light touch. As the story begins we find them living in solid bourgeois comfort in Los Angeles, along with their two children, Jacques and Claudie. It is the perfect family. Except that it isn't. Edmée has begun to suffer sudden attacks of anxiety, "for no reason," as we like to say. Something is wrong, but what? The curious answer to that question makes up much of the novel.

The crisis is treated almost humorously. *Crisis as comedy* might be a good way to put it. Without doubt, Edmée's plight is a cri de coeur: there is real crisis here, personal crisis for all concerned. Yet the tone is so light, the play of wit so continuous, that we often seem on the edge of high comedy.

Pierre the engineer embodies the best of European and French culture, but he is not Edmée, he is not of the elect. This is shown clearly in their separate and crucial visits to Washington Park, which to Pierre is nothing more than a banal city park in Los Angeles. But Edmée sees something different, something beyond the city park and humdrum reality. She is of the elect, as is her daughter Claudie. They share an exalted communion with nature and between themselves.

Edmée will later learn that being of the elect means pain as well as exaltation. In the language of Parsifal, we might say that Edmée bears the wound. And the link with Parsifal is not so inappropriate as it might seem. Giraudoux was a student of German literature at the Ecole Normale before the First World War and spent time in Germany in 1905 and 1906. One may sense the influence of the German romantics in the mystical quest of this novel despite its tone of French urbanity. It is a little as if one of Hermann Hesse's novels had been written by a Frenchman. The search for the Blue Flower—*die blaue Blume*—has been brought up to the 1930s. It is not hard to see *Choice of the Elect* as the French mate to *Steppenwolf*, both of them voyages of discovery, trying to chart unknown territory of the self. Nor, to use Nietzsche's terms, is it hard to see Edmée as the Apollonian counterpart to Hesse's more somber and Dionysian Harry Haller. Giraudoux, then, is drawn to the mystical German romantics but at the same time remains the debonair Frenchman and man of the world.

It may help us put things in perspective to compare the dates of several writers of the period. Marcel Proust was born in 1871 and Hermann Hesse in 1877, while Giraudoux, Virginia Woolf, and James Joyce were all born in 1882. It is easy to forget that these writers were roughly contemporaries. And each member of this remarkable group has at least one thing in common with the others: they are all navigators of the inner world. Yet the voice of each remains utterly distinct. The whole fanciful dialogue that Pierre has with himself in Washington Park is of a subtlety worthy of Proust, but there can be no mistaking the two authors. It is not only that Giraudoux depicts a different era and society but also that he is less didactic than Proust, at times even casual and offhand. He may like to play a bit more than the others in this company and he often wears a smile. But in the end he is no less serious.

Despite the light tone and light touch, the novel has been serious all along. Edmée is very close to many another hero and heroine in Giraudoux's plays and novels, and she shares some of the same themes. Edmée has had her season in Eden, a long flirtation with divine and mysterious forces, and her strange affair with the elusive Abalstitiel. For years she has devoted herself solely to the daughter she adores. Then, as Claudie grows up, Edmée finds this daughter rejecting her. What is worse than to lose the person you love most? Or is it just what Edmée deserves? For she has herself abandoned an adoring husband and son. Now she is living alone in San Francisco and the prose takes on a darker tone, even a little bitter. The scene of the distraught and opium-muddled Edmée sitting on a street bench at dawn as she watches the lights on a billboard flash on and off, imagining that she sees Claudie's name appear there, Claudie whom she thinks lost to her—this is wonderful writing, sad but magical: there is depression, rue, filial love lost, and all the alienated beauty of the modern city as the sun comes up—a lonely cityscape as painted by some Gallic Edward Hopper.

To readers brought up on the economy of a Hemingway, Giraudoux's style may sometimes seem a little discursive, perhaps extravagant, even perverse—his sentences full of digressions, rich in clauses and parenthetical asides. With his recherché vocabulary and metaphors, Giraudoux presents the most disarming combination of sophistication on one hand and extreme innocence on the other, as if he were an adult inhabited by an erudite child. Whether the reader is diverted by the continuous banter and constant play of wit is probably a matter of taste. It may irritate some yet hold ineffable charm for others. There is no doubt that Giraudoux writes for a highly literate reader of wide culture, and at times his sentences require the same close attention as those of Proust or James. But the reader who is susceptible to his charm cannot fail to be rewarded by the many moments of striking insight, wit, and poetic beauty.

Early on there were those among the French critics who called him précieux. That may offer a convenient label, but how much does it illuminate? To lean too much on précieux misses a lot. Instead of *précieux* I would simply substitute *playful*—a continuous effort to *lighten the load:* Giraudoux is acutely aware of the ideal and the beautiful in life as ever penetrated by the ugly and tragic, aware of the inevitable compromise. His worldview has room for tragedy, for comedy, and a certain mysticism, from the German romantics to the Hindu idea of the world as Maya, illusion—the world as seen from a distance, like a cinematic film of the experience of everyday life, the world as training ground, a school in the long education of the soul. Perhaps a need to lighten the load is always with us.

The English world has been translating French novels of penetrating psychological analysis from Madame de La Fayette to Benjamin Constant, from Stendhal to Balzac, and from Proust to Colette and on. How is it possible for us to miss Edmée's flirtation with the divine, for us to miss *Choix des Elues?*

# Choice of the Elect

# 1

No! This was unbearable. She could no longer simply ignore it.
. . . If, on the night of her birthday and in the middle of dinner,
surrounded by those she loved, concealed behind laughter and
happiness—if tonight this anxiety managed to find her out and
take hold of her, then this thing was turning into a real mystery.
Or perhaps a sort of sign? She would have to think about it.

She thought about it right then and there, in that nimble
yet reliable way of thinking that her husband used to compare to
her fingers, kissing the fingers because, as luck would have it,
they were the only things he really could kiss, though the two
terms of his comparison were equally dear to him. . . . For it was
always to her that the children would bring the buckles that
were too complicated, the shoelaces that were tied in knots, or
the jump ropes that were all tangled up: no matter, in a minute it
was all set right. Her son—no doubt studying Alexander the
Great at the time—had managed to tie what he called the true
Gordian knot; she undid it with one touch, and the original, his-
toric one, so the child insisted, had been perhaps even easier. . . .

Yes, she had to think about it, confront the attack head on, face up to it. Until now she had been able to avoid the question. Each time the anxiety had appeared there seemed to be a more or less valid explanation. The first time, in that hotel in Santa Barbara, where a blond woman covered with emeralds had a nervous tic of the jaw, there was a high wind and her husband had been absent. Perhaps in the catalog of anxieties, an anxiety produced in the wife by the combination of an absent husband, emeralds, nervous tics, and the rumbling of thunder might well be the most normal sort of anxiety imaginable.

The second time had occurred as she opened her eyes in bed one morning. She hadn't really thought much about it, supposing it to be the end of a nightmare whose beginning she couldn't remember. The third time, the most recent before today's experience, her son and daughter were in Arizona, and everything seemed well explained by a vague sense of dread, a gift of second sight, since that morning, at a turn in the path, they had barely missed setting foot in a nest of rattlesnakes—the latter being the kind of knot where even the nimble fingers of a mother are of no avail.

Everything had happened, in short, as if absence itself were the cause of the trouble; as if she could no longer bear the absence of those she loved, no, not a one of them. She had given in. She had sacrificed a sort of taste she had for absence, for absences. For she bore the absences of her own family serenely, with a kind of modesty; it was not as if they had gone away, but rather as if she had disengaged herself from them, out of discretion, as if she were relieving them for a few days of their mission as children or husband. At train stations or on boats, when they were going away, she felt inside, along with the sorrow, a kind of peace to know them relieved of a weight, the weight of even the dearest wife or mother. She felt them released from her care, from being looked after—that is, freed from all the dangers and ills that may befall us. Her son once absent, even at the age of three, was for her what would have been for a pious mother a son freed from the burden of life on earth, a son safe in heaven above. . . .

Very well then. Turning her family over to a divine guide, to a divine kitchen and laundry, which was what absence meant, well, there would be no more of that; she wouldn't leave them anymore, she didn't want to suffer anymore to that degree. . . . For this was real pain. Like a terrible wrenching, like a collapse. . . . What you might feel on escaping from the embrace with a demon—yes, that was it: the very opposite of pleasure with a human partner. In any case, it was quite beyond her strength. All the more so as there was a sort of remorse mixed up in it, what she imagined she might have felt if she had cheated on her husband. . . .

Very well then! . . . There would be no more question this year of separate outings, of anyone taking a trip alone; she would simply suppress her little seasons of maternal lethargy, and the other three would be denied their bit of freedom with the angels of absence. She had told them. They had jumped to hug her around the neck. And she had been moved to see that it was only for her sake that they had ever accepted her convention of happy separation. They had stampeded her. It had really taken all the indifference of the fabrics she was wearing or her own skin for them not to remain forever riveted, clinging and stuck to her. From that day on it seemed as if there were no longer any appreciation of distance between her and them; they would run into her, they couldn't pass near without brushing against her, without shoving. The natural order of the family had become both free-for-all and procession. They would gather round her all the time, in her bedroom, in the kitchen; they followed her wherever she went, as if she bore both the food and the heart of the house. Yes, she was bearing it, and it was her heart indeed. From that day on they had all begun to be in perfect health, as if that variety of absence that is called death had been also definitively set aside. Thus had taken shape the family that would have had the greatest chance of being wiped out in case of a catastrophe, a plague, or flood.

This evening of celebration, this anniversary of her thirty-third year, was really the celebration of a presence heightened even more by separation from France in this city in California where the father was an engineer. Each of these four beings was with the three beings that he or she loved the most. Each one was taking soup, laughing, and having fun with the three beings that he or she loved the most. The evening, the night, the day after, the life of each one—and all that this included, waking up, meals, working, and in the children's imagination, marriage with its retinue of other children who would marry and have other children, not one of whom would ever leave the others—all this would go on and on with the three beings that he or she loved the most. And the most loved of the four beings was herself. And she was almost sure that she was also the one who loved the most. And now suddenly this pain that she thought came about from their absence was coming back in their presence. . . . A sharp pain went through her. . . . Heavens above, she only hoped it wasn't all because of their presence!

Mealtime, which in other families is the most intimate time of coming together, was in this family almost an hour of separation, since it put spaces between them that could not be reduced. She took advantage of this moment when she wasn't being caressed, embraced, or clutched, to come to terms with this threat, to find a word for it. . . . It wasn't a sense of impending danger. There was no sort of peril floating over these heads; they were quite glowing in fact, sending out a signal to happiness like the beacon from a lighthouse, each one with his or her own special beam: Pierre the husband with his two smiles, one big, one little, succeeding each other a second apart every minute; Jacques the son with his open and frank face itself, which he would raise and lower; Claudie the daughter, a more sensitive lighthouse, with the mere blinking of her eyelids. . . .

No, death was not present, not the death of any one of them. Edmée would have sworn that this was no threat about to fall due. She was sure that she could sense the approach of death, not as some brutal blow one might feel deep within but rather by a feeling of renunciation, by a kind of giving way. She had felt it in the case of a cousin, in the case of her own father. At that time she had sensed death in the lightness of the curtains, in

some pattern in the carpets, in the very cheerfulness of the pa-
tients, in an ever so slight reduction of the amount of oxygen in
the air. When her father had said to her, "I am cured," she had
understood, "I am dead." She had taken him in her arms, but he
was already gone.

Nor was it a question of her own death; the doctors she
had consulted after the third attack were unanimous. Everything
about her was in perfect shape: "If you were to feel any better,"
one of them had said, "then there might perhaps be a little something wrong." Unless by an odd chance of creation she were
linked to some creature unknown to her who inhabited another
world and who was thus notifying her of a death about which
she would otherwise neither hear nor grieve, then death was
very far away, she was sure of it. Today, on the contrary, she had
a feeling of absolute security, an absolute assurance that the
ancestors of the germs and viruses that would one day bring into
this house scarlet fever, the mumps, and inflammation of the
aorta had not yet been born, that asphyxiation by gas or collapse
of the house due to termites had never been farther from any
group of human beings.

Nor was it one of those anxieties that run in families and
accompany you throughout life, which have come down to you
from your grandmothers, like dowries and anxiety assets. That
kind of thing she was familiar with and wouldn't have given up
for anything in the world; anxiety over the war, for example, in
which her brother had died, and which she felt sometimes, not
as a memory, but fresh and new, as if the battle had taken place
yesterday. She valued, she took pleasure in mourning anew these
deaths from the past, feeling despair afresh over things given up
long ago. No. Everything that sanctifies anxiety—the family,
both the future and the past, none of it had anything to do with
her trouble. The only truth that really emerged tonight, where,
for a moment, the children had been unable to disturb her
thought with their magnets, the solemn occasion preventing
them from hopping up from the table at every possibility, was
this feeling of some kind of fault, some kind of deceit. It was as

if she had betrayed their trust, as if she were hiding some misdeed that would cause them to suffer or to blush. It wasn't easy to see herself as the adulterous wife returning home, but this evening she had to admit that in spite of her virtue, her loyalty, and her love, she seemed to bear the shame and the remorse—when there is remorse—of the adulterous wife.

There they were now, offering champagne to the adulterous wife. Her husband came up and, unable to resist, hugged and kissed her. The children rushed at the adulterous mother, with the added problem of putting their arms around her with a full glass in the other hand. Then they got back to their seats for the serving of the cake. To see their three faces lighted up by the thirty-three candles, for Pierre had had the electric lights put out, their joy more real and even more glowing in the candlelight, Edmée was overcome with rebellion against this suborder whom she didn't even know. She felt the deep shame and indignation of a woman taken during her sleep. She wasn't responsible, but there it was all the same. For all three believed her to be the very model of that purity which is the greatest in the world, and which is happiness; and what did this stab of pain in her heart mean if not that she wasn't really happy?

The others were thrilled because they believed themselves at the supreme moment of this happiness, and because they modestly thought themselves to be one of its causes. The lights had now been turned back on. Pierre was cutting the cake on which was written the name of his wife, Edmée, the name of his own happiness, on a beautiful cake in big white letters that stood out as if on a tomb. The children were fighting to see who could eat the most letters of her name, the generous husband reserving for himself only the very last one, the mute *e*. It was a cake also stuffed with raspberries, the first of the year.

"Make your wishes, children."

Both were silent for a second, obeying their father. They were too young to make a wish other than in silence. And one could guess what those wishes were. They all concerned her: the wish that she might always remain the most beautiful, that she never grow old, that she never die, that no one else in the family should ever die either so as to spare her grief, the wish that they might always stay just as they were, without having any need to make any further wishes.

"For you to have the most beautiful car," Claudie said out loud.

"Beautiful cars don't make you happy," said her brother.

It was at that moment that they all plainly saw two tears in her eyes. She was looking straight ahead, almost without expression, the face of someone who feels a sneeze coming on, and two tears appeared, welled up in the pupils, right in the center: one sensed behind those tears a thousand more. Why not the sneeze, why the tears? Why did the words of the children release those tears from a reserve she believed so secure? If all it took to start crying from now on was to hear the word *happiness*—unless it were the word *car,* although that didn't seem too likely—well, this really wasn't very serious. The worst of it was that they had seen them, that they were all deeply moved, that they thought those tears were due to the evening, to this truly beautiful evening, due to happiness, as Jacques would say. She felt those two tears were her very own blood, but for all that they were no less transparent and pure. Six tender glances reached out to them. A little calmer now, the children were eating the first name of that mother who, before their eyes, wept for joy to be their mother. The husband himself had tears in his eyes. "It's a fortunate woman who has the right to weep from happiness," he was thinking, "for she doesn't use makeup." "Of course," he thought next, "if there was one thing more that could complete this evening, it was for her to shed those two tears. I'm such a fool for having planned fireworks. Indoor fireworks, with nothing more than pinwheels, for rockets are impossible inside an apartment. And now my beautiful fireworks are all damp. . . ."

As soon as Jacques had seen the tears appear he had lowered his head and didn't raise it again, calculating, in his boyish discomfort, how long it would take for the tears to fall and then evaporate. Only Claudie didn't miss a single detail of what was happening. It was the first time that she had seen, not just her mother, but any woman cry. She was savoring this forbidden moment. She was staring at the tears themselves and guessed that when Jacques nudged her with his elbow, it was only to distract her from all this and so didn't respond. Poor Jacques, only last week he had seen someone hurt in the street, and when the wound started to bleed, he had tried to stop her from looking at the blood! Why are boys so embarrassed by blood, so embarrassed by tears? Now he was giving her a pinch. And neither was the father going to leave her alone:

"It's time for the fireworks, children!"

At least the stir this caused allowed Claudie, under the pretext of giving her mother a kiss, a chance to see the tears up close and dampen her own cheek. Jacques gave his mother a wide berth.

The children had long since been in bed. Pierre was going to bed. Edmée waited a little before joining him. With husband and children in bed, Edmée loved to live a moment of life in the vertical, beyond the reach of anyone. It was her life outside the living, her life with objects. She didn't talk to them but would go from room to room, touching them for a while and looking at them. There was a sort of nocturnal order required by picture frames and ashtrays. One had to straighten pictures that had slipped just a bit during the day. She would touch brass, silver, and pewter. She would touch cherry, rosewood, and ebony. She didn't avoid the mirrors. She would leisurely offer them her dark reflection, as a sort of nourishment that they were to slowly absorb. Tonight the great mirrored wardrobe was taking more of her time. She was really going to have to feed it by hand, breast-feed it. . . . Perhaps have to press her whole body against it. . . .

"Mama, are you hunting the pickles?"

Only Jacques's head was still awake. His lips were all that

he could offer to embrace Edmée. Any other movement was out of the question. She bent over him. She rubbed his forehead with her own. She nourished him like an object.

"Are you hunting the pickles?"

One night, two years ago now, her husband had surprised her in the pantry with the pickles. He had not found her beside him on waking up, had rushed off to look for her, and had suddenly come upon her, like a little child, with one pickle in her hand and another in her mouth. Early the next morning, the children had found out what happened. It had become a legend that they liked to recall on days when they felt really close. A mother so beautiful, so perfect, who would leave a deep sleep just to fish pickles out of a stone jar—now that was something to warm your heart! Jacques was smiling. For this evening of happiness to end in such a favorite episode—well, it was too wonderful. . . . Edmée was again on the verge of tears. . . . Why, yes of course she was looking for the pickles!

"I want one."

"Go to sleep now. . . ."

"Go get two. One for you. One for me."

She went. In the pantry she opened the cupboard. The dog stretched, an old dog of some eight years, with a worn-out nose, who no longer recognized dishes except by seeing the plate and who now turned his head away when she took down the jar. . . . No, no, he didn't need to worry about it. The pickles were there all right. And those little hearts on the paper, they were cloves. And that little branch, as worthy as a sprig of boxwood, that was the thyme. And filial love and maternal love and conjugal love, they were there too and should have added their salt and pepper and a lovely scent to the whole day. And yet everything was flat and tasteless. The night was flat. The dog, who had gone to sleep again, was a bundle of tastelessness. She took a pickle and ate it in order to taste its bitterness, its vinegar, so that her life might be acidic for a moment.

"Open your mouth."

Jacques opened his mouth, a surprised mouth in spite of

the wait, and in a clumsy way; it's hard to open your mouth and smile at the same time, especially while sleeping. For sleep had already reclaimed him. And hard to speak at the same time, for he wanted to say, "Thank you," and "Till tomorrow," and "Good night." And he had also decided to tell her at long last and fully what he hadn't been able to tell her during the day, that nothing was more beautiful than she was, that he adored her, that he could kill himself for her. He suddenly had the feeling that it must be extremely rare for sons to tell their mothers that they adore them. He must take advantage of the opportunity. . . . But already Edmée was sticking the pickle between the half-open lips. He crunched down, and his eyes closed.

From her bed nearby, Claudie called out and demanded her share.

"Wait for me, I'll be right back."

The girl waited, half asleep but happy. She enjoyed these absences of her mother when she really knew her to be present. The idea that her mother, in the kitchen or the pantry, was lingering over chores humble by day but noble by night—putting away jars in the cupboard, washing out the sink, setting the table, sorting the forks and spoons of the silver service—these things filled her with a mysterious expectation and confidence in life. That a mother so beautiful, with hands so fine, not in her bathrobe but still fully dressed, with her hat still on and all her rings, should be rummaging in the icebox and checking the garbage pail, Claudie relished this with a strange, almost sensual delight. Now and then a sound would reach her, some slight sound, a dish that slipped, the distant pop of a bottle uncorked— her mother no doubt wanted to see if a bit of wine was still good or had turned to vinegar. . . . Sometimes there was a real racket: her mother was moving the sideboard, for weak during the day, incapable of lifting anything heavy while the sun was shining, in the middle of the night Edmée would become stronger than a furniture mover, changing tables about, sometimes giving herself over to a complete rearrangement of the furniture, settling domestic arguments of ten years standing over where a marble bust or a secretary ought to be, and all this without so much as a spot or wrinkle appearing on her dress.

Sometimes, like tonight, there were interminable silences during which one might believe that her mother had passed from their apartment into the invisible apartment. Claudie alone knew of this invisible apartment, alone, that is, along with her mother. It was easy to gain access. Opening the door to the back stairs, her mother, in a low-cut gown, merely had to take the big fire-escape ladder and go up a thousand rungs and she would arrive at that house up in the air where hosts who were more intelligent and less blind than those of visible apartments would receive her and tell her that she was the most beautiful, would cover her with pearls and flowers and sweep her off in a whirl of dancing and pleasure. When she came back down at last and embraced her, Claudie in triumph would grab her around the waist as you do a returning hero of whom you are very proud. She would kiss the hand that had been kissed by all those extraordinary invisible friends; she scented on her mother all the unknown flowers, she felt new jewels scratching against her. . . .

Surely she was up there right at this moment. This very evening, after the family party, that crowd of splendid men, that throng of superb women had waited for Edmée above the iron ladder and had pulled her up to them by both arms, way up above the city, above the eaves and the night. . . .

Why hadn't her father gone up? Claudie had a thousand answers to this question. Father was someone that Claudie put to bed in the evening like something you might take to the post office and get back with the morning mail. Father got dizzy: he would have fallen to the ground before reaching the thousandth rung. Father would have looked ridiculous in his pajamas on the ladder behind his wife: Father didn't put on evening clothes to go to bed. It wasn't for sure either that Father could breathe at that altitude; already he had trouble flying in an airplane. . . .

So Mother, at this moment alone up there, was presiding over the cutting of a cake where the giant letters of the word *Edmée* were at the center of fierce competition, especially since whoever won the first *E* got to kiss Edmée herself. . . . How quiet everything was. What a beautiful party it must be that her mother would soon return from, without being out of breath from dancing, without her triumph affecting her heart, with the little pickle that she had snitched from the midst of all that caviar and champagne. . . .

Meanwhile, Edmée was sitting on the pantry steps, arms hanging down and yawning there in front of the spice cupboard as if in front of a window. . . .

"Open your mouth."

Claudie opened her mouth. She received the pickle as she used to receive the bottle, sucked on it, and fell asleep. . . . "And there is the milk, Lord, with which I now nourish my daughter."

"Edmée!"

She was now being called from the bedroom.

"Me too. Pick me the best one."

Her husband also wanted a pickle. She was touched. He who never had a kind word for mustard and preserved and spiced delicacies was giving in tonight. She went to look for a pickle. Although one may not select pickles so carefully as a rule, she obeyed him; she picked the one which by its architecture, sculpture, and contrast seemed to lay claim to the title of pickle of the head of the family, and, with the tips of her fingers, carried it back through hallways and drawing room. Pierre regarded her with tender eyes to which the shadowy half-light gave the secret and the charm of unknown eyes. And for him too, only the lips were able to move in a body that was paralyzed: he opened them, his face serene and grateful, with the faint pout of young communicants when seen from profile in country churches.

And she gave him this bitter communion.

# 2

"What was I like when I was two?"

"Very pretty. Very nice."

"Do you have any pictures of me when I was two?"

"Why don't you talk about someone other than yourself sometime?" said her father. "Neither your mother nor I are going to answer you anymore when you ask questions about yourself when you were little."

"I'm eight years old. I have a right to know myself."

"You have a right to be quiet."

Claudie was quiet. She had to be quiet for ten minutes: Father was leaving for his office in ten minutes. But the injustice of it made her red in the face. As if it was out of selfishness that she liked for people to talk about her. There had been a hundred, a thousand little girls who had succeeded each other day after day in order to create the Claudie of today, and her father refused her the right to know them, to love them! Did he ever suspect, poor Father, that she never loved the father of today, whereas the father of yesterday, so clumsy with his fireworks inside apartments, the father of the other month, so helpless over his broken-down radiator, filled her with humility and obedience? All those little girls who had disappeared thanks to whom she was able to get along in life: the one who had sacrificed herself for her scarlet fever, the one who had taken her place to let her finger get caught in the door, that multitude of Claudies, Claudettes, Claudines, even a Clo-Clo—for there had been a little country girl Clo-Clo—well, she liked to collect all their photos, not as photos of herself, but as family portraits. She didn't descend from Eve, but from the little Claudie of one week old whose picture opened the album, strangely nude and maternal. She would find out later if it had been of any benefit.

Jacques of course descended from Adam and not from Jacques. In the pictures where he appeared with his sister he never dared look at himself. He believed that the little Jacques of three months, sucking his toe, and the Jacques who was piloting a cardboard plane was himself. . . . When they were really everything that was no longer himself. When it was all the dead brothers of Claudie, her thousand dead brothers that Claudie adored, whereas she had some pretty mixed feelings for the one who survived. The latter would lower his eyes in false modesty, like the other evening when he didn't dare look at his mother's tears. Men never dare look anything in the face, not even those who cry and who don't see us. To have the luck of seeing your mother cry and to turn your eyes away! She, Claudie, hadn't blinked once, from the moment she had guessed what was about to take place in her mother's eyes. The tears had gathered, had glistened, had trickled, trickled down on the tablecloth. Claudie had touched them with her hand, without seeming to, as she left the table. They had been distinct and precise, like the drops for your cough when they come out of the dropper. There had been two of them. . . . It was a two-drop remedy. . . . The one on the right had fallen first. . . .

Her father kissed her good-bye, saw that she returned it, and went out. . . . If he had known that the kiss Claudie gave him was not for the father who was present but for the father she had thrown a boiled egg at three months ago, he would have avoided bending down so low to receive that kiss.

"Where are we going, Claudie?" asked her mother.

"Let's go to Mr. Warren's, for my portrait."

"All right, we'll go to Mr. Warren's."

Edmée was at times terrified by Claudie. There was in this girl of eight an instinct that she could not help but admire; she hoped it was an instinct, for if it was reasoning or feeling, it was better not to think about it. Claudie, with all of her little body, if not her little brain, nourished a determination that was calm, concealed, and discreet, but also tireless and quite obstinate: to make sure that her mother was able to see and talk to other men. It didn't seem to matter with whom. Whether her mother talked with a friend of her father, an Irish policeman, or a gardener, Claudie pretended not to be there; indeed, she really wasn't there: you would find her behind some trees reading something or slipping pennies into a piggy bank. She wasn't curious, she didn't listen. A sense of duty ordered her to leave her mother alone with other men and that was all. Alone with men who were themselves alone, even the ugly; Claudie was already informed, heaven knows by whom, that the ugliness of men is only a mask. . . .

Alone with all men except her father, that is. Of him she was jealous. When her parents went to bed, she didn't accept the idea that this father had the right to be quietly alone with his wife. She sensed by signs that would escape Edmée herself those evenings when Father's tenderness took on a threatening guise. Then there would always be an incident, caused by herself, with the help of a storm, or a rat, or the colic, on one night with the help of a real but very slight earthquake, some incident that would allow her to break into the duet of calm and understanding that prevailed in the office or living room. How many times, moreover, when it was still night, had Claudie not slipped into the bed of her parents to prevent their attempt to come together at the break of day, to see that between her parents there would be no special awakening, no first words, no conjugal dawn. Edmée was amused at this obstinacy and sense of perfect timing. This appearance, as sudden as a birth, of the little girl after the slightest kiss, after the slightest embrace, this little girl who persisted in being reborn every time her husband made a tender move—this gave Edmée the very same pleasure as had the first arrival of Claudie eight years ago: a feeling of repose, an easing of the marriage bond which was dear to her, but a bond nonetheless. By her inaction she was abetting this third party who was causing caresses to regain their forbidden nature, who organized throughout the house a ruthless pursuit of marital tenderness and its sudden consequences, and who returned it to the bed and to the middle of the night.

This suited Edmée. But her husband was furious. He didn't accept the idea of having his wife only at midnight—the only hour at which one could be sure of Claudie's being asleep—and in the dark, when their two bodies had become anonymous. He was annoyed at the little girl, and at his own mistake in giving in to her—but what could he do?—annoyed at having so little presence of mind in his response to her one day when he was trying to kiss his wife in the hall, only to find Claudie born suddenly there at their feet and staring them in the face:

"Your mother has something in her eye. I'm trying to find it."

"Yes, that hurts a lot," Claudie had replied. And she had added, "You know, you have a right to kiss Mama."

But with a tone, a face, and a soul that said just the opposite, and as she remained there, it was the father himself who had to leave. . . . Whereas, as soon as it was a matter of some other man, it was Claudie who would stay out of the way. She hadn't been born. She wasn't being born right then. "I'm going into the library," she would say if her mother had a visit from a friend, and off she would go to the library; she would settle in the only spot in the library from which one could see nothing that was going on in the living room, from which one could hear the front door open, and she would not stir from there. Teatime might pass, the telephone might ring, but she stayed at her post, unless by chance Father should return. She was the first to hear him, and would cough loudly—a cold taken no doubt in a too chilly library—and would rejoin her mother, climb up in the lap of the visitor, give him a hug, and smooth his hair as if to change fingerprints or divert suspicion. Edmée, intrigued, had tried in vain to understand this puzzle. She could only ascertain that Claudie was naive, pure, even a little backward, and extraordinarily open except for this piece of comedy. So she didn't hold it against her. Her own honest nature adjusted to this natural complicity as if it were a sort of game or pledge.

Frank Warren had no sooner opened the door of his studio than Claudie disappeared into the kitchen.

"Isn't Mother beautiful?" she had found time to say as she passed by.

"But we've come here to finish your portrait!" cried Edmée.

In vain. Claudie slipped away from Frank's kisses as if she had stolen them from someone more deserving than herself, slipped away as if she knew what real kisses were, in a hurry, without letting her hand, arm, or coat be caught, just like that spy La Païva would have done, just as if she knew that a woman held back even by something so slight as a bit of lace trim or her purse is lost. . . . And already in the kitchen, she was latching on to Blanche Pearl, the black housekeeper, who asked nothing better, on good grounds, than to leave Edmée and her employer to themselves. In a sudden impulse of good behavior, meant to counterbalance heaven knows what folly, Claudie demanded of Blanche Pearl that she teach her how to crochet, knit, and iron. What Edmée and Frank might have said to each other mattered very little, but at the day's end Claudie would know how to darn her socks. She would also have learned, through practice, that one should wash plates twice, first in hot water and then again in warm, and that it is a good idea to line the china cupboard shelves with paper. Edmée observed moreover that it was only these dubious situations that she was pushed into by Claudie that inspired her daughter with such a frenzy for housekeeping.

With his palette on his knees full of those colors meant for Claudie, Frank was now looking at Edmée, the ravishing colors of Edmée, with emotion and restraint; they seemed to him the only colors beyond capture in a studio where the most beautiful girls had at least left behind a bit of their ochre and their red. Edmée felt at ease and was smiling. She loved light chitchat with men. It was enough for her to be in a room alone with a man for her to be on an island with a man. She had a natural inclination to feel intimate with any companion, even transient. She didn't hide from herself that she was easy prey for using *tu*, for dancing, for long walks arm in arm, for trips at night. It had required the dignity of her husband to return some gravity to danger and a sense of ambiguity to male companionship. The admiration that Pierre had for her had not taught her to admire herself, to place more value on sharing her intimate moments, but obliged her to assume the rather formal relations with most men that made up her life with Pierre. However, the education that her husband had tried to give her about men had not been fully successful. In spite of the lessons, Edmée was unable to distinguish, as clearly as he, men who were cowardly, lazy, or hardworking, or even—and this was the distinction that perhaps meant the most to Pierre, who was tall and good-looking—the short from the tall or the ugly from the handsome. She felt for one and all a kind of goodwill and fraternal affection that, on moonlit evenings, was easily translated into a walk with the biggest potbelly or (in spite of the moon she didn't see it) the shiniest bald pate.

Pierre suffered from his wife's inability to distinguish him from his subordinates in looks and strength even more than from her ignorance—which nothing had been able to remedy— of his merit as a top student and engineer. He felt himself loved, he felt her to be faithful, but the idea that she would have loved the first to come along, that she would have been faithful to the first to come along, exasperated him to the point that the complete satisfaction in life to which he was naturally inclined was often compromised. This woman loved him not because he was handsome, courageous, and intelligent—exams at the Ecole Polytechnique are not infallible proof, but if you're ranked first on entrance and first at graduation, one can hardly speak of coincidence—but because he had been the first to ask her hand in marriage! It was there that he was first among men to this extraordinary young woman: the first to ask her into his bed. If he, Pierre, had arrived one month later, it might have been the bed of a stutterer or a humpback! . . . What made this perverseness still more surprising was that Edmée was sensitive, was educated. She read Nietzsche in the original, would read him without any pretension, alternating Nietzsche with the memoirs of Madame de la Boigne; she had written a thesis on the idea of repetition in Gide; she could have been a virtuoso on the piano, and would play with him, four hands—the four hands of the couple suddenly untied and separated by Liszt or Brahms—the very hardest concertos. She would sing, though never by chance, only on days when the acoustics of the world or of the family demanded a human song, those days when the female would sing in the cage of the canaries. She was discerning, she was witty; she judged events and people with such sureness and freedom that her words seemed spoken by chance but hit their mark every time, like the words of clerks of the court and of the gods. Why must she reserve her ignorance, her incapacity for the one subject that mattered most to Pierre, the subject of men?

Pierre, who, through the lessons of an arduous life and his magnificent responsibilities, as a result also of an innate sense of tact and nobility, saw men as they are, in their physical and moral hierarchy, saw them as if each one had his price marked in chalk on his back, saw them ranked for entry into the great schools of Centrale or Polytechnique, into the Pantheon, into heaven or hell—Pierre had reached a point of not tolerating, of not admitting as equals any except those who seemed to him touched and moved by honor. . . . He was even broad in his discrimination: he could admit the honor of thieves, the honor of the dishonored. . . . But he was sure, if one met some vague acquaintances on the beach by chance or should happen to dine out in the city, that sooner or later he would find his wife in friendly debate with some guest without honor. Everything about her that should have been reserved for honor—her smile, her lack of reserve, her talkativeness, and her undivided attention—she would lavish it all on someone utterly worthless, someone truly rotten.

With the result that at night, once in bed, while he would become in the act of love a being conscious to the utmost of the nobleness of his life on this earth, conscious of what his family, his country, and his home really meant, and that all of his treasures and personal resources were gathered around him for this marriage, and that the pleasure of love gave him, in every sense, his highest and most precise likeness to himself, he sensed, on the contrary, Edmée liberated by love from everything that was her class, position, and purpose, from everything that was outside of love, and first of all, from himself, Pierre. It was from the union of this paragon of human virtues and this woman without name or face, from this husband to the highest degree and this fallen wife that the two children had been born. This immediate sleep which took Edmée right away, impossible to avoid or to disturb, while he on the contrary felt wide awake, good humored, and inspired, while he would have been the wittiest of engineers after making love, while he would have talked endlessly about the future of their son, of the virtues of the country, of the need to change the wallpaper, and that feeling of infinite peace and happiness had him telling stories from yesterday all the way back to Plutarch—this deep sleep sometimes made him fear that by the next day Edmée would have forgotten everything of their life together, everything of life itself. He risked nothing of course, he thought, furious. . . . She would take him back again since he would be the first to come along!

This was the way he found himself every time, stretched out beside her: father of a model family, esteemed musician, department head paid in dollars, and engineer a hundred times over, lying there facing her back in a motionless march which could only have led him to where she already was, to nothing. Sometimes he wished he could see her take notice of a man, be attracted to another man. Then at least he would have had an enemy. He might have won out. Probably he would have won out. But what could he do against this vast throng where he was the first to be confounded and where he deceived himself with himself?

In Frank's silent studio, Edmée gave herself up to the feeling that she felt every time she was alone with a man in a place that was closed, walled in, or locked up tight: a feeling of security. The presence of men, of any man, from the locksmith to the window washer in the empty apartment, protected her instead of worrying her. If this man, as Frank was about to do at the moment, drew the curtains halfway and came to sit down at her feet, what did it matter? She was someone that you protected by taking her hands or getting down on your knees. She didn't even hold it against those who had tried to protect her by taking her in their arms, by offering her a string of pearls—certain protection against the spirits—or by trying to embrace her. Her faithfulness to Pierre was so complete and so natural that these attacks were not even insults. Besides, she didn't believe very seriously in abductions, kidnappings, or rape. . . . If Frank let his head drop back on her knees, on the hollow between her knees? Fine. She accepted this head as a head by itself. She took it as a present, the sort of present that a decapitated Saint Denis might have offered to his favorite female saint. Frank's body had disappeared, but this head that talked by itself, that opened its eyes, a head covered with lots of hair of the finest quality and lashes a bit too long for the eyes of a man—this head, for an hour, was a charming present. She wouldn't take it with her of course; on the trolley or in the street it would be rather awkward. But she was glad to have it there for a moment. . . . Meanwhile, out in the kitchen, Claudie was explaining to Blanche Pearl that one shouldn't serve tea unless it had been requested, even requested twice.

Frank's head appealed to Edmée. For among all these countless innocuous men, Edmée couldn't help but prefer one category. One day she had tried to find out once and for all which one it was, and she had stopped midway in her research, a little ashamed, for she couldn't deny that the ones she preferred belonged to a variety completely different from that which had produced Pierre. They all shared this same characteristic: they were light. It was not only a question of lightness of language or of conduct. It was a question of their weight, of their density. They didn't weigh on life. They had, in their bodies or their souls, that pocket of air that enables the birds to fly. They were not all like Frank, easygoing and bohemian; some of them had an occupation, a trade, a faith, but they were light nonetheless, because of that lesser density that endowed them with a certain ease, gaiety, and humor. They were senators who were light, arms dealers who were light. As she enjoyed waiting for men and spending some time with them, she liked them not too punctual, on the idle side. As she was offended by any obliga-tion, she liked for men to be changeable. She fled any sort of argument, whether it was about the house or was didactic or re-ligious. Through a contradiction which used to make Pierre furious, this highly literate woman hated any sort of literary de-bate, and when the club would invite Sinclair Lewis or André Siegfried to a dinner in their honor, when it came time to toast them, he was sure to find her out in the garden, playing table tennis with some stout gentleman who weighed well over two hundred pounds but who was nevertheless one of these crea-tures of least density.

This woman who was music itself, once her piano was closed would reply only reluctantly to those who wanted to talk music, and when Pierre played four hands with her, even though she had expressed all the gaiety or passion of the piece, and often added her own bit of irony, he knew that he wasn't supposed to say a word after the last note, and they would find themselves face-to-face once more, silent—she smiling, and he bitter, just as they were now after making love. It made him grit his teeth. You struck the final chord, you stopped the drama right there, stopped the tug at your heart and the beauty of the world, and it was over, and she was setting a vase of roses down on the lowered piano lid. What did he care about pianos with roses on top? What he longed for was a conversation on the pillow, at the keyboard, about the sons of Bach, about Goethe's letter to Schubert, or the despairs of Berlioz. She would decline without a word, smiling. "But see here, you little donkey," he felt like telling her, "it isn't just the music of Bach or Schubert! There is Bach himself, Schubert himself! There are thirty men who lived a life of delight or hell in order to leave you this magnificent gift! You surely don't mean to turn *Armide* into an anonymous opera! When Gluck, on September 3, 1780, . . ." But already she was no longer there. . . . You might have said that the name of Gluck had made her disappear. . . .

For Pierre, who thought of Eiffel when one spoke of the Eiffel Tower, of Pasteur when one went by the Boulevard Pasteur, this lack of aptitude for calling humanity by its great names was a denial of justice. He, who felt inside himself endless gratitude for those who had invented the motet, the serenade, the string quartet, the vocalize, the use of portamento, who would have been delighted to invite out to lunch the first person to use the sharp sign over a note, he couldn't accept the fact that Edmée considered music as an anonymous harvest, like hay or mustard.

"Why don't you want to talk about Mozart?" he had asked her one day when she had played one of the concertos as never before. . . . Do you have something against him?"

"What would I have against him?"

"To be the acknowledged composer of *The Magic Flute,* of the *Requiem.* It bothers you to talk about him. But there are witnesses. The works really are by Mozart."

"All right. Let's talk about him."

"Do you think one can talk about Mozart, just like that?"

"All right. Let's not talk about him."

"You have some secret with him. You have a secret with each one of your composers! You're cheating on me with them. You don't want to share them with me. That's the real reason."

"Pierre, darling, if I gave you a kiss, would that help you get over this?"

"I don't think so. You'd be kissing me so as not to talk. That upsets me very much."

"Let me try. We'll find out! . . ." And the kiss came. And it went on. And when it was about to end, Pierre would no doubt want to talk about the kiss. But the kiss that now filled him already no longer existed for her. She saw that he was going to speak. She kissed him again, seriously and hurriedly this time, so that there could be no further question of the kiss.

Thus it was that little by little, in he knew not what sort of defensive instinct, he had been led to take the side of the great men against this woman, who, in some inexplicable silence, persisted in not acknowledging their presence. The walls of his office were lined with authentic portraits of great musicians, great writers, and one could even find among them, less authentic of course, the authors of great works that Edmée, in triumph, would have declared anonymous: the *Odyssey,* the Bible, and the *Song of Roland.* He had even added a portrait of Charlotte Corday, to prove that there were great women. This was the only sort of betrayal that he had ever allowed himself; he deceived his wife with Charlotte Corday, with Louise Labé, and with her colleague Madame du Châtelet, the mathematician. Edmée accepted this gallery—they were the portraits of her in-laws; the intelligence, boldness, and inventive side of humanity, those were the ancestors of Pierre, and for her they were mothers-in-law; whereas in her own gallery she had only the *Gilles* of Watteau, not because it was by Watteau, claimed Pierre, but because it was *Gilles.* At the dinner table, while the husband and son talked only of Gandhi, of Racine, of Stevenson, Edmée and her daughter held forth on the proper place for saltcellars or whether the oil cruets were clean, a dialogue that seemed to turn sly and mischievous by its very poverty.

For Claudie was her accomplice. She hated the heads of the portraits. Though it scandalized her father, she called them by their first names, as if they were servants, and this included Charlotte. If Pierre sometimes suddenly asked Edmée a question about Voltaire or about Beethoven, Claudie would find a way to overturn her glass, or to ask what she had been like when she had the measles, and so change the conversation. She would leave her mother alone with men, never with great men. But perhaps Pierre was even more irritated by the scant interest shown by mother and daughter in the living great. He himself still felt the honor of having been the godson of Marshal Foch, of having had his ear pulled in the Tuileries by Georges Clemenceau. He used to recount the scene to Jacques, who would listen with throbbing ears, and whose greatest happiness would have been to have had his ears pulled by Jeanne d'Arc. "Did he hurt you, Papa?" Claudie then asked, in a clear little voice in which Pierre could hear playing that which he hated most of all: a child's mocking irony with regard to the world of men. Jacques couldn't stop himself, he got up and was about to pull her ear, pull both ears of that little heretic. Claudie began to insult her brother by using his favorite name: "Dirty Georges! Dirty Clemenceau!" Edmée stopped the fight. But as he left the dining room, Pierre distinctly heard the little girl's voice, and, every now and then, a voice graver, sweeter, and more tender, that of his wife, crying out behind him: "Dirty Voltaire! Dirty Descartes! Dirty Lavoisier! . . ." Lavoisier was his favorite scientist, for he was a chemist. To shout "Dirty Lavoisier!" An unforgivable injustice! He was glad that Claudie didn't know Lavoisier's first name. All the more since it was Antoine.

"If only," thought Pierre, "this insensitivity to human values were due to a taste for the fantastic, or due to naïveté!" This was not . . . the case. Edmée was not the gushy sort, hadn't the resources, had no gift for inventiveness. Nothing bored her more than telling children's stories to the children. She would tell them all wrong. She would alter characters as clear cut as Puss in Boots or Cinderella. She would even mix up the details, making the princess feel the sting of an asp, though everyone knows for which very unanonymous personage the asp was intended. Pierre was obliged to intervene in order to restore the right number of years of sleep to the Sleeping Beauty, to give the correct kilometric span of what Edmée called the four-league boots. His exactitude as an engineering student suffered still more perhaps from the assaults carried out on fairy measurements. But the interest of the story was only shifted around. Pierre couldn't keep from listening without interrupting as soon as Edmée spoke of what was not legendary in the legends, of the silverware of the lady woodcutter, of how very smooth were the feathers of the Blue Bird, or when she described the weather, for she had brought into the stories the elements of rain, wind, and mud. Her description of Cinderella's snow boots, of the ogre's umbrellas, and everything that made up the everyday, prosaic, and real life of these false creatures filled him with admiration. And also a new uneasiness.

For if this woman had such talent, if she perceived, if she felt things to this degree, then her antipathy to what he himself considered the very joy of life arose from a deliberate obstinacy or, even more frightful, arose from instinct. This woman, whom he had chosen above all others in order to complete himself, was she in fact his opposite? Half of the couple, was she, for the other half, just plaster, a fake? At night, to such an extent did he feel that his son was himself and that his daughter was his wife that he would linger about to watch the children sleeping. What mirrors they were! Jacques would sleep with his fists clenched, like he did when nursing, drinking in long drafts the milk of sleep that would make him strong tomorrow for his life as an industrious little boy, with his three names of Jacques-Thibaut-Alain floating like a nimbus around his head, his whole consciousness given over to unconsciousness, his eyes invisible but frank beneath their lids, future man, future father, future great man. Claudie, on the contrary, anonymous, her face obstinate, hostile even in deep sleep to all those missions that were piling up around Jacques, sexless and barely human, quite ready, if anyone pestered her with these stories of men, war, porridge, the nation, or Clemenceau, to change biological kingdom or function and to become a plant or a faun. Awake now besides, beyond a doubt, but pretending to be asleep before her father, like you play dead before a grizzly, and for the same reason—to escape his embrace. She didn't even take the trouble, she, so uncompromising in her modesty, for fear of being embraced by her father, to pull down her chemise or to pull up the sheet. With her whole body bare, with her mouth shut tight, she said no to Pierre.

He regarded with fear this little creature born of himself, of his innocence, of his devotion, of his friendship for mankind, of his accord with nature, of his contract with God, and who was bringing into the house the opposite of all these virtues. If some unknown man, cynical, devoid of any grandeur of soul and bereft of trust, had found the way into his bed, this is precisely the daughter he would have had. To what end, for what vengeance had she been set down in this heart of the bourgeoisie? And yet there was nothing monstrous about her. She was in the same class, took part in the same games, the pleasures of her own age. She never spoke of anything unsuitable for a little girl of eight. But sometimes it seemed to Pierre that this might be by some convention, one that she could give up at any time, and that one would then be free to address her in any language whatsoever, be it brazen or serious. He remembered the day when she had first opened her eyes, those eyes still without color which had cast on him a look that was dull and worn out, almost like a judge, as if he were the one being born and she had nothing to do with it. Yes, that was what Claudie's first look had said: her father was in the way, any father for that matter. . . . It really wasn't what he had expected from Providence, to find once more the age of the world itself in his own little girl. "I am now punished," he said to himself. "Every crime deserves punishment. I have committed the crime of believing that life was beautiful, that with honesty, work, and faith one might manage well enough on this earth. I believed myself above the others who don't have autographed copies of Beethoven and who don't know Vigny by heart, including *Les Amants de Montmorency.* I believed myself good, without guile. And really, I am. I am even generous. I am not afraid of death. I would throw myself under a train to save an old lady. It would be a stupid gesture. The death of the old lady would delight her heirs, while mine would blight the fate of the three people I love. But that is the stuff I am made of. To be confident of one's own goodness, one's own perfection, is to take account only of oneself. Egotism to this degree is intolerable, and deserves its punishment. And here it is: brought to me in ribbons and swaddling clothes, a little creature who would disturb the whole house, and who would introduce, not faults, for faults go hand in hand with virtues, but rather scandal. Or perhaps I am exaggerating. . . . Perhaps little girls are all like that. . . . But what affects me the most is that even if she is perfect, she demeans me and I feel tainted. She has made me suspicious of life, of herself, of my wife. I'm becoming just the opposite of what I would have liked to be—I'm too fussy, I'm jealous. When she goes out alone with her mother, I have the same impression as if Edmée were going out with someone who might lead her astray. . . ."

Meanwhile, at Frank's studio, Edmée was discovering that not only was Frank light, but that his head was light too. A head like that would have been no bother in life. With a head like that on a silver platter, Salome could have danced her famous dance on one foot. Maybe Frank had a heavy step, a heavy foot, but as far as the head was concerned, it was perfect. . . . Pierre's head was heavy. . . . This wasn't a reproach. She loved Pierre and not Frank. But it's no less true that weight is heavy in itself. Perhaps some women need for their husbands' heads to be heavy, like the weights they put on hampers of oysters to keep them from opening, or like a paperweight. "How can I follow you?" they

may say to seducers. "My husband's head weighs me down! ..."
And yet Frank's skull didn't sound hollow, it was full of brains,
the jaws didn't lack a single tooth. And the few words that came
out of this head were also light. Frank lived with himself and of
himself. Never in his conversation did an anecdote, a story, or a
joke appear that seemed ready made. His words, like his culture,
he created on the spot. Not that he never seemed like himself,
but he didn't give the impression, like most men, of being a simple gutter spout of humanity, put up to shed knowledge,
thought, or moods. Like most men. Like Pierre.

The problem with Pierre was that by wanting to be humanity's representative, that is what he had truly become. Each
of his acts, each of his words, was no more than a sort of worthy
sample of human gesture and speech. He was the traveling salesman of humanity. He dealt in the sublime like others deal in
sugarcane or in nickel, in really good sublime, but you had the
unfortunate impression that this sublime needed a dealer and
that without the fierce efforts of similar publicists and without
the passivity of their clients, one could have conceived of a
humanity without conscience, without invention, and without
pride. The head of Pierre, in length, in breadth, whether vertical,
horizontal, or reversed, was adaptable to the bodies of all human
beings in work, in gestation, in inspiration, and in love. But from
Frank's head no lesson emerged, no kind of blackmail. She was
ashamed to think of that word. But it was the right one. Pierre
demanded blackmail, the blackmail of perfection. . . . Deep
down, like all women, she didn't hate blackmail, but is there any
kind other than imperfection?

"Where were you today?" Pierre asked at dinner.

"At Frank's," said Claudie.

"Is your portrait coming along well?"

"No," said Edmée. "We didn't work. We talked. Frank has
such a nice way of talking."

That wasn't quite the truth. The truth was: Frank's head is
so light. . . .

It was then that the attack returned. Like yesterday. That tension, followed by that anxiety. That weariness of everything, of all that wasn't there. Of all that was there.

"Was it interesting, Claudie?"

Oh dear Lord! How clumsy he was! Why must he persist in pushing that little child into a lie? And why, at the moment when she was suffering intensely, add this further pain? . . . She couldn't keep silent. . . .

"Claudie was in the kitchen. She was helping Blanche Pearl."

"Oh, is Frank doing your portrait too? That's very good."

If he thought she was going to lie, he was mistaken.

"I told you that we had a talk."

"What can one talk about with Frank?"

With Frank, he was thinking, who didn't know a single famous name, who had no profession, who would use colors without knowing what made up their base, who, at the university to get a degree and forced to pick three subjects to write about, had chosen flowers in spun glass, the swastika, and European cultivation of the grapefruit. A three-year course of study where the only human mentioned, and barely even then, turned out to be Otto Meyer, the herbalist of spun-glass flowers of Regensburg. With Frank, who in his whole life had never earned a penny, and who was eating up a small fortune. With Frank, who had neither knowledge, imagination, nor talent.

"About everything," she said.

"About everything?"

"About everything!" she was thinking. With Frank, who knows how to breathe, who knows how to close his eyes, who knows how to sew, to remove spots with benzine, to fix the faucets in the kitchen. With Frank, who answers the front door himself, who doesn't know how to speak, who, when he talks, is like a puppy dog, putting his head on his master's knees. And, when you came down to it, it was true. They had said nothing. She would have been quite incapable of recalling a single word. But what an easy hour it was! They had said everything there was to be said between them. Whence that beautiful silence.

"Did he wish you a happy birthday?"

There. That did it. She was going to cry again. She tried, as she used to chase away useless tears when she was little, to think of the worst misfortunes, the dying moments of her father, the death of her children. It was too late, her eyes had already misted over. Pierre and Jacques looked on fascinated: in those eyes where they thought they had seen two tears of happiness the night before, now emerged two other tears, about whose nature there could be no mistake—just as pure to be sure, but through them the purity of the earlier tears was now lost. Pierre watched them steadily, as he watched his experiments at the factory, so as not to miss one detail of the process by which the watery humor that ran throughout Edmée's body was able to distill the water of the tears and the end of the world. He noted the false serenity of the brow, the unhappiness of the temples, the utter desperation of eyelids and lips. He restrained an impulse to kiss those eyes, out of the qualms of a scientist, and from an awful fear of displeasing her. He had understood his mistake, his insistence; a first-year engineering student would have understood it: when you press too hard on the weak spot, even if it is steel, the steel breaks. There was a break in Edmée.

He didn't make another move, he stopped eating, to breathe would have been almost to insist. Jacques, like the naive little boy that he was, equally shy before joy or sorrow, had at once turned his eyes away from his mother; he was eating his custard, his favorite dessert. "It's so good, my favorite dessert!"—trying not to look at her. But how hard that was! He hadn't realized before today that he took his views of life, like his pictures with his Kodak, always with his mother at the corner or in the center. The best he could do right now—"Yes, Mother, I'd like some more, it's perfect"—was to manage not to see the eyes; he could still see her dress, her arm, and her chin. . . . They must never again make egg custard at home, otherwise life would be unbearable! . . .

Only Claudie seemed natural. She didn't look at her mother, and she didn't have a second helping of custard. She had seen her mother cry yesterday for the first time, but already inside her there was the habit of seeing a mother cry. . . . No custard, but an apple instead. The lack of attention that she was being paid even gave her enough time to achieve what Pierre had never before allowed, peeling the apple in a circle, at one go. As for Edmée, little thoughts were going through her mind for which she didn't feel responsible; the most precise went like this: "At two tears a day, it will take me a century. . . ."

They went to bed early. Claudie had already found a cure for two problems: she went to sleep while going to bed. It took Jacques till midnight to find the same cure. . . . In bed, Pierre asked her pardon, asked her mercy, asked for happiness. Edmée granted all. Of course she loved him. Of course he was the only one. Of course she was happy. . . .

He was heavy, very heavy. . . .

# 3

It was really just chance, indeed, quite by chance, for Edmée had vowed to think of nothing henceforth, to scrutinize nothing, to look into nothing anymore. She no longer concealed from herself that at each turn in a new path there were individuals and dangers awaiting her. Within the family there was growing, beneath the appearance of tranquillity, dignity, and enjoyment of life, a tumor whose nature it was really best to leave unknown. Tumors pass. The greatest ills in life disappear by themselves—wickedness from the heart of the wicked, cancer from man, and that is all they have to do, simply disappear. And everyone else at home was like Edmée. Happiness had fled the house, yet its inhabitants acted as if they were happy. The same happy smile on the lips of Jacques leaving for school, or on Pierre leaving for the factory, the same, except that they were unhappy. And a quarter of an hour apart, for the son left and returned a quarter of an hour before the father. Edmée gave them back the same false smile. The threat would pass. The smile would remain. . . .

It was the laugh whose rapid return seemed less probable, that laugh you couldn't stop that used to seize Pierre on occasions that seemed the least likely to inspire laughter, when he was reading, in general—when he read that Aristophanes had died laughing on seeing a donkey eat a fig, or that a seaside hotel advertised "an atmosphere of calm dignity," or that the pope had received from the Catholics of Wisconsin a pair of ebonite shoe trees. This sort of sonorous braying, which went on for several minutes, instead of irritating Edmée as it did Claudie, gave her some comfort, gave her the impression that there was a real little donkey in the house, and that this little donkey, shaking its ears, twitching its nose, forgetting everything in its laugh, and making everyone forget that there was anything else but donkeys, this was none other than Pierre, and she was even rather touched by it. Pierre had sometimes wondered, when he was laughing, why Edmée would come up to him, pat him on the shoulder, and embrace him. She was simply taking advantage of his transformation, simply patting her donkey on the back, embracing the muzzle of her donkey, ever so much more cool and silky than his cheek as a man. It was the only way to lift Pierre out of that "atmosphere of high dignity" which he did not laugh about and which he had wanted to make that of the family. But now it was over, that laugh was heard no more, the great chamberlain could try out in silence his shoe trees on the slippers of the pope, Aristophanes's donkey might eat his figs in peace, the little donkey inside Pierre brayed no more. She would not hear Pierre's laugh anymore unless a real donkey began to bray. Pierre had given back to the animal kingdom the only sign, alas, that he had ever received from it.

Guilty? Concerning Pierre and Jacques, certainly she was guilty, since the feeling that their presence stirred in her was remorse, awareness of some betrayal. But guilty of what? Guilty of not observing strictly the laws of this little republic whose civic duty was happiness? Yet never had the most frivolous of her thoughts betrayed Pierre. Guilty, in order to be tender to him, of first turning him into a beast? Guilty, the other day, of having taken Frank's head on her knees? The gesture had been so innocent. It was easy to see herself answering Pierre as he interrogated her about this crime:

"How is it that you came to take it on your knees, this head?"

"It put itself there by itself. I didn't seek it out."

"You could have put it back down on the floor."

"I would have had to take it in both hands. It seemed out of the question."

"You could have gotten up."

"The head would have been no better off. Nor I."

"In short, it appealed to you?"

"No, it didn't bother me in any way."

"Your specialty, in order not to be bothered, is to have a man's head on your knees?"

"I suppose it is. Until today I was unaware of that."

He kept insisting. For some time now he had been very insistent. . . . Why did Edmée so obligingly prolong the dialogue?

"Men's heads don't exist by themselves. Where the head is, the man is not far away."

"In general, yes. But yesterday, definitely not. If Frank had been so near, I can assure you that I would have seen him. I would have quickly given him back his head. I know myself."

"Did it stay there without saying anything?"

"Oh yes, it talked. But Frank didn't say a thing. Not a single thing. It was the head talking."

"What do they have to say, these heads?"

"That the weather is beautiful. That it's really nice today."

"There's nothing like heads for kissing."

"Maybe so. I had no idea. I'll see. This was the first one."

And this whole explanation seemed so natural to her that one evening, when, barely in bed, he returned again in his clumsy way to the visit to Frank's studio and forbade her to go there again, she couldn't keep from steering him toward the debate already composed in her head and from saying that she didn't see what harm there was in taking a head on your knees. And the explanation began, the real one.

"What head? Frank's head? You put Frank's head on your knees?"

"It put itself there all by itself; I didn't look for it in any way."

The first line of the first version would do all right. But already Edmée realized that it was the only one that would.

"I didn't know you had reached that point."

"Reached what point?"

"The point of taking men's heads on your knees. . . ."

It was not nothing that he accepted the fiction of the separate head. But the hour didn't allow time to settle the theoretical debate over politeness that had been in Edmée's thoughts. Inasmuch as the couple was lying there immobile and stretched out, anointed with their creams and lotions for the evening and offered up to the night, the debate took a very different turn. In the summer they would often sleep nude. Pierre, for whom nudity in itself had nothing anonymous about it, was in the habit of saying, "We're going back to Adam and Eve. . . ." Tonight, with this new reserve and the apprehension that the ambiguous nature of the recent days had lent to things, Pierre had put on the pants to his pajamas and she was wearing shorts. "The offense is there," Pierre might have said, "Eve has discovered shorts. . . ." But despite this veil, the operation that consists in putting a man's head on your knees took on at this moment a very special intimacy. It really didn't seem right to ask a woman whose legs were uncovered, her belly and bosom bare, and coated with a thick layer of night and sleep and moonlight—for naturally the moon was mixed up in it—just why she had taken Frank's head on her knees. It seemed deceitful to talk about the incident at this hour. One might as well ask Edmée at this moment, when she felt her two hands like the dual slaves of chastity and pleasure, why she would give them in the street to men who were almost unknown, men who liked to squeeze them or lick them.

Let him get up, this clumsy husband! Let him get dressed! Let him put on whatever men need to get dressed, his trousers, his drawers, his suspenders, his garters, his pullovers of that spongy material, his vests, his jackets, including his fourteen pockets and his three handkerchiefs. He should let her get dressed too, and they could resume the debate over the head with their clothes on. Then he would see how silly it all was. Besides, if it meant that much to him, she wouldn't do it again, she wouldn't touch another. The best-groomed heads always leave a slight trace on dresses of delicate fabric. Even that of Frank. She was at the cleaner's with the dress of the other afternoon—at the cleaner who asked no less than four days to remove that tiny smudge which was the impression left by the lightest of men.

"What charm do you find in Frank?"

His head propped up on the bolster, one knee raised, his pelvis sheathed in light blue, Pierre had become one of those acrobatic family fathers who stretch out on their backs in the circus to toss their sons up in the air. Why did he only appear that way? How she would have preferred to see him juggling with his feet tonight! With what care she would have brought him the children gotten up as toads and set them down on his shinbones. Jacques would have been a little afraid. Claudie would have at last understood fathers. . . . And she, husbands. . . .

No such hope. He went on with it:

"Don't see him again. Or I shall have to speak to him."

With that, jealousy entered this bed for the first time. And yet it was Pierre who had always laughed at jealousy, made fun of the jealous. The last time he had brayed a bit like a donkey had been on reading that a jealous husband, suspecting that his wife had cheated on him with a prisoner, had spied on them by sticking his head through the iron bars and couldn't get it back out again. It was Pierre who, overflowing with irony, had taken Edmée to the aquarium to show her the famous pink fish. Bright pink, such a pink as gave him the right to reign alone over all the female fish, and who—when a young male was swimming among the females and gradually changed color from the white that he was to a pale rose—provoked him, faced him head on, and confronted him until he turned back to a dull white. . . . Let him get up, let him go confront Frank. Let him look Frank in the eye until Frank turned white again, and let there be an end to it! She asked only to remain faithful to the bright pink one. What more did he want? . . . She turned her back to him. . . .

"I love you, Edmée."

She loved him too. She loved him for his goodness, for his intelligence, for his braying. She loved him for a thousand, a hundred thousand reasons. But not one of them tonight could get her to tell him that she loved him. She didn't turn to face him. She held out a hand to him behind her back. He took it. . . . Since these beings had been living piecemeal, the head apart, for some time now, a single hand could suffice, a dead hand: for already the ants were at it.

On the morning of the next day she went out with Claudie. Truly, nothing announced what was about to happen. A breeze was blowing, but not one of those that carries you away. The sun was shining, but not one of those that burns right into you— rather one that ripens sensible fruit like pineapple or peaches. It wouldn't ripen anything in a woman. Nothing to buy, no errands to run. For the first time it happened that nothing needed doing concerning wardrobe, pantry, or desk. The gas was paid. The soles of Claudie's shoes were brand new. Not the slightest debt was owed humanity, or inside the house. She wasn't the least bit behind about anything. Equidistant from hunger and from mealtime, from birth and from death, Edmée found an hour that could be stolen from the sum total of all the hours, that did not belong to it, that did not have to be returned to it. That advance in time over others that is gained when a traveler going round the world starts out toward the east, she knew not what special favor in life was granting it to her today. The thing was not to waste it.

"Where can we go, Claudie, someplace we've never gone?"

"To Washington Park. . . ."

Claudie never hesitated. To all questions, even the most awkward, she had her answer ready. Always satisfied apparently, comfortable with everybody and everything, eating at any time, unconcerned about her clothes, she would respond, if one ventured to consult her, with astonishingly precise answers, which indicated that her choice was forever made concerning fruit or colors or the best places to take a honeymoon, about the jet black trimming for evening gowns, or about the relative value of the Dutch cut or the French cut for rubies, or about the need for the death penalty. Edmée sometimes found it frightening, and for nothing in the world would have questioned her about religion, about suicide, about the resurrection, or about her father. Claudie, who for three years now had let herself be taken to Central Park or to Builtmore Square, really had only one thing on her mind, and that was to go to Washington Park. This was the day.

Once there, a surprise awaited Edmée: the park was small, but it too seemed outside of time. The path for walking was narrow but imaginary. They first went through a grove of giant magnolias, whose flowers were small; then past dwarf camellias, whose flowers were huge; then came a wild area where cactus almost five feet high surrounded a lake, a real lake. The city had been built without paying any attention to the lake, and they had found it there one day, without any name, when even the smallest reservoirs had already been baptized. Nor did the park seem unknown either: all the little occupants, all the small shrubs from her father's garden at Montbrison were there, but had grown a hundred times larger, had now become sequoias and baobabs, and gave Edmée the impression, not that her youth was gone, but that she had grown a hundred times bigger. In a choice to be explained only by the perverseness of the landscape gardeners and a bit of competition they meant to offer the Creator, the avenues of flowering trees ended in a vista, the avenues of fruit trees all ended in an impasse, the avenue of banana trees ended at a statue of Pithecanthropus—absolute impasse—and the avenue of date trees led to a cemetery of rolling lawns with tombstones that went different ways, each one already leaning according to the pull of gravity of that world where its deceased now was. Edmée was alone with Claudie. What a happy inspiration to have chosen to come there the very moment when public gardens were of no purpose to humans! ... Alone with a raven or a finch. The moment when public parks were indispensable to birds. A swan even came along on foot, from some unknown pool, wandered about, pecking at the grass, nibbled at the remains of an apple, seemed to turn into a goose, then suddenly left, became invisible again, turned back into a swan.

Edmée had sat down on the bench that seemed the most free among all those free benches, beneath the tree that seemed the most rambling of all those trees. A great lookout mast rose up on her left, now with its own name tag, and quite beyond use, a beacon only to interior sailboats. Two cannons threatened a past long since out of range. Beds of plants, filled with high and ambitious flowers, were hemmed in by barbed wire or sentinel flowers that kept them from spilling over en masse, as their arrogance might lead one to fear, onto any humans that were passing by. That so much beauty and fragrance seemed contained and did not overpower you was very moving. ... A gothic tower crowned with a virgin projected above the palms; after a moment, one realized that it was the Virgin herself, rising above the palms. . . . An immense feeling of rest overcame Edmée. Not a rest from the day itself: she wouldn't have known what to do with it, she wasn't tired. But rest from an immense fatigue, that she herself had not yet suspected, that had accumulated over her with the years, from her childhood. A rest that softened the contrast between that Edmée so very fresh, ardent, born of the day itself, and that Edmée weighed down and bending beneath a burden she was not aware of.

There was no doubt: she was now on the only parcel of earth that was hers. The only feeling that these flowers, so public, municipal, and national, inspired in her about the world was a feeling of strange possession that she had experienced only when her children were still inside her, and Claudie, at the center of this park, was once more at the center of herself. She didn't stir. All the clocks of the city sounded ten o'clock, eleven o'clock, then noon, but at this prime moment today accorded to Edmée, there was no time, and she was unable to be in any way concerned. She had no fear on finally looking at her watch. She felt incapable of leaving this place. She couldn't make up her mind to get up. When Claudie came to sit down near her, tired from playing, intrigued by an indolence that she had never noticed in her mother, even more aware than Edmée of the distress that their absence would cause at home, Edmée was amazed at the words that came to her lips, for they were surprising, but she was even more amazed at the need for the phrase than of its monstrous side. . . .

"What if we stayed here?"

"For the rest of our lives?" said Claudie. "Oh, Mama, let's stay!"

"Go phone your brother first. He'll likely be very upset. Say simply that we're going to have lunch out."

"Quickly!" said Claudie.

Every word Claudie uttered had a meaning. "Quickly" meant that in a quarter of an hour it wasn't Jacques who would answer, but rather Pierre; Pierre would have returned, and what explanations would not be necessary with him!

"Quickly, then we'll go buy something to eat."

The little girl went into the telephone booth. She knew how to phone. She also knew what Edmée had never known, had never been able to do, if not today for the first time—how to free herself. In ten seconds she had overcome fraternal love, for at the other end of the line one could imagine a little Jacques who didn't understand and who was struggling to regain his usual lunch, his mother, his family. He talked about his father, but filial love was overcome in three words. The contest was uneven with the daughter that Edmée could see through the glass booth, so definite and merciless. The wire that connected her to the two men at home was truly only a wire. And she cut it. Then quite flushed from having canceled the father who was waiting, the son who was waiting, the husband, the lover who were going to have to wait, she calmly hung up the phone and carefully closed the door of the booth so as not to be held back by her family by so much as a hair or the tip end of a belt. Edmée mused that for the first time in her life she had before her five or six hours free, that she was free herself. . . .

They bought their food of freedom. Edmée expected that Claudie might charge for her services, that she might lay claim, in a natural kind of blackmail, to that which was normally denied her. She was mistaken. Claudie on the contrary was surprisingly undemanding. She passed up the crab salad and the whipped-cream dishes without a word. It led one to think that she too didn't count on being able to pay too much to be free. The first lunch of freedom was that of any escaped prisoner, of any explorer, of any soldier in war: bread, ham, and fruit. They had lunch on the bench in the bamboo grove, feeding the birds with their crumbs, except for one suspect who was there to watch them instead of eat, and who flew off during dessert for some distant engagement. They drank at the water fountain, American style. The water came out in a jet from the three mouths of three reclining heads. Claudie drank from the man's head, disdainfully, affecting not to see that it was a man who offered her this cool water, with no more gratitude, thought Edmée, for this mouth of a man in marble than she would have later on for the mouths of men who were not of stone. Edmée chose a gentle woman's head, almost her own head. She drank little. It seemed decidedly too much like a kiss.

A fir tree provided the shade for Claudie's nap. She went to sleep right away. She, who would struggle at home since she was one year old to escape taking her afternoon nap, laid her head against Edmée's shoulder and closed her eyes, opening them again for a second to reveal eyes that Edmée did not recognize—wider, older, and brighter—then went to sleep. Edmée, supporting this envelope of her child and this unknown person that it suddenly contained, wondered what this strange submission meant, an unruly Claudie now docile. What had the child understood, what was she trying to make clear by thus turning the obligations of her small life into spontaneous acts? What promise did she mean to make by refusing whipped cream, what sort of yes was she saying to her mother by saying no to lobster, by instinctively going to sleep on time? Her head rolled over onto Edmée's bosom. Very light too. Edmée began to question it, making up both questions and answers after her fashion.

"Do you know what we're doing here?"

"Of course. We're running away."

"Do you think we'll go back home?"

"We'll go back today. We'll leave another day."

"Why did you eat your ham?"

"For the first time in my life I wanted ham. Just a coincidence."

"Why did you go to sleep at the right time?"

"For the first time I felt like sleeping."

"And those eyes you showed me—where did you get them?"

"They're my spare eyes. Do you like them?"

"We're not supposed to have spare eyes. That's lying."

"Very good, Mama!"

"It sounds like you're saying that I have spare eyes too."

"Me? How could I say that? I'm asleep."

"Of course. But since I'm the one giving the questions and answers, you can tell me."

"You have spare eyes. The ones people never see. I see them often. You have a spare soul. You have a spare body. . . ."

With that, Claudie stretched, opened her eyes, and her real eyes appeared, with their color of steel blue, uncorrupted by either truth or lies.

"Let's go to work," she said.

And now it looked like work too had become a need for Claudie.

"Where are you now?"

"I'm in catechism, at the Creation. In reading, at italic script."

"Did you have class today?"

"It doesn't matter. I'll have class with you."

"What will you tell your teacher?"

"I'll tell her I had class with you."

This was consoling. In vain did circumstances, threats, or temptations crowd around Claudie—she never lied. It wasn't that she was incapable of lying: deep down Edmée thought she was false. But some force—Edmée didn't know if it was contempt or a superior form of lying—allowed her to tell only the truth. She declined to lie, like a girl who is noble, her senses already half awakened, turns down risqué books and naughty shows, not out of respect for decency but out of a higher idea of pleasure. Claudie had a higher concept of the lie. She held back the lie as she would hold back her virtue, for whatever or whomever should be worthy of it. Instinctively, she kept away from the first lie as from a first offense, not because it was a lie but because it was the first. Edmée had worried about this frankness, which created between them more difficulty than glossing over things or excuses. She asked only that all this frankness in Claudie should not itself, someday, turn into one enormous lie. The child lied only during her lessons. She would bring into the life of the Chevalier Bayard, of La Fayette, or of Christ episodes or remarks which could in no way be ascribed to the imagination but which were simply lies. To say that Jesus was left handed, that Lincoln had one red eye, that Bayard as a child had knocked down and trampled on a little girl—those were lies, nothing more. But today she introduced neither scandal, slander, nor errors of chronology into the Creation. She recited it without a mistake and in a straightforward way, or so at least judged Edmée, who was no longer any too clear about it all. She recited it in a low half voice.

A sailor had sat down at the other end of the bench and turned his ear to catch a few bits of the secret. For all around the child giving this recital, little by little the park had become peopled with a kind of chorus. Lunch was over; as an intermission, or as a practical exercise, the Creator was causing to march past those humans recently created, in an order whose secret seemed to belong to himself alone. Typists, Negroes, rheumatics, and patrons of the sparrows—all stirred about the lesson in a sort of ballet, some stately, some frenetic; then, when the factory sirens sounded, they disappeared, leaving here and there only a few scattered couples of talkative old ladies who would stop at nothing to bring to light the story of the Creation, as well as that sailor, who was no doubt waiting for the flood. The reading lesson was no less simple. On the labels for trees or plants, the park furnished their names in magnificent italics, in the very language in use when italic script was invented: *euphorbia splendens, opuntia semperviva.* Like a tree that produces resin, each tree appeared to secrete, at the height of a little girl, its very noblest name for Claudie, its name at Creation, its Latin name. . . . "Amen," she said when the lesson was over. There wasn't any arithmetic lesson, or geography lesson, but one sensed that the park had at its disposal secret multiplication tables, magic formulas, an equator, a magnetic pole. Just a sign, and a zebra would arrive for a riding lesson.

At five o'clock they went for a snack. Claudie drank her tea with perfect posture, without any need to warn her that she was going to become round shouldered. She finished her toast, without any need to make her fear that she might become a dwarf. For the first time she ate her snack like the sort of girl who will turn out to be slender, tall, capable, and, one could see by the way she juggled a cup, very clever. What was she aiming at by showing such perfection? To thank her mother? To embellish an adventure? Edmée was inclined to see in it a childlike instinct that both touched and alarmed her, a kind of responsibility for the nobility of this day, so different from the others. It meant not only "see what I am like on this unusual day" but also "see what I might be like in a new life . . . see how I obey, how I can juggle with cups, how good I am, how well I would understand in a new life." For already it was no longer a matter of a single holiday. The word had been passed to Claudie. She was an accomplice in this crime that was still not clear to Edmée herself. From having seen throughout the day the sort of person that her mother was—always up and about, ever active—now turn into this woman who was nonchalant, idle, and quite absorbed by the beauty of the birds and the black people, Claudie must have understood. Did not her perfection stem precisely from the fact that she had the advantage over this transformed mother? But transformed into what? How then was Claudie seeing her now? Where did this happiness come from that filled Edmée and that, so much more than the happiness of being free, resembled the happiness of being enslaved?

Being enslaved to everything and everybody. It wasn't because Claudie was her daughter that she obeyed Claudie, but because Claudie was a child. This stay in the park, it was submission to the magnolias, to the conifers. It was more—it was surrender. She gave up her arms, she didn't know which ones. A long siege had taken place, by she knew not what enemies, or rather what friends, and today she had capitulated! What she had given up to them, she still didn't know. But there was much reason to suspect that it was herself. All these objects and creatures that she had unconsciously refused to be familiar with up to now had become conquerors. They had rolled her in the gravel of the park, they had overcome her with the shade of the fir tree, with the shiver of the bamboo, and they had defeated her. The sun was part of it. The clouds were part of it: from now on things would be done according to their will. Pretty soon, when night had fallen, the moon would be part of it, and the stars—for the sun had also fought on their behalf. A young man from another table asked her for the sugar; she passed him the sugar not as a neighbor but as a servant. The sun had also fought for that young man. . . . Servant, yes! How noble the word *servant* seemed today! How close it was to the word *priestess!* . . . She was a servant of the parks, of Claudie, of the young man, of men themselves too. A servant consecrated to an unknown sacrament, but one as broad as the sacrament that called her to go home at this moment now seemed narrow.

Not that Pierre, whom she could see coming home early from the office, stamping about in ignorance and rage, was not to her a master, head of the house. . . . But he was too much of one. . . . My lord Pierre, your servant is weary. Don't hold it against her if for one afternoon she serves masters who are more unconscious. . . . If Pierre should suddenly turn into some savage chief with blue stripes on his cheeks, then she would smooth out the feathers of his headdress and the fur on his cape, rub his buffalo leggings with the palm of her hand, and trace the tattoos on his back with her own tongue. . . . Or perhaps Pierre would let her prostrate herself before him. She would be glad to wash Pierre's feet or anoint his thighs with scented oils. . . . That was her secret! That was why she loved—which Pierre had moreover quickly forbidden—to cut his hair herself, to remove the tiny blackheads on his face with a watch key, to give him shampoos, or rather one shampoo—Pierre had not authorized a second. With what ardor she had poured shampoo on his head, rubbing his scalp and hair with unleashed hands, having fun letting the foam get into his ears and nose a little, adding to the oil the first liquids that lay within reach, lavender or eyewash, concocting an infernal formula.

Yes, that day Pierre had been her lord and master. She had rubbed his head like that of an idol on the eve of a procession. Their club was giving a ball the next day; she had been very proud of that head washed by herself. She would pinch his ears when no one was looking, she would pull his hair, in an exclusive familiarity which depended only on Pierre's back, Pierre's neck, and Pierre's feet and to be rewarded like his head and receive the same loving washing. But the rest of Pierre's body had resisted these demands. He hadn't allowed her to give him a second shampoo. The servant for his head was once again Monsieur Julien, the French barber at the hotel. . . . And now Jacques was like his father. She felt that he was unhappy when she supervised his bath, in a house that feared Mary Magdalene and accepted only Mary. Poor loved ones! Still, she could hardly ask them to dress in kiwi feathers and have lunch in the nude! Yes, she had deceived Pierre the other day when Frank had put his head on her knees. There really had been a temptation, a desire to commit that sin, that indignity that Pierre disapproved of so much himself—to give Frank a shampoo! Why make such a fuss about it? A shampoo never does any harm.

"Where are we going now?"

"Why, back to the park," said Claudie.

That was what Claudie had understood: that there was no longer any home, any brother, any father, that there was no longer anything but a park.

They shouldn't have gone back. Habits that were stronger than any of those from their former life were waiting for them there. . . . "The first apartment where I really feel right, . . ." Edmée was thinking. "For the first two months of the rainy season we'll go to the hotel. . . . Not only where things suit me, but where they do everything for me, and everything in my size, from the heliotrope to the giant rubber plant. Everything there is what I love or appreciate. There is even a cemetery where they can transport me without having to put my body—my only phobia—in a freight elevator. . . ."

The sun was setting on Edmée in its color of victory. The petunia, the fuchsia, the daisies—flowers that were frugal during the day—hastened to spread the perfumes which they had been saving up to that minute and, alarmed, threw them overboard on entering the incorruptible night. A quarter of an hour's duet between the birds of the day and the birds of the night started things off, those American birds of night whose song contains a laugh, a flute, and four notes of the voice of the nightingale. Those four notes were quite enough for today. All the new masters of Edmée's twilight began to stir. Her master the wind, who liked to caress each leaf of her master the bamboo with a different caress. Her masters the shadows, still held in check by the electric street lamps. Her masters who were men too, in the flattering light of the setting sun, passing by in tints and hues that she knew very well to be false—purple, glowing yellow, and vermilion—but she affected to believe their definitive hues. They might well be so. Maybe all you had to do was paint them that way. . . . Alas, Pierre would never allow himself to be painted like that, with an emerald face, a reddish forehead, and golden hands. Nor would Jacques either, who had cried the day his mother had put a little rouge on him. . . .

There was no hope left except for Claudie. . . . Yes, she had the right attitude at Frank's place: she posed not as if Frank were painting her portrait but as if he were painting her herself. . . . What a sad life with skin the color of human skin! How was it that one single day of retreat, of absence, had been able to give her such an apprehension of creatures without colors, without tattoos? What had she come to? Was she going mad? In any case she wouldn't see Pierre tonight. Their dinner would be a sandwich. . . . They would go home when the others were in bed. . . . And besides, why go home at all? She didn't have the strength to go home. . . . Claudie had always wanted to spend a night at the hotel. . . . This was a good opportunity.

"Telephone Jacques, Claudie. Tell him that we've been detained. That we won't be home this evening. He mustn't think we've been kidnapped."

"All right," said Claudie. "But Father is the one who will answer."

"What does it matter?"

"Oh, it doesn't matter."

Edmée followed the dialogue from the door of the telephone booth.

"It's me," said Claudie.

From the receiver she could hear an exclamation, then a worried voice.

"We haven't been kidnapped," said Claudie.

The voice was shouting, furious.

"We'll be back tomorrow morning," continued Claudie.

The voice asked a question:

"Where are we? I don't know myself."

The voice implored.

"Without fail. The only thing I can tell you is that we'll be back without fail."

The voice. . . . But Claudie had hung up. That was all.

Why did it occur to Edmée to go spend the night at the Ambassadors? Why did all her new masters lead her to the hotel of the stars and their retinue? Why did she sense it the thing to follow the men of silence and the shadows, penetrating this haven of noise and light?

They arrived there without handbag, without luggage, not as at a hotel but as at the home of some host. They had a room with a large bed carved from a wood whose label gave its name: Nigerian cherry. Claudie caressed it. Never before had she caressed a tree indoors. From downstairs the distant sound of the orchestra reached them. They had come at the right time—it was a gala dinner. The maid told them that all the stars were there: Garbo, Claudette Colbert, Miriam Hopkins, Merle Oberon. . . . When one of them would arrive, the first clamor would reach them through the window, from the crowd below, and soon thereafter, depending on how long it took to check her furs, a second uproar from her peers and colleagues would reach them through the door to their room. Claudie ate her sandwich, then undressed. At the perfume shop downstairs, Edmée had bought soap and toothbrushes; she would have had to buy them even if they had slept in the park. She gave Claudie a bath. Her hair in ringlets, not quite dry, like God loves them, the little girl then said her prayers. But what a strange sense the words today had for Edmée. . . . "Our Father, who art in heaven," Claudie was saying, "thank you for this bread which is not daily. . . . Make of our life a life of repose, of tenderness, and of nonwork," Claudie went on. And it concluded, "Make me always happy and I will not be tempted. As for these stories of trespasses, they aren't very interesting. No one takes offense in life. Except the susceptible. Too bad for them. Thy will be done. . . ." But their room was over the orchestra, and the prayers had to give way to the music.

"Go down and see them," said Claudie.

For the first time the things that Claudie had imagined became reality. All those persons that her mother went to see at night above the twentieth floor at home, they were all there, together, downstairs on the main floor.

"Go down there with them, I'll be good."

Edmée went down. The banquet hall was open. From outside she could see the dinner. Claudie was right. They were the very friends who received her mother during her sleep—the happy of the earth. They were just about all there, boisterous, relaxed, familiar. One of them even motioned to her from far off, one of those no doubt with whom she had danced such a long time on the night of the pickles. She recognized all of them— Gable, Powell. "See, you don't know the names of great men," Pierre would have said, "and you know by heart the names of these actors. . . ." And to be sure, she did know them. And, sitting at a desk, where she pretended to be writing, a whole series of proper names came back to her, her own series, collected in her memory since childhood, the names of mediocre singers, mediocre painters, proprietors of mediocre establishments, names that didn't mean much, of no glamour, names that made you feel neither anxiety nor humility, but that urged you gently toward life—the name of the tenor Blomingham, whom she had heard sing in *Manon* at Forges-les-Eaux, of the painter Roulafeu, who had exhibited a red-headed harem girl at Vichy, of Maria Camaska, her neighbor in the hotel at Biarritz, who had two Afghan hounds. Were those then the saints and heroes of her own Gospel? They were, in any case, the ones she liked to meet, the ones she liked to see on the nights for pickles and those parties attended by way of the fire escape: her brothers, her cousins, her sisters. . . .

She had made a mistake tonight. She couldn't drink and

dance with them—she was wearing a suit instead of an evening gown. She went back upstairs. Claudie was asleep. Edmée took off her clothes—there was a moment when she was nude, and, in a pinch, that too might have made a suitable costume to rejoin the party below—but she lay down, and by means of a sleep that was new to her, reached an unconsciousness that was newer still.

# 4

Life had resumed in the house shaken by the storm. Pierre had not understood. He had not understood that there is a need for vacation, vacation from everything, even from the most patent conjugal love, even from happiness. That it is a fine day, that a wife might go out, that she finds it a fine day, that she might not return home that evening, this seemed to him inconceivable.

Pierre had not become an engineer by chance. He was truly one of those human beings who arrange the earth, who construct, who invent cellars and sewers, who think in floors and elevators. He had an innate horror of the nomadic life, and a sort of scorn for whatever may still exist of it in this sad world, such as the restaurant or camping. For him the hotel fell under the category of vagabondism. That his wife should have spent the night in a hotel when she had an apartment less than half a mile away seemed to him not far from madness; she might just as well have spent the night on a bench in the famous park. He had not questioned her when, the following day at breakfast, he had again found this new wife, who nevertheless very much resembled the old one.

He had kissed her on the forehead. . . . A good thing there are foreheads on human faces. . . . He had talked about the nice weather, about today's nice weather, which in a moment of secret panic struck him as very much like yesterday's nice weather. Because of the children he had been forced to appear to find it natural that their mother should stay out all night. The words seemed sordid, but how else to put it? Edmée might find other words for it, but not he. If staying out all night was ever to have its proper meaning, this was surely the time. This wife had fled her own bed. She had gone off and stretched out between sheets that had covered dozens of unknown men and women—bald heads, redheads, and, given the hotel in question, no doubt both at the same time. The home of which he was so proud, this house where there were no lies, no deceit, where he had thought to have all possible insulation against that cesspool that is the world, this untarnished home, his own wife, by means of this escape without escapade, had brought it down to the level of the usual ménage, to a ménage itself in short. She hadn't gone to spend the night at Frank's, but the household was none the purer. It was home and hearth that had had her escapade. . . .

Pierre had tried to tell himself that he was exaggerating, that in America an act of independence is easily explained, that Edmée's hands even on a camping trip had touched human hands less than in her own home, that Edmée's skin was pure, that Edmée, since she had not been his own companion that night, had gained a night in purity. Nothing worked. The home was sullied. He was eating his braised beef in a sullied home. For today was Saturday, the day when he insisted—so that his children should be nourished on French food, should have French taste buds—insisted on one of the dishes from his side of the family. This offering to the ancestors was usually carried out in the midst of exclamations, of enthusiasm, and wine was taken with the meal. But today the braised beef called only for water, like a plate of noodles.

Pierre wondered if he wouldn't have preferred it if Edmée hadn't returned the way she had, would have preferred her to pose conditions, to make complaints, would have preferred himself to concede or to pardon. The children would have understood. He too moreover. One day of disagreement doesn't take away the purity of a house. He was even at the point of wishing for one of those spats between ordinary couples that the tabloid press thrives on. Yes, she would have her fur coat. . . . Yes, they would go to Hawaii for their vacation. If Edmée had only demanded a car for herself, all the joy of her return would be there at this moment. The spat would even have left behind a son, a charming son: the little car whose make and color they would be debating over lunch right now.

But what were the children to make of the fact that their mother had suddenly become a stranger to the house, that she should forget that they took lunch, dinner, and slept there? Above all, what was one to make of the very naturalness of her manner toward him, the way she seemed to consider with apparent satisfaction this sudden abandonment of a duty, the highest duty: to be constant and steadfast? That a wife may deceive her husband concerns the two of them, and concerns only them. But for her to deceive the entire house extends the wrong to everyone. Jacques's eyes were very informative in this respect. The eyes of a little Latin, a little Roman, lighted by a civilization where a wife who returns home in the morning is punished by death without explanation. Now they were full of fear, fear that this death penalty might really be applied. And shame too; his father and mother were no longer models. It was awful.

For the first time little Jacques was having lunch between parents who were given to the ills that afflict other parents: to compromising, not paying attention, to fault and blame. A dreadful resemblance between his parents and the parents of his schoolmates appeared today. It was the first step down. His parents were like the ones his friends would sometimes talk about in class and as they left school, fathers of easy morals, mothers too often absent. The original sin of children, which is to be born of parents who are not models of the world—he had it. Braised beef is a heavy dish when your parents have just lost their crown. Only Claudie asked for more, but of course there was no reason, thought Pierre, for it to have lost its taste for her. She was the one who stood to gain everything in this scandal. She had become their equal. Through the part she had taken in the escapade, a sinister advantage redounded to her. An advantage that her father, she was certain to think, could not help but hold against her. She looked at him for the first time with a kind of fear, as if in this calm house where no one lifted a hand against anyone, they were about to come to blows. She was getting ready for it. As Pierre abruptly raised his arm to pick up the carafe, she protected her face. Whoever, during that awful night, had taught Claudie that fathers strike their daughters in the face? A fear full of contempt. There was arrogance in that very fear. It wasn't from Claudie that one would hide that there had been deception on the part of her mother, and that he was forced to admit it and accept it in front of the children. The truth for Claudie was that he was a husband who turned a blind eye when it came to Washington Park, and that hotel, and that bed where Edmée had slept with Claudie. Yes, that's the way Claudie was, that's what Claudie was thinking. Her mother had deceived Pierre, had deceived the house with Claudie herself. . . .

"I know why it isn't as good as usual," said Edmée. "I forgot to put in a spoon of olive oil."

It was all clear. Not a spoon of olive oil. Pierre had recognized the mistake: a spoon of pure bile.

"Do you know your lessons, Jacques? Do you want me to go over them with you?"

"Oh no, Father. I know them."

Poor Jacques! It was surely the first time that he felt that lessons were not made to be repeated but rather to be kept deep down inside himself. The lesson today was the hundred days of Napoleon's return and Waterloo. Yesterday he would have pressed Pierre to question him, in his fervor not to admit defeat, certain that his father would be able to show that Waterloo had been a victory, better than a victory, the mere defeat of one day in the mud and cobblestones of Belgium, the supreme moment in the camp of the archangels. Pierre had the ability to perform these transformations for his son. Whether Agincourt, Malplaquet, Trafalgar, or Sedan, he would find a way to remove any suggestion of panic, of a rout, or of any error on the part of the general staff. Or it was just a question of mercenaries fighting amongst themselves, and the honor of the country was not at stake. Or the enemies had had recourse to an act of treachery, and the disgrace fell on them. Or that the death of Nelson was for England the worst of defeats. Or even if a military defeat, the combat turned out to be a civil victory. All those names became no longer infamous, but rather religious and sacred, like the names of feast days in the calendar when one must fast. Any other day with what rapidity he would have given little Jacques for his class recitation a Waterloo that was all new and shiny, a Waterloo that made Blücher look ridiculous and from which Wellington himself—a lot of merit there was in waiting an hour for reinforcements, at Sidi-Brahim a section of cavalry had waited for them for twenty-eight days!—from which Wellington himself had little cause for pride.

But today Jacques would have nothing to do with such doctoring of history. On the contrary, he felt a sadness inside that moved him, not to mitigate Waterloo, but to make of it the supreme defeat. We had lost everything at Waterloo, save for that honor we were to lose at Metz. There was even on the part of names once deemed to have a certain luster, such as Austerlitz or the Marne, a sinister tendency to pass over to the side of the disasters. Pierre wondered what that sad smile on Jacques's lips could mean. It was that this little schoolboy understood for the first time the meaning of disaster, panic, and capitulation. . . . This afternoon he would tell the story of Waterloo the way it had to be told: the French army had been badly beaten there. And beaten himself for the first time, he got up from the table, and, as one defeated, he embraced his father and mother. He didn't embrace Claudie—there was triumph on her face. . . .

Fortunately no one questioned him. You question the little Englishman, who lights up and, beaming, never stops talking. . . . Poor little English, who believe in victory!

That afternoon at the office was hard for Pierre. Not that it was really any different from the others. On the contrary. All those operations to which he felt so passionately bound—the drilling of oil fields, siphoning oil at sea, putting out oil wells that had been burning for centuries—today they were still giving up their secrets and revealing their patterns. And yet they were no longer the same. He was concerned with them, he discussed them with both subordinates and chiefs, but they were dull; they were like the braised beef, without taste. Edmée had forgotten to pour her teaspoon of olive oil into the oil deposits of the world. Prospecting, siphonage, and the business end of things didn't give him that euphoria, that general feeling of ease which allowed him to separate his profession from his life. What was his life up to now? An abundant flow of petroleum beneath a sun that was the happiness of his marriage. But today, on one side there was Edmée, and on the other there was all the rest.

Yes, that was it. Instead of being its creative spirit and its motor, Edmée, by means of her little spree the evening before, had released from her person everything that was not herself. That Edmée, who in this office presided over the drilling, over the pumping and flooding, that Edmée was no more. She had not broken with Pierre, but rather with everything that was Pierre's very life. The oil wells, the bridges, and the fiery towers were without Edmée. The watermarks of the graphics were without Edmée. It was with them that Edmée had broken. Therein lay the divorce, therein lay the division of property that her flight was bringing about: she would no longer have anything to do with all those objects and those creatures that she had perhaps never seen, but which Pierre for eleven years now had connected to her. She had undressed away from home, and she had undone everything. The thought of Edmée that permeated his work, that love of Edmée instilled in every minute of labor, every drum of oil, every underground deposit, every word dictated to the typists—it was all withdrawn forever. What odd creatures they were, those typists, since Edmée had evaporated from the scene! Miss Lily Smith, with her eyes of faience, the long fingers of Miss Smith, which she managed to cross between every word that was dictated, for she had been told that she had the hands of a Pre-Raphaelite; the heart-shaped lips of Miss Robinson and their shadow of mustache, the hands of Miss Robinson, which she would hide after every word dictated because the thumb was splayed—what curious, animallike creatures they were since Edmée had been exorcised from the scene! . . . Not that there was any question of no longer loving Edmée. But it was clear that the same soul would no longer be able to serve everything. This whole marvelous achievement that he was so proud of, this unity of life, action, and love, he would have to get along without it—it didn't exist anymore. Two souls were going to be necessary now, one for the use of Edmée and another for all the others. There would no longer be one happy soul for all, noble for all, but a first soul for the business, for his work, happy and noble, and, for Edmée, a second soul where Pierre already sensed that, along with suffering, compromise and unworthiness were going to find a place. This is what was happening to him in that office where each colleague who came in thought to find the Pierre of yesterday, master of his life, at one with his life. The colleague found instead, separated forever, the soul of petroleum and the soul of Edmée. It would be rare luck indeed if the second soul should not one day corrupt the other. And, as he was thinking about Jacques, about Claudie, and he didn't see them either, dissolved as usual and diffused throughout his work, he wondered if it wasn't going to take a soul for Jacques and a soul for Claudie. It was definitely going to take a new one in order to dictate the correspondence to Miss Robinson. . . . That's where pride leads, where the desire to have one single soul, one great soul will lead: to all this parceling out!

"Don't exaggerate," said a voice inside him. "You exaggerate."

"Me, exaggerate?"

There he was talking to himself now. What people call

talking by yourself, and which happens, on the contrary, only when a man's been cut in two. New proof that there were two voices there where formerly there was no talking at all, where everything operated by reflex and without discussion. In those few minutes each one of the two souls had already found its voice. Yes, the duets were going to start between the Pierre who was unhappy, bitter, and suspicious and the Pierre who would pretend that nothing had happened and consider of no importance the absence of his wife, the Pierre who would appreciate next Saturday the omelet fixed country style and who would again take, when the cycle of family dishes brought it back to the table, his part of the braised beef. For that one, yes, of no importance. But the other one knew very well what that escapade and that return resembled—like the act of a woman who had gone off to put her bonds and jewels in a safe place. If Edmée had carried off some treasure from the house before a divorce, if she had stolen and put the treasure of the house into the hands of those who receive stolen goods, she wouldn't have shown any different face on her return home. How wrong he had been to let this dubious state of affairs be prolonged at all with the children! He should have taken her in his arms and said to her, "You were quite right to get out of the house a bit. You're going to sleep better tonight, . . ." then kissed her, and in such a way as to tell her that her running away was everything, and yet nothing, that he had believed everything, feared everything, but that he now believed and feared nothing. And to tell her, herself, when it came time to go to bed—offering her his humility, not continuing to believe that he was the ideal husband because he, had he been a woman, would have married only himself—that he could understand that she might grow weary for a moment of this domestic life, of the long days, of all these domesticated objects, and since the bed was right there, that she had, after all, been right to look for an undomesticated bed for one night. The one in the house had become a sort of chest, a buffet table, a pack bed. . . . That she might have wanted to get back to a real bed, new, not to be trusted and hard to manage—it was very understandable. A hotel bed, that was the kind of bed you couldn't

tame. The one here really smacked too much of the family. . . .
So passed the afternoon, between the two busts—deprived each
second of an arm of Miss Smith or Miss Robinson—an afternoon spent in a struggle against an undomesticated bed.

And so he found himself again that evening, at bedtime, in
the chest bed. As usual, he was the first to take his bath, the first
to bed. All the other nights he would be reading his paper. With
his elbows on the pillows, there on his marital platform, he
would let the exploits, rumors, and cataclysms of the world
unfurl like a harmless swell in the sea, at the foot of this plateau
where he was invulnerable. He who was without vice, without
sin, faithful to the most faithful, happy with the happiest, and
ready to receive—he never took a tisane—the homage of that
humanity where a husband puts the foot of his wealthy wife in
a box full of cobras, where the vice president of the stock exchange goes to Sing Sing, and where mothers kill their seven
children because they saw their husband kiss a loose woman.
The news of fires, of a crash on the stock market, of death in
Hollywood, with his left hand massaging lightly his left knee
where he was beginning to feel a touch of rheumatism, he would
read them with sympathy, affable about the murders, indulgent
about the floods, with the godlike nature of those who read a
letter that has gone to the wrong address. All the more so as his
reading was punctuated by successive apparitions of an Edmée
ever nearer to the night and to love. Fire devastated Atlanta, and
Edmée appeared already in her dressing gown. Jean Harlow was
dying, and Edmée went by with her hair unpinned. A struggle
had begun about concessions over Shanghai, and this time her
feet were bare. At last the moment came when he had to put the
papers aside, to exchange all the news of the world, and the
world itself, for Edmée in her pajamas. She took her place beside
him, sitting up also, sharing for a moment his royalty. He himself felt generous, kind. She was fresh, ardent. Their apartment
was an apartment of pardon to humanity, to the universe. The
rheumatism was cured, the hands of kings cure rheumatism. He
put out the lamp. He forgave the world for being the world, for
being cowardly, for not wanting to suffer. Sometimes Claudie

was born there between the two of them, and he had to turn the light back on—was born before he could touch Edmée, before he could give her a kiss. Sometimes Edmée would escape, for her voyage of exploration in the kitchen, so as to tidy up something that had been put off for years but was urgent that night. She would come back lighter, more gentle, her waist more supple, her breasts more distinct: his wife had changed into a woman.

But this evening, no newspaper, no royalty. He had read nothing, and he had stretched out right away. His head alone stuck out of the bed, and never had there been so little question for her of a crown. It was a bed high on legs. As an enemy of no- mads, Pierre admitted neither the sofa that turns into a bed nor the bed that folds up out of the way. What had he run across today that this bed resembled? What sort of apparatus had he seen a picture of in the papers? Now he recalled: the sort of apparatus you set up and tuck people into whose lungs are par- alyzed and who can't breathe without its pressure. He was breathing himself not without effort. He had closed his eyes. He wouldn't reopen them. It was the first time that Edmée had un- dressed without her husband's eyes being open. Did she know that she was invisible, that she had for the first time a separate bedroom? The apparatus was a good one. Pierre inhaled. . . . He exhaled. But without seeing her, he was observing Edmée, he heard her, he followed her in her itinerary, in her ritual: he rec- ognized, by the sounds that only a husband of ten years can recognize, each little bottle, each tube; he sensed, by a lightness, though almost unrelated to her weight, the progress of her un- dressing. And even though it might have taken the same time, and this ballet, this dance might have included the same steps, the same long delays as the other evenings, that was what seemed to him so heavy. The sounds of Edmée getting ready for bed he had believed to be the murmur of fidelity, the echo of joy, the sounds of their union, and, doubtless, if one judged by tonight, it was only the comings and goings of a wife who is getting ready for bed. . . . This straying off to the pantry, these inexplicable stops at a window or in an armchair, these sudden and complete disappearances of an Edmée on her way to bed were not merely the preparations for a blissful night, were not what he called her night hunting, but simply the stages and routines of the end of a day.

For, if not, Edmée this evening should have torn off her dress without unbuttoning it, not undone her hair nor taken off her stockings, but rushed ahead, as had he, in that false race toward sleep which provided for each of them the only possible impetus to reach the other. He would have forgotten everything in finding an Edmée who had run away and was regained before she could put back on the makeup of the nice and reasonable Edmée. All day long she had had on that color of rebellion, that scent of something foreign. There could be no question about it. . . . Her night at the hotel could have continued here, the Edmée who had run away could have been the one who had returned, the poor bed, both ridiculous and presumptuous, could have become the untamable bed, if she hadn't begun to undress in this way as if following a timetable. And everything she was doing right now to her body and her face was against herself and against him. . . .

He recognized this silence among silences: it was her silence when she was looking at herself in the mirror. Once, each night, there was this halt: sitting at her dressing table, Edmée looked at herself. For her it was the critical moment of the whole day: someone, who was not herself, considered Edmée at length, very close, got right up to the glass to get a better look at the eyes, the lips, the eyelashes of Edmée, the eyeteeth of Edmée, so distinctly eyeteeth, so as to see deep down in Edmée, the surface of Edmée, now drawing back so as to see only the archetype of Edmée, and this someone was Edmée herself. She was looking at herself just to check, he used to think, so as to be only Edmée, to bring to him presently only herself. Just the opposite of Psyche. . . . Sure of Pierre, of that rock, of that paragon of the stable and faithful, she would verify her own reflections in this glass, would assemble them in this mirror. She saw herself as glowing, and when the glow seemed true, she was ready to plunge into the night. She lighted up a truth, which was the face of Edmée. On this body that the fatigue of a day was already dissolving and melting, she would attach this precise face. It was the grace of this first stage of sleep: he would receive love, and the head of Edmée.

But today, what was she doing? What could she be doing, if not looking at this stranger, whom she knew only from yesterday, who had run away, who had gone to bed alone, who had not gone to bed with the king, Pierre, propped up on his elbows there in bed . . . and trying to find out her secret. That's what this silence was: the confrontation of the two Edmées, drawing lots as to which one was going to come sleep with this man, which both of them, moreover, by a common mistake, thought to be the same as the evening before, intact and unalterable. Which one would win? The old Edmée, whose gentleness, weakness, and consent would henceforth be hypocritical? The new Edmée, with this tenacity, this unknown life, these evasive acts, this passion perhaps? He waited, anxiously. All his former love, his devotion, his pity, were prepared for the old one; and, if it were the new one, then so be it. He accepted what he foresaw now in a sort of frenzy. For it seemed to him that he could never imagine, after her retreat the evening before in that park, after her solitary sleep with her little girl at her side, that Edmée would not have brought back forevermore both passion and abandon. That was the alternative that faced him, as the prize of honor for a perfect life, as recompense for his admiration of Edmée, he had to choose between all the women that he had made of her: to keep the old Edmée in duplicity and ambiguity, or to accept the new one in an act of betrayal, betrayal of the children and of those habits that were more precious than life. He waited, guilty, ashamed of feeling this evening, instead of that Pierre so complete who usually stretched out to go to sleep, only part of a Pierre who he didn't suspect the evening before and who was already familiar to him, a Pierre of capitulation, of anguish and desire.

One is always mistaken in this sort of calculation. Edmée came to bed very sweetly, sat down for a moment beside him, embraced him, and asked his pardon for the pain that she had caused. From her night with the demon, she retained no sign, in any case no memory. He was amazed to discover, both disappointed and relieved, that he expected her to be rough, crude, brazen. She seemed to him on the contrary more fragile, more open to a set of ills to which he would never have believed her vulnerable—insults, ugliness, death. She came to bed as if to a refuge. She had everything that provokes ugliness and death: glowing color—one of her knees provoked the worst insult— beauty, and life. And that he might be able to keep these threats away from her forever for the first time he was led to doubt. If he could manage just this one night to get her to the next day intact, to get her to the dawn alive, was all that he could ask.

The whole night he kept watch. There was an alarm. Disguised as Claudie, those who wanted to give Edmée white hair, loose teeth, and tough skin tried to penetrate the bed by way of the alley. It was necessary to accept their convention, take them by Claudie's hand, lead them back to Claudie's bed, and threaten Claudie with having to go a week without dessert. Heaven knows whether it had any effect on them, but bound to their disguise, they had to obey. It was necessary to comfort Jacques, who couldn't sleep either, who, instead of being tucked in and snuggled up, was lying in bed almost nude, showing arms that looked a little thin and a chest that seemed to stick out a bit, and who, so as to keep watch over his mother, had assumed the most touching appearance of Jacques. . . . The two of them were enough. By daylight, Edmée was still there, without a wrinkle, not a smudge on her face, and the long night that had just passed even seemed deducted from her age.

The house was not set right. The alarm had been too real. Every night Edmée seemed willing to rely on the guardian who wards off all harm, but the guardian was not sure of her unless she was there beside him, clothes removed, as with prisoners who cannot be freed on their word. At night Pierre felt less uneasy: Edmée could only have run away with no clothes on, and that was unlikely. At least it appeared unlikely. But during the day it was another story. About Edmée, he could guess nothing, it seemed there was nothing to guess; she didn't stray from that same obedient sweetness from before her flight that he had so long believed to be her transparency. Perhaps his uneasiness would have weakened without the presence of Claudie. With her it was hard to rest easy. He couldn't remove the thought that this little girl was unconsciously the reflection of her mother, that she would announce moves before they came from her mother. With sidelong glances, and sometimes directly in the face, he would scrutinize her as a witness of the life of Edmée, or like those mirrors of German sorcerers in which they follow the changes of a world that for others is immutable or inaccessible. At times Claudie was calm and serene; she would be laughing and lift her forehead for a kiss from her father, without emotion but without embarrassment: Pierre would then leave confidently for the office. But another time her apprehension of the kiss was so marked, her voice so penetrating, her good-bye so distracted and at the same time satisfied, that he began to be afraid all over again. He surprised himself examining Claudie's homework and the way she dressed as barometers, as indications. Claudie would intersperse her dictation and written work with personal remarks; he would read her notebooks on the sly, fearful of finding phrases like this: "That's the last subtraction that my father will ever make me do. . . . There will not be another dictation in this house on the cow. . . ."

If not today, then tomorrow? There was one of Claudie's dresses that he couldn't see on her without anxiety, a little Scotch plaid which it was so easy to imagine the child dressed in, in a car, in a train, sitting on a trunk, in an empty hotel room, a little girl's dress for a mother who is running away. He left for the office defeated when Claudie had that one laid out to put on. A Scotch plaid so easy to imagine unbuttoned down the back, the little girl asleep almost upright in a Pullman, and just like the ones those little girls have on whom a tall, mustachioed stranger takes in his arms at the station and kisses, not daring to kiss the mother, who knows nevertheless whom that kiss is for and who smiles looking straight ahead. By adding to the picture a linden tree in bloom and a tilbury, on the folding seat of which the Scotch plaid was sitting, Pierre would arrive without hindrance at the depths of unhappiness. He had to stop himself not to hide the tam-o'-shanter that went with the dress. Edmée was still in bed, leisurely taking her coffee, but she might be like those women who jump out of bed as soon as the husband is gone, since the little Scotch plaid was laid out ready. Still, you couldn't hope for Claudie to be sick, for her to come down with a pain in the hip. . . . He left. . . . If a big wind was blowing when he got down to the street, he sensed upstairs an Edmée lighter still. . . .

Jacques had always been back home for a long time when Pierre returned. As soon as class was out, the child would rush to get on the bus which, without any discernment moreover, would bring the children home. It was a bus that made detours without any reason, that gave priority to a child whose mother was a sort of newsstand that couldn't move, or a pharmacist who couldn't leave her pharmacy, to Phil too, whose mother was dead. Any mothers who bore some impossible burden or who were ugly were delivered their sons before Jacques was delivered to Edmée. Under a pretext, he had swapped his seat at the back of the bus, so hard to obtain, for a seat near the exit; a child of eight, during the Civil War, had jumped off a train in flames, so he too could jump off a bus, even when running, if he caught sight of a certain woman or a certain little girl in the street.

It happened in fact that one time he thought he recognized a hat and a dress; the bus was going too fast and he didn't dare jump. He returned home humiliated by his fear, and it was his mother herself who opened the door. It was as if she had come back for him faster than the fastest car. As if, even in case she left home again one day, she would come back to welcome him faster than any bus, than any plane. Then, reassured, he would go off to work in his father's office, assuming an air of the most complete calm, as if it mattered very little whether his mother or all the mothers in the world were there or weren't there, opened or didn't open the door to you, sang "Mon enfant, ma soeur" in the dining room or didn't sing it on the other side of the world, came to lean tenderly over your head to see how your home-work was coming along, or stood stiff and indifferent over a map of the coast of New Zealand (capital, Wellington and not Auck-land). Then, with his written work done, he would go to study his history lesson in the drawing room, with the door open to the room where his mother was finishing her check of how the table was set, with his legs crossed in false indifference, his col-lar unbuttoned, a shoelace half untied, just as if mothers setting the table never left home, as if putting out the mustard, the sugar bowl, and the vinegar cruet were an operation that would stop them when the idea of leaving struck them and made them for-get a husband or son, a son already quite bored with the Restoration and Wellington. (Wellington again! Was it going to turn up also in biology?)

He had read the evening before that good dogs were those who stretch out with their paws crossed, because the bad ones, with their paws uncrossed, can thus spring immediately on their prey; he looked at his legs crossed and his knees loaded down with books with some shame: he was a good child, he was the son who can't spring immediately after his mother when she runs away. Sometimes his mother would touch him as she passed by, would stop and embrace him. Tense, he received every kiss like a last kiss. There was not one gesture, one touch of endear-ment of his mother that might not be understood as the last, that might not appear in itself as something final, that might not be a good-bye. He was getting thin. It is hard for a child of twelve every day to have his last lunch, his last dinner, to go to bed for the last time as a nonorphan of his mother. Was he looking poor-ly? So much the better. He could make use of it. He lied one day, complained of having a headache. "No, no, surely not!" said Edmée. "What's that you're telling? Your head is perfectly cool! . . ." As if his mother understood that he could never be sick and meant to remain completely free to leave, without the measles or typhoid fever ever getting in the way. She had taken in her hands that head where Jacques felt a volcano and that managed only to remain cool; she had given it a kiss and looked at it. "How much like your father you look!" she had said, and his heart had skipped a beat.

He had had the feeling that to be like his father at this moment was maybe not the best remedy, that the face of his father, that two, that twenty faces of his father were not exactly what would hold back his mother when the day had come. That if he had looked like no one it might have been a lot better. That if he had looked like that heroic little drummer boy, or like the brother that Mother had lost when he was so young, too young—when you're twelve you can't look like an uncle who died at three—maybe that could have helped him out. Mr. Florey, from Metro Goldwin, had said one day at dinner that he looked like an angel from Chartres Cathedral, the one with a band over his eyes. He felt like putting a band over his eyes, but keeping a watch over your mother with your eyes banded doesn't help out with the problem. In his distress and pain there entered no resentment. It didn't occur to him to judge or to accuse his mother. He feared that she might leave again, but it was as if she weren't responsible for it, as if she were under a spell. She was the most beautiful, the best of mothers, but she was of an element which, without one's knowing why, becomes diverted, is made volatile. There was a name, it seemed, in chemistry or physics, used to designate metals that have a tendency to change nature suddenly. He borrowed the textbook of an older student. Nobody at school suspected that it was to find out the name of the metal his mother was made of.

Like Pierre, he clung to the presence of Claudie, a presence which seemed however to defy him. Claudie had over him, since the escape, a sort of right of the elder, a superiority that she rendered suspicious by her very bearing, as if that day she had seen things beyond her age. She had told him nothing about her night at the Ambassadors. But if, in the course of that night at the Ambassadors, a little girl of nine had approached all those mysteries about which Jacques, in his modesty, didn't even dare think, Claudie would not have acted in any other way. She would have assumed that same vanity, she wouldn't have answered the simplest questions about her lessons or her classmates, as if she were no longer free to use, for the most natural things, anything other than a forbidden language; in this way would she have cared for her nails and hair, whereas before she had been rather careless. Jacques could no longer get her out of the bathroom, where, for the first time, she would shut herself in and lock the door, and, when he threatened to break the lock, instead of opening the door to him in the briefest attire, she would appear wrapped up to the neck in a dressing gown, and, if in her haste her knee was exposed, she would turn her head away. This affectation of having returned from some forbidden country irritated Jacques. He felt like telling her: "Stop putting on such an act! You've spent the night in a hotel with traveling salesmen and the delegates to a convention of the Masonic lodges of California. That's no reason to powder and perfume yourself for life. . . ." He didn't dare. He realized that it wasn't true. His little sister had spent the night with every freedom, with all manner of daring, with adventure itself.

In the little bedroom where she had been put since last spring, next to that of Jacques, she also wanted to lock herself in at night. Jacques had stolen the key, and as soon as Claudie was asleep, he would get up and open the door a bit. For him, as for his father, she was the witness, the pledge. As long as she was in there snoring, for she snored slightly—he would tell her so tomorrow, that would get her off her high horse—he knew there was nothing to be afraid of. She slept without a smile, seriously, without the sheet showing one wrinkle. Whereas the bed of poor Jacques, so straight and meticulous in life, was by morning a disorderly bed, a field of battle; Claudie, who by day was negligence and disorder itself, seemed not to have touched her pillow, and her coverlet was as tight and neat as it was when she had been put to bed. She did not give herself up to the night as did Jacques—who before falling asleep would go over his lessons, his long days, his past life, who liked to imagine and act out his future life, bring to a victorious end the conquests of both

Alexander and Napoleon, pursue the career of heroes who had died too young, and really execute the only thing that one can do in a bed: dive like a submarine, and then during sleep, dream nonstop—no, with Claudie it was more like giving herself up to a Frigidaire entrusted with conserving her until morning, without adding another minute of age, and without any further change in her thought either. Thus both durable and permanent, she seemed to Jacques less a little sister than a sort of hostage charged with linking him to a forbidden world.

Kinship with that little red mouth, those little hands, and those blond curls was for him the tie to a whole order of events and beings from which he thought himself removed, with that which in life knows its lessons poorly, with that which lies while saying words that are true, with that which seems selfish even in the act of giving, without seeming to value any of it (that was Claudie's way), its pen, its Erector Set, its part of the tart; also with that which is unstable, that which gives away its house, its own room, its family, perhaps with that which gives away its mother. . . . Oh yes! Maybe he wasn't ready, but his sister surely was: with her legs uncrossed and so distinct, her arms stretched out! He wouldn't go to sleep. . . . He would watch her all night long. . . .

A loud cry woke him up. It was broad daylight. Claudie was calling for her sandals. She watched her brother bring them out from way back under his bed and toss them to her, without understanding. . . . Without seeming to understand. . . . That was exactly the kind of honesty, the kind of sincerity she would have feigned in her lack of understanding if she really had understood.

So, that was where she had spent her day! This then was the famous park! It was for this that Edmée had exchanged the house that it had taken thirteen years to build and the world that had taken a thousand. . . . Pierre had not been able to keep himself from coming to see it, as he would have gone to see Frank if Edmée had taken refuge at Frank's place. Seated on a bench, the bench that seemed to him to have been that of Edmée, an explanation was what he asked of this happy rival. And the other responded. Pierre sensed a general response in the form of beautiful weather and laziness, and a hundred detailed responses in the form of the trees and the flower beds. A bed of purple and yellow flowers even monopolized the answer. It was all you could see, you couldn't hear yourself think. But Pierre didn't understand. He was expecting to see a vast park, a certain nobility, a sense of distance, and through every branch you caught sight of advertisements from the street or from windows. . . . He thought that Edmée had been seduced by some promontory above the city, some spur of land above the world of men, and all he saw was a public park, just an anonymous public park.

She had deceived him with an anonymous public park. This place that had made her giddy, in order to excuse Edmée, he sought to embellish with California's most beautiful redwoods, with slopes covered in rhododendron, but it was in fact, if there were nannies in the United States, a simple park for nannies. Flowers of course, but, if one may use such a word with flowers, vulgar flowers. Not that aristocracy of flowers which Pierre might have accepted as a frame for the image of Edmée, no roses, no lilies, no peonies; a host instead, an anonymous host, it too of creeping, climbing, rippling flowers that seemed to flourish, not by special attention of the Creator, but by a fatal proliferation of the plants, and also out of the satisfaction, rather cheap, of being in a public park. Out of the question of entering with them that symbolic domain to which the least rose could lead Pierre. They didn't speak a language of the flowers, but that of sterile vegetables, vegetables meant for the eyes. They did not say to make haste and enjoy the day: they were hearty perennials without the slightest wish to be found dead the following day, like the magnolia blooms fixed there on their branches with the nails of the Passion; they were arrayed on the trees without

the appearance of ever needing to make way for any fruit. There
was really no moral at all to be drawn from this mistaken apartment of Claudie. The few monuments and statues were also
banal: an Indian, holding a little bear in each hand, dancing a sort
of saltarello, a bronze bust of Mr. Joshua Hall, with a goatee and
décolleté. . . . You could see the nipples on his chest. It wasn't
that Greek statues could have excused Edmée, but at least they
might have raised the pain of Pierre to a level where he sensed
very well that she was not present. Since it was a question of
deception with objects, trees, and statues, one had to recognize
that she hadn't deceived him with accessories of the highest
quality. As for himself, if ever an attack of madness or nostalgia
were to lead him astray, one would be able to find him high
above the far end of Corfu, at the corner of the Parthenon, or in
front of the great door of Chartres. One would find Edmée in a
small park, furnished with this bronze bust and this dancing Indian, which would also furnish the mantelpieces and serve as
bric-a-brac for bachelor flats rented by the week. . . . Pierre understood that you might conceivably come here to find your
watch or a toy that belonged to your daughter, but not really in
order to rediscover your true life. . . . The cemetery itself—no
one great buried there—wedged between bottling plants and the
Kodak warehouses, gave a sorry idea of death, no elbow room
for it or its relations. . . .

Suddenly he stood still. That young woman who was wan-
dering through the park, about the same size and age as
Edmée—was she going to give him the solution? Less beautiful,
but with a sweet look, along these byways that barely criss-
crossed, she nevertheless found a secret path, invisible and
treacherous, a path for a labyrinth. Surely it would be enough to
keep an eye on her to the very end in order to keep an eye on, in
order to understand, Edmée. One couldn't have wished for a
more perfect reconstruction of the crime: Edmée had barely
looked at the people passing by, Edmée did not smile once at the
sight of the nipples of Mr. Joshua Hall. Edmée had rubbed with
her glove the bark of that tree on which an orange tag, the one

for poisons, indicated that it was toxic and that it was dangerous to touch it with your finger. . . . Claudie had probably gone even closer to it and touched it with her tongue. . . .

If one were to lend complete faith to this reconstruction, Edmée had at last sat down, put her handbag beside her, and, with hands crossed, legs crossed, and a sort of smile on her face, had lost all notion of time and hour. The young woman wasn't reading, and appeared to be waiting for no one. Despite all evidence that she was coming for the first time to this park, she was being treated as a regular, the gardener greeted her, and the man watering the plants began the same conversation with her that he had perhaps started with Edmée. The flight of the birds, the hopping about of the squirrels, students walking by, or workers trooping off to lunch, all seemed to incline politely in her direction; one would have said that it was customary and to be explained only by the continual presence on this bench of an Edmée who came there daily. Bells were ringing where the trams stopped, whistles blew from the factories. Deaf to this timetable that concerned her no more than it had concerned Edmée yesterday, the young woman remained there, like the sentry on duty mounting his guard, who has nothing to worry about before his relief appears. . . . That was it. A relief guard. Why such a drama over the absence of Edmée? All in all Edmée hadn't done anything so very serious. She had carried out for a day, in a park, that relief, unconscious and the one best carried out, if he now recalled Versailles or the Luxembourg Gardens, that is mounted by the heart of a public garden in the form of a distracted heart, the distracted body of a woman. It so happened that regulations were that it should never be the same woman. But Edmée would never come back anymore. And if some relief duty later on should carry her a whole day to Central Park or the park of Pasadena, he wouldn't say anything more, he wouldn't worry anymore, for women have to carry out missions of a general nature in our lives. . . . All that husbands have to do is to accept them. . . . Where could that young woman be led this evening by her reverie, if not far from her own home, if not to a

hotel? . . . He left the park by a new path, the one that was as-
signed to him by the presence of the false Edmée. He took a
drink of water; it was surely the first time that he had ever drunk
that way in public, but it was in order to taste Edmée's potion,
at the fountain of the three heads. He was almost reassured.

In his car he got the answer. It had, alas, nothing to do with
relief duty, nor with the general duties of women. It came to him
suddenly, like a revelation. What this park was for Edmée, in re-
lation to Edmée? This park that was mediocre, banal, without
fame, without ambition? It was the opposite of their life, of her
life. Edmée had escaped in order to go the opposite way of her
own life.

It was two o'clock when he arrived. Jacques was waiting by
the elevator, very pale. He looked at his father with alarm in his
eyes; he grasped his hand and wouldn't let it go. He had feared
that this half hour of being late might be drawn from the same
time that his mother had used to take her day of absence.

# 5

"You should go," said Pierre.

"I don't really want to."

"Yes, go ahead. Take Claudie with you since they invited the whole family."

"Then why don't you come too?"

"You know that's impossible. But you should go. You need distraction. Both in the singular and the plural."

How stupid Pierre was. For a week now he had been trying to get her to accept an invitation from the Seeds. The Seeds were in fact four Seeds, two couples who at first sight seemed alike, although alternating: two husbands of forty, blond and brunet, tall and short, and two wives of thirty, brunet and blond, short and tall. All four of them spent money by the millions, money that the two men seemed to produce out of nowhere, for they were specialists in deserts, wastelands, in business deals with nothing behind them, and the team maintained a terrible virginity to match. The two couples had met Pierre and Edmée at a reception of the president of the petroleum company and had swooped down on them. Every month they unleashed themselves in this way in a collective assault against some fellow creature or family who, besieged day and night, even if they resisted the blond man and brunet woman, ended by giving in to the two others. Thus they conquered friends, enemies, secretaries, peers, lovers, and mistresses—all four of them conspiring to acquire that human being who would be of use to only one of them, not knowing moreover to whom the victim would belong, once defeated, until the evening of their victory. Who would win Pierre, who would win the beautiful Edmée, once they were captive in their estate at Santa Barbara, mattered little to the pack, but there was no bush not beaten, no trap that they had not already made use of in common. Gifts descended on the modest home, in the still timid form of orchids and hundred-year-old sherry, but ever ready to change into sapphires and gold fountain pens. For the appetites of the Seeds created around their favorites a magnetic zone where the impossible became possible: whoever among their friends liked to swim, after two days away from home, would find a swimming pool in the backyard, whoever liked to go riding would find a complete stable. Already they were looking about, eager to fulfill whatever might be the unobtainable wish of their future guests; they looked into trips and tours, looked into motorcars. . . . Pierre turned away, out of pride, so that everything would go to Edmée.

The latter was finding it hard to pack her bags. Never had she had such an impression of packing for a trip. She would have preferred not to leave, not because a visit to Santa Barbara didn't appeal to her, but because she was afraid. When a threat like the one she had caught a glimpse of is prowling about you, the best advice that anyone can give you is not to make a move. Since the day of the park she would hardly make a move, she would hardly even think, insofar as thinking meant making a move. Her only chance of escape was to observe in regard to fate the sort of prudence that emigrants show before the police: avoid conversation and meetings, avoid talk and people. Besides, the very sight of whatever makes up our human police already alerted in her she knew not what defensive instinct—a guardian of the peace, a police dog, the siren of a police car, this she already found disquieting. It was as if she must someday come to blows with them or seek to escape them. Never had Pierre found her so reticent, so unwilling to join in the sort of conversation of unlimited horizons that continued to entertain him. At dinner he liked to talk about the immortality of the soul, in terms that were slightly different depending on whether the children were in bed or not, or talk about other countries, or war, in terms that were completely different depending on whether war was declared now or after Jacques might be facing his military service. Edmée was silent, as if she felt compromised by the slightest word; she was no longer among those who could talk casually about the afterlife or about Europe.

On Sundays Pierre liked to take the children down to the ocean; he would lift them up onto the rock from where the sea was the bluest, or the waves crashed highest, or the water was of a calmness recognized miraculous by maritime records; he would point out to them the cape where the most ships had gone down and the bay that had had the most drownings. Edmée no longer went with them, and this distressed her. For to her it was as if suddenly words, whether abstract or common, had taken on their full meaning, as if those entities which for Pierre were only so much decor, or poetic vocabulary, had become for her as real as the modest personnel of her everyday life. The world continued to be for Pierre a book, not the world. But for Edmée, shipwreck, drowning, war, wealth, and volcanos were becoming as real as her daily companions, as real as getting up, washing your face, and getting dressed, as motherhood or dinner. Her fear of going out, her apprehension in accepting an invitation didn't stem from a fear of boredom or of rain, but from a fear of being led back to a series of crimes, of sensual delights, of earthly or mental eruptions which she could escape simply by remaining in the abode of honest affection and long, commonplace days. She gave herself over to this reserved and restrained existence, which Pierre and Jacques distrusted, not in order to prepare anew some

flight, but in order to try to become again what she had been before, an Edmée who was anonymous, in a world where she felt
that some all-powerful voices had called out her name. To be
sure, she couldn't hope to give back to the mountains or the sea
on Sunday Pierre's kind of varnish, which rendered them benign
and noble: no, she saw them raw and in all their cruelty, and, in
the first blaze of summer—to Pierre a Bengal flare—she felt that
for her the light and warmth went just a bit beyond the degree
of heat and light necessary for her peace and quiet. It was really
hard, when she crossed the avenue at noon, without the slightest
shadow falling on her face or dress, hard not to say to herself,
"Why, there's Edmée!" But she lowered the risks by going out
as little as possible, by avoiding that world which in one month
and since her stay of one day in solitude had become peopled in
a diabolical way, to the point that she almost expected, in the
street, for someone suddenly to take her hand. When Pierre the
other day had caught up with her on some sidewalk and had
taken her by the arm, she had cried out. . . . The truth was that
she had at last been discovered, that she had been recovered for
death and for life, that the unknown was there, and insistent,
that nothing would be thrown off the track anymore. . . .

But no, it was Pierre. It was only an illusion, it was only
Pierre. He didn't ask her why she had cried out. A real cry of ter-
ror. People passing by had turned around. They had not said,
"Why, there's Edmée." But each one had pronounced inside the
name that he gives to a woman in anguish, a woman frightened
and guilty. "Why, there's Emma. . . ." "Why, there's Olympia. . . ."
Pierre had only been able to say, "Why, it's no longer Edmée. . . ."
He had smiled and seemed to find it natural that his wife should
appear everywhere so distressed, a sort of victim of having been
flayed, crying out in pain if a hand so much as touched her. And
now here he was forcing her to leave like this, with her flayed
skin, off to the land where they take hold of you around the
waist to dance, to dance the tango or the waltz, to lift you up
onto a horse, or to crowd six deep into the backseat of a car—all
fatal occupations for anyone who has been flayed. At the Seeds',

people also went around a lot almost nude. She was already fearful when it came time to take a bath. However would she manage, with flayed skin and nude at the same time!

So she was packing her bags, but it turned out, by her very choices, that she seemed to be preparing not so much a trip as a departure. She was packing her bags for another life. She picked out the new from the old, what had been a success from what made no effect. It was the final judgment among fabrics, among the colors that would find themselves at home with the Seeds, and other colors less fortunate. Those of her shoes that made her foot look small. Clothes she had bought on a whim, when they had seemed to her of no use and even scandalous, in aggressive colors that clashed to this day with her life and that were waiting only for this invitation from the Seeds now to become her very well. Lingerie unknown to Pierre, hidden in a corner of her wardrobe and which would have surprised Pierre, and—she found them with an ironic smile of recognition, for she had completely forgotten them—the famous black silk pajamas that she had dreamed about as a child and that she had insisted on buying when passing through New York two years ago, the only forbidden item in these conscientious closets; it really seemed as if this departure were taking place on their account. Edmée's budget had been thrown off balance at the time by the purchase, her wardrobe had been deprived of some very necessary items because of these pajamas she would never use, and now they were the very thing, the only thing really suitable for her week with the Seeds. It was they who were to decide all of Edmée's accessories; everything that didn't go with these pajamas that no one would see—aside from the chambermaid—would stay here with Pierre. Here with Pierre her dressing gowns of Japanese silk and their stupid embroidered dragons. Here with Pierre the cheap stockings, the resoled shoes, the mended underwear. Pierre would keep everything required for a servant wife, a wife who doesn't weep on her saint's name day, a placid wife, a good wife. If he should happen during Edmée's absence to open the wardrobes and the drawers, to push aside the silks, he would see nothing there but gray, drab colors, nothing but sadness. She was bequeathing him—in truth he wouldn't see much of anything there, he would see love and happiness, he would embrace her— she was leaving him only her sad skin. . . . He would find there nothing but the metal flasks, that worn-out pen, and a whole mess of buttons, gloves worn through on the ring finger and pushed out by the ring, some hairpieces and tubes. . . . Very well, then. She was going off to the Seeds'. She was packing her bags for the Seeds', without pity. She accepted only that which belonged. She was breaking with mufflers, with belts, even though they meant devotion, meant safety itself. She was breaking with friends who were poor, breaking with fidelity. She was breaking with the old frame that held the photo of Jacques; she pulled out the portrait that it had held for three years so as to give it to a silver frame. She broke with little boxes and cases that had accompanied her since childhood and which, deprived of love, had become sinister. To the extent that she didn't dare leave behind such colorless remains. She put back on the dressing table a few articles from her silver toilet set, and among the drab robes she hung back up a bodice of gold lamé. Besides, it was a bit vulgar for the Seeds; here, it restored a touch of youth and sparkle. Pierre came to attend the end of this choosing what to take. He saw nothing. She was picking the hats. He didn't understand. He didn't see Edmée's head leave with the cerise toque, Edmée's head with the blue beret, with her Greek coiffure. He didn't see Edmée's head stay with the wide-brimmed hat, with the cocoa-colored cloche, with all the failures. He didn't understand when he closed the suitcases himself, the only two handsome suitcases in the house. The whole rainbow of his home was inside this coffin. He buckled the straps carefully. He insisted on her putting the silver flasks and the lamé bodice back in; he was ready to repack the bags if necessary.

No. She wouldn't let him open the bags. He cast an inquisitive glance at the wastebasket, anxious to see boxes crushed that were like old friends, or friendly cartons torn up. Despite all, he had a suspicion of the carnage they were the victims of. Sure enough, once Edmée was gone he started to busy himself at saving the less wounded. Poor Pierre! If it had been up to him to make the same kind of selection, he wouldn't have had anything left to take to the Seeds' except his blue tie with the golfing figures and his twelve Vittel handkerchiefs. That's the way the couple would have arrived at the Seeds', Pierre nude with his tie and his twelve handkerchiefs. At least he still had all twelve. He defended them tenaciously against Edmée's absentmindedness and Claudie's covetousness. And they were new; he would have used them only as pocket handkerchiefs, a substitute handkerchief in one of his pants pockets. . . . What insincerity lies inside even the most honest human being; he called them his handkerchiefs but they were his treasure. . . . She snitched one of them from him, and when she was all alone, put it inside the suitcase. Probably he would recover it from her handbag.

The house wasn't as kind as Pierre. The house no longer knew her. Everything that Pierre didn't say to her, everything that she was betraying and giving up, the smallest piece of furniture was shouting out loud. It even proclaimed some unexpected news, wrong no doubt, the main item of which was that she wouldn't see them anymore. Provisions in the kitchen and pantry, in their jars and their saltcellars, were becoming detached from her, were no longer her food. They didn't accept any word of affection, any excuse. . . . "We're the coffee," said a pound of coffee from behind its glass pane. "Leave if you want! We don't have to be sentimental. We have to stimulate people. If we're not there, another coffee, a better one—so they claim—will provide your stimulation. . . ." "You won't have to bite us anymore," said the pickles. "We're the pickles, just simple pickles. Be unfaithful if you want. We're not concerned about people's souls, but rather about their tongues. Other people will eat us if you're not there. You'll see how delighted we are. . . ." But this kind of talk was wrong too: the coffee and pickles used to like to be ground up and eaten by her; they had been her pride and joy, and now they had fallen out with her, they were rejecting her. They were even going a bit too far with their insinuations about her future coffee in its tortoiseshell container, about her future pickles in jars with gold lids; that way they were just proving that one can be a first-class condiment without the least talent for predicting things or the least bit of good taste. . . . Thus the whole week was a series of denials and insults. The damaged coatrack would say: "Of course a pretty woman can't sacrifice herself for a damaged coatrack!" Everything that was chipped, soiled, or cracked was becoming at the same time whining and disdainful, like poor relations. On the last night the bed allowed itself an unbearable monologue. With all her lingerie packed, Edmée had decked herself out in a nightgown that was a sort of cream with Valenciennes lace and yoke, a real horror that she no longer wore; she got into bed, already a bit ashamed of her costume, and the bed started insulting her. . . .

"It's perhaps very feminine," said the bed, "to put on a nightgown that one describes as a horror, so that your husband, who has only the opinion of an oil prospector concerning lace, may believe you to be dressed as a sort of fiancée deluxe. But we beds call it pure hypocrisy! . . ." To explain to the bed that when she returned, Pierre would get to know the black pajamas might have appeased it, but that would have been lying to the bed. In any case Pierre would never know the black pajamas. "It's disgraceful," resumed the bed, when Pierre came to join her. . . . "You're disguising yourself as a fake bride. You put on a wedding garment that you find ugly and ridiculous, because you think your husband won't see it. . . . Listen to what he says: 'What a beautiful nightgown!' Listen to what he's thinking: 'What a ravishing wife in that superb nightgown! . . . '" And the abusive monologue went on like that, without mentioning allusions that would make you blush, until Edmée jumped up and got out of bed, until she went off and shut herself up in the bathroom. Pierre heard a piece of fabric being torn from one end to the other, a piece of linen, he didn't know what, he didn't ask what. . . . Already Edmée was back, with a pair of his own pajamas on. . . . The bed was quiet. . . . So passed the night. With the same kind of nightclothes on they were like a team. Those who can see in the dark would have taken them for twins, for bicycle riders in tandem. Deceived by this sudden mimicry, the objects gradually calmed down, the voices faded away. Toward dawn the garbage collectors passed by, emptied the cans, carried out a final sorting among Edmée's victims, and with their hooks picked up the pieces of the cream-colored nightgown. Already the cream-colored nightgown had passed into the lower order of elements, at the disposal of that metempsychosis that would turn it into powder or pulp, unless the garbage collector should decide to take the tattered pieces home to his wife, who would then exclaim, "What a superb nightgown!" Then Edmée got up. . . . She had always liked to sleep at the edge of the bed, even though Pierre usually got up first. She had often wondered why. . . . Pierre would begin his day by crossing over his wife, or by crushing her, or, as on the anniversary day of his promotion, by jumping over her with both feet together. Edmée would then immediately and greedily make for the middle of the bed that she had refused during the night. . . . And this morning she understood why: it was because all the other times she had gotten up didn't count. Getting up this morning was the only time it mattered. . . . It meant freedom. To be able to get up one morning, when the cock crowed, without crossing over the other. And so she got up. Because Pierre had not gotten up before her, she dismissed him from her whole day, from her life. . . .

The car sent by the Seeds was to pick her up at eleven o'clock. Pierre refused for anything to be changed about the family schedule: Jacques would leave for school at eight-thirty, he would leave for the office at nine. The more painful of the two departures was that of Jacques. He was having breakfast in the dining room, as his father usually insisted, and as the solemnity of the occasion demanded today. It was different from the other days in that he used to have breakfast alone. Claudie—who knew why?—was refusing this morning to eat the usual dishes, taken by invincible repugnance for the plates, the toasted bread, the honey they had there at home; and this time his mother, still in bed the other mornings, was serving him herself. She was watching him eat, sitting there beside him, and when he needed more bread or sugar, she got up and would serve him. He could have endured eating alone, like the other days, alone with Claudie, though solitude was no longer something you could share with Claudie, but this maternal presence changed everything. The result was a sinister misunderstanding. It seemed as if he were the one taking the trip. . . . Edmée had come to his bed when it was time for him to get up. She had helped him get dressed, had put on his stockings, had sewn on two buttons missing from his pants, had put his shoes on without using the shoehorn, hurting her finger between his heel and the leather; she had washed his face. It had been the scene of the son about to enlist, the boy who goes off to serve the troops. . . . Of all the little boys in the world that morning, he was the one that a mother had looked at the most, washed the best, embraced the best. He was covered with the fingerprints of his mother. Claudie had been there too, and that wasn't the least of it, acting as Edmée's double, ahead of her in holding out his sweater, his belt, terribly aware of the order in which you put on clothes when dressing boys. He felt confused between these two extraordinary servants. He blushed at being served like a child hero, like a child god. . . . And he was the one being left behind. He felt the injustice of having to be the one who leaves, of seeing piled on his shoulders all the responsibility, all the guilt of leaving. He was leaving the house at eight-thirty as usual, for a few hours, and they were organizing on his behalf a solemn departure, affecting to fit their own long trip into his very slight absence. There they were, his mother and his sister, busy telling him not to rush, to take his time, saying he looked well, as if they were going to have nothing more to do in life than await his return, while in fact, as soon as his back was turned, they would hurry back to their bags once more, and back to the wardrobes where they would pull out whatever they might consider too beautiful for his father or him. . . . For he had spied the frame of his portrait empty, he had seen the wardrobes bereft of color, suffering a frightful anemia. . . .

And now these women wanted to make him think that this trip off to school in the bus was thrilling, dangerous, that it was a real trip. . . . The only thing he dared tell them about this was that he wasn't taking a suitcase, not even a school satchel, not even a small one, that he was only taking a single book. For this huge trip he was about to undertake, there was need for only one book. "What! You're taking only one book?" his mother actually said to him. . . . Yes, despite all the hours, years, seas, and mountains, he was taking only one book, and one book was already too much. What's more, he had made a mistake: instead of *Two Children on a Tour of France,* he had taken *Principles of Geometry.* It didn't matter. He even forgot it. Claudie caught up with him on the landing, handing him the book with importance, as if it were a great suitcase. . . . He didn't cry on leaving them, since he was the one who was the traveler.

Pierre's departure was more rapid. He took his breakfast standing up, in a hurry; his car was in front of the door and he risked a trip to court if it was parked there more than twenty minutes. Fear of a police sergeant prevented him from taking Edmée in his arms, from telling her what he had been preparing to say for a week; he knew it by heart, it began with "The important thing in life, Edmée. . . ." And it ended with "Your happiness. . . ." Neither did Edmée dare pronounce the words that she had repeated all night long. They began "Pierre darling, listen to me. . . ." And ended "That's why I'm not going to go. . . ." But fear of the police officer, fear of having to send back the Seeds' car, of appearing impolite to the Seeds, all four of the Seeds, stopped both of them. There are always reasons of civic or worldly courtesy which push you into your true life. So it was that Edmée and Claudie served Pierre standing up, like those officiating at mass. He too took his departure on himself, but voluntarily. He was doubtless, he explained, going to have to go down into a coal mine. . . . The deepest kind, a real hell. . . . He was leaving for Hell! . . . They were turning around him in their morning garb, the grayest, the most out of date—clothes they had been able to find left out of the suitcases, clothes that women wear who go for fifty years without leaving the house. A drop of coffee fell on Edmée's dressing gown. Pierre excused himself. "Oh, it doesn't matter," she said, and, to be sure, milk, grease, and beer could attack at leisure whatever now remained of her dressing gown, the moths could eat it up. It didn't matter, not anymore. . . . Underneath the gown with a spot on it, Pierre noticed his own pajamas. This sign of fraternity was enough for him. . . .

As soon as he had left, they got dressed—one in red with gold, the other in blue with a thread of emerald green.

"What can I write her, Frank? What can I do? She won't come back! I don't believe she'll ever come back. You think I'm crazy, don't you? Crazy, indeed! When she left she thought the world of me, she cherished me. It was her wish that we spend our last night together wearing the same kind of pajamas. If that doesn't tell you something, I'm certainly not going to try to explain it. You can ask those who invented cross-dressing and twins. Ask Shakespeare. In order to really show me that she was also my sister, that she had on the same color, that we had the same body—well, more or less—in order to show me that to us two we were only one, she tore up the most beautiful nightgown that French fashion can create and put on a pair of my pajamas. And a single pair of pajamas would have sufficed, where she would have worn the top and I the bottom, or vice versa, where everything that wasn't covered up would no longer have been anything more than a sort of annex, the domain of one perfect body dressed this way. You can see the kind of nightgown and the extent of her sacrifice by this wonderful bit of lace that I found in the hall. . . . Last year I gave a talk at the club on how Calais was ruined by a drop in the sales of lace in America. This is my reward. . . . She has never complained once. There were two tears one day that I didn't understand. Or perhaps I did understand:

two tears of unhappiness. What I didn't understand was where they came from. Why I wasn't able to understand, you can guess, can't you? But I simply thought they were the last of the unhappiness. In our oil fields we have wells that we believe flooded; we have giant pumps at our disposal, we connect enough hose to drain the world dry, and the most that comes out are two buckets of water, two tears, to pick up my metaphor, the well is no longer flooded, and happiness returns. . . . But her, she won't come back. I had said to myself, 'Why don't you return from the office, under some pretext or another, a few minutes after the time that the Seeds' car has picked them up? If they aren't there, themselves returned, under some pretext, if the Seeds' tires haven't blown out, if Claudie hasn't suddenly had an attack of her hay fever, it's because Edmée is not going to come back. . . .'

"I waited for her all day long. It was as if she had the option of the whole day in which to choose, but only that day, up to midnight. Since she didn't come back at noon, braving the blame of the Seeds' chauffeur, nor at five o'clock, the hour when the Seeds take tea, telling the female Seeds they could stuff it, nor at nine on going in to dinner, suddenly removing her arm from that of one of the male Seeds, well, it's because she's not coming back. . . . Midnight struck, option canceled. Midnight, one minute after, two minutes, three minutes, . . . sixty minutes after. And the option of the option is canceled. . . . For twelve years she was a perfect wife, and now she leaves me. She's a wonderful mother, and she leaves a son alone, him alone with me alone, doubling our aloneness by two squared. . . . Too bad for our tech students, who like unlimited possibilities for the calculations of their souls! No doubt she imagines that she can come back one day; she doesn't know what an option is. When Pierpont Morgan was asked for a typical example of an option, he replied, 'The guillotine, there's your example of an option. . . .' She used to like to hold my hand, Frank. I assure you that when her hand held mine, her hand wasn't distracted, wasn't trying to check my pulse; she was holding it so as to hold me. She used to like to part my hair; one day she curled a lock of my hair with the curling

iron—the curling iron was too hot, but she has the most wonderful pomade for second-degree burns. . . . When tying my tie,
she used to like to hang onto it with all her weight, her tongue
stuck out a bit as if she really meant to hang onto me, as if the
best thing in the world would be to go to my office with my
darling wife hanging around my neck with her tongue stuck out
a bit. She liked everything I liked, and liked me to boot, who am
only a friend of myself, and since midnight a friend to be pitied.
She liked it when we would rest with our elbows at the window
in the evening and the frogs from the wholesale fish market at
Builtmore Place would start to croak from their tank. She loved
the croaking of the bullfrogs. She loved Schubert's *Shepherd on
the Rock,* she loved all those who love Schubert's *Shepherd on
the Rock,* she knew that I was the one who loved it the most, and
as a result she loved me. And I won't tell you the days that she
embraced me when I was saying nothing, when, with a smile, she
turned over her life to me, at a time that I asked for nothing,
when she hit me with her whole body while I was motionless,
hit me with her whole life at a time when I was dead. And now
she doesn't want to see me anymore. There has never been any
disagreement, never a scene, never a word in anger. We respect
each other, as if each of us were the hostage or the ransom or the
reward for the other. I can assure you that there have been days
when each was the mirror of the other, when she saw herself in
me, when she not only embraced me, but she embraced herself
as the mirror of me. And I'm as certain as can be that she has
gone. . . .

"That she may have been too fine, too sensitive for me—
this is stupid reasoning! However much of an engineer I may be,
I'm no more insensitive than the painter that you are. What affects you affects me too. Whatever affects you in the fine arts affects us engineering graduates. If I'm out swimming and a fish
touches me lightly, then takes off like a shot, I'm affected too.
I'm just as affected as you if I'm out in my car and a river that
has been running alongside the road for a few minutes or a few
hours then changes course and leaves me. I cite you these two
examples. I have a hundred more. I too am affected if in the sky,

as I saw yesterday, a large bird flying above suddenly changes its mind, gives up trying to set a record, to heed its call, forgets, and lets itself glide. I have a thousand examples. . . . In the middle of the sky, if we were both large birds, rushing toward the bottom of a pocket of mysterious air, toward the nest of air of the big birds, toward the aerie of the airs, as my director, General Poloillet, who was fond of wit, would have said, I'll bet you, no matter how much of a painter you are, that I am the one who would stop short, struck by some human pain, the one who would let the world or the sea beneath me go on at its own speed. Insensitive! Even turned into a machine, into particular machines—I'm thinking of our freewheel bikes on the road to Senlis when we were engaged—I would feel moments of intense joy, shed tears of joy! She understood everything, forgave everything, loved everything. And yet suddenly, as a result of this blow that you can't explain any better than I, she understands everything, apart from me, she loves everything, aside from me. We loved to read together at night, we were in such accord over the speed of our eyes that neither one had to ask when the other wanted to turn the page, and suddenly she has stopped reading: because every book, whether an English novel where they mortify souls in the dead leaves or on the lawns, or a French novel where the struggle between thought and style is each time taken up anew— you can see that I'm not insensitive—every book became our book, the book of our life. . . . She is pure, she believes in duty. The only time I ever had a word with her, Frank, was over the subject of your head. I've tried to explain everything through your head. In vain. Try it yourself. That your head should have seemed to her so different, that she should have noticed that I'm not the only man in the world, this is the stuff of novels. That the head of a vaguely intimate friend, very vaguely intimate, should be at ease on your knees, that this should have given her the idea of trying the same thing with the heads of utter strangers—just absurd; I feel completely reassured at this moment about the respective position of Edmée's knees and the four heads of the Seeds.

"That the act of putting your head on her, as on a block, of seeing that head all by itself, detached, should suddenly have changed her whole view of men and things—that too is far-fetched, 'pulled by the hair,' as we say in French, if you'll pardon the joke. You don't have a head that suddenly turns into a gorgon's head, the kind suddenly crowned by banners with flaming inscriptions. Your head, on the contrary, is the very model of the sort of head that makes us human, kind and helpful to all heads in general, even to the heads of others. You have surely put your head on the knees of other women. One doesn't make one's debut in that exercise at the age of forty-two, forty-one and a half, if you wish. And these other women, I'm quite sure, did not one fine day disappear, not as if they were absent, but as if they had been erased. *Erased* is the word; I'm not only sensitive, I choose my terms carefully: Edmée has been rubbed out of our bedroom, out of our dining room, by an eraser gum that even pulled off the wallpaper all around the outline of Edmée. The other women who have taken your head didn't refuse to return to a perfect home. They haven't abandoned a child who has to be given plausible reasons every evening as to why his mother is late. I have no doubt that you yourself could find a lot of plausible reasons! I'm going to soon be like our dear old friend in the Latin Quarter who was seduced by a sergeant on leave from the Senegalese riflemen, abandoned when pregnant, and who, to the questions her son asked when growing up, replied that his father was in Oceania and couldn't come back until he had killed a hundred elephants. Every month the son would ask how the hunt was going; in her desire to ease the wait she had very quickly arrived at the number of ninety-nine elephants that had been killed. And since that time, she would reply, 'We're still at ninety-nine; hunting hasn't been good this year.' And a woman friend told her one day that there weren't any elephants in Oceania, and she made her son skip geography class, and at the zoo they wouldn't go past the giraffes. . . . Well, that's the point I'm at. The child looks at me as if he suspects a secret cause for our separation. He wonders if I am guilty of that excessive haste that suddenly isolates the males in our family from the women. All day long he watches me. He's looking for the vice in me, the flaw that has ruined everything. Oh, Frank! What did I ask for in life? To live with the most beautiful woman, the most loving, the simplest, the sweetest, the most intelligent. And I had her.... And, since an hour ago, I don't have her anymore.

"And I'm obsessed by an episode from my childhood: we had a filly that one day refused to pass through the doorway to the stable. We built a model stable for her—exposed to the light, no rats, no chickens in the hayrack (she hated chickens). But one day she refused to go through the door. We put sugar in the hayrack, we got out the sulky whip; it was all of no use, she lay down, she trembled all over, and she, who was so gentle, even tried to kick.... A little while ago, in a dream, I saw Edmée, like the filly, refuse to go through this door, lying down like the filly, darting little kicks at both Jacques and me, obstinate to the death.... For the veterinarian told me that we would have to kill the filly...."

That's what Pierre was telling Frank, who didn't answer one word, who, moreover, wasn't even there. For what in the world would Frank have been doing in the bedroom and bed of Pierre at three o'clock in the morning, with a storm beating down on Los Angeles, flooding Los Angeles, blowing down trees in Washington Park, setting fire to twenty houses? . . . Twenty houses burned down.... It was always like that.... But why did Pierre feel, on reading the next morning that not a flower, not a shrub remained in his enemy the park, the park that had deceived him, why did he feel something close to despair?

Pierre, at first, had written. Three times. Carefree letters; the third a little less carefree of course. At least he had tried to make it as carefree as possible, as carefree as his life; full of fear, anguish, and a remorse which he really couldn't quite understand, he gave them to believe, to read these letters, that the house, even in the absence of Edmée, was a refuge of happiness. Disaster already dwelled there, insomnia and renunciation, yet Pierre went on awkwardly dancing his dance. . . . Pierre had never danced very well. . . . Aside from the simple step for skaters popular at the Latin Quarter ball. . . . But for a dance before the Ark, for an entrechat before the beatitude, he definitely wasn't the one. Jacques too, if the letters were to be believed, was living a charmed life. Pierre related its ups and downs and its adventures with a mischievous pen: there had been a mouse, they had bought a new record featuring an Australian lyrebird. "The time just flies by, dear Edmée. . . ." Each hour lasting a century, if he had told the truth. Neither did he tell that, at the sound of the mouse, he had raised up in bed, had thought for a moment that Edmée had returned, had gone back to sleep, and had dreamed that Edmée had come back changed into a mouse. It had been quite an affair in his dream to let Jacques know that his mother had turned into a mouse. The child refused to believe it. He said it was impossible, that metempsychosis had its own laws, that for a woman to be changed into this creature or that, it would have been necessary for her husband or her son to have such a creature in mind when he saw her one day, that for himself he was sure that he had never thought of a mouse on seeing his mother, so all the fault was due to Pierre. . . . What madness had ever come over his father to compare his mother to a mouse, to an animal with tiny eyes and whiskers and four paws? . . . What a bad father! . . . And yet, he had to admit everything when the mouse had turned into a mouse with huge eyes and soft skin, and had taken him into her arms, all the while calling him her little Jacques. . . . He had dried his tears. . . . What difference did it make if she were a mouse as long as she was there! A mouse mother who is present is surely worth as much as a nonmouse mother who is absent. They would simply conceal her existence. Their friends would say, "Jacques no longer has a mother. Pierre no longer has a wife. But they have a magnificent mouse. They're really very lucky. . . ."

And the episode of the record of the lyrebird hadn't been much more amusing: one might have expected, considering its name, that the lyrebird would sing you a song somewhere between that of a bird and that of a human being. "I think it sings and accompanies itself with its beak as if it were a guitar," Pierre had informed. But the lyrebird, like some musical clown, would only give imitations. In the first part of its recital, it imitated the birds of its region—the whipbird, the doorbell bird, the smack bird, the handbell bird, and the sparrow; in the second part, it imitated whatever had struck its ear in the approach of civilization: the carpenter's plane, the buzz saw, the hacksaw, the motor or horn of a car as heard from a distance, and the bellows used to make charcoal. Pierre and Jacques listened, disappointed, hoping to the last grooves of the record that it would imitate the nightingale or some human voice. But no woodcutter had whistled that day. It had been necessary to replace the record with a better-named lyrebird, with Liszt in fact. . . . Those were the events that Pierre tried to dress up with smiles. He had even, in the margin of the letter, drawn the mouse and the lyrebird, regarding each other amicably, one on the bed, the other on the sideboard. He had also drawn Jacques and himself—facing the head of a calf that had turned out particularly well. He drew well. You could see the eye of the calf. . . .

"I think our men are putting us on!" had said Claudie.

To the first letter Edmée had written two replies. One of them accepted Pierre's theory, according to which they were the very model of the happy couple. The other revealed to Pierre that the couple was dead, that between them there was now only empty space. She wrote the first under a sort of slavery, not to Pierre or to public opinion, but to habit, to the easy way out. She accepted the convention of the mouse and made some joking remarks: it was very naughty of Pierre to receive nocturnal visits during her absence. . . . She looked forward to hearing the lyrebird—they must treat the record with care, it ought to be like brand new for Claudie and her to hear! She told them not to change their places at the table so as not to take on the ways of old bachelors. A jolly remark about the calf's eye, she covered them both with kisses, and if she'd been able to draw, she would have drawn the eye of the giant ray captured by the Seeds on their boat, Claudie on its back. . . . Then five minutes later, that letter torn up, she wrote the letter that a wife leaves out on the table the day she leaves home, with the full name of her husband written out very neatly, as if she were going to return it. . . . She thanked Pierre and told him good-bye. . . . She loved him, for nothing in the world would she have wanted to cause him the slightest pain, she knew that she was going to kill him by sending him this letter, and she was sending it: she had been dying at home. She didn't know from what, but it was as certain as if the gas had been turned on. Had he really never seen, never understood what she was suffering? If she could draw, she would have drawn herself on a cross, with nails through her feet and hands, refusing the sponge held out by her husband by turning away her head, with eyes that were glassy, dead. . . . It was also necessary, no sooner than signed, to tear up this letter. . . .

And when she had to answer Pierre's second letter, she started over. . . . She thanked Pierre for all the news, and everything was going well at the Seeds'; a Dutch singer had sung one evening and it was a pity he couldn't have been there. Claudie was getting along fine with her pony, she would stick him with a pin to make him draw in his belly when they were saddling up; from France the Seeds had learned by way of friends that all was going well, despite the talk. In short, everything, between the lines, told her husband that she was attached to him by all that unites two people forever—music, children, and country. Between them there was nothing trite, nothing selfish, nothing unnecessary. To the point that the letter became an eternal promise, a song of love. . . . And at that point she really had to tear it up! . . . And to write the second one: that she didn't know when she would return, that some charming people were taking her on a cruise, that if someone could bring her little Jacques for a few days—oh, not himself, definitely not himself, she didn't want to see him at the moment. . . . It was the letter of a divorcée, a woman in revolt, a woman who will never forgive. . . . Poor Pierre! She tore the letter up. And it appeared to her little by little that silence could spare her this awful treadmill. She committed her cause to silence. For her part, for the part of her own soul, she would be unaware, unintelligent, myopic, in a word, deaf. Where Pierre was concerned, so attentive, always on guard—one could judge by his story of the mouse—she would be mute. If he woke up at night, on the alert, it surely wouldn't be from any word of Edmée, not even the echo of a word of Edmée, nor from any thought coming from her, but rather by way of a mouse . . . by way of the mouse itself, for the creature, through Pierre's gift at mythmaking, must by now be legendary in the house. Let the mouse wake him up, talk to him, console him, caress him. . . .

For he shouldn't count on Edmée too much anymore. Each day of silence was going to slip between them, the first like a folding screen, the second like a partition, the third already in the form of stones that no sound can penetrate—modern stones, particularly soundproof. Five days. Ten days. At Carcassonne, when they visited the chateau, he had put her on the other side of the wall and had tried, in vain moreover, to make her hear him by tapping against the wall with a key. . . . In case she had been a prisoner. . . . In case they had lived in the Middle Ages. . . . She imagined him tapping now against this wall of ten days of silence, with his key, his hammer, his drill pump. . . . In vain. . . . She heard him only if he was tapping with Jacques's head. . . . Most likely Pierre already felt there was something impenetrable between them, since he no longer wrote, since the only times he tapped with Jacques's head now were very far apart. . . . Every night would sanction, would iron over, would glaze over the omission of every day.

Without taking into account that Edmée was changing herself. Pierre would hardly have recognized her, in dresses that he had seen before but which would have seemed new to him now, that Edmée had told him were out of style so he wouldn't notice them but which now appeared stunning; in a beauty that had blossomed here at the Seeds', that had taken on an air of professional beauty due to one of those miracles that can happen to any being suddenly plunged into idleness or egoism; in a head of hair out of which Pierre would not have recognized a single strand, along with that new rouge, that new powder. The powder of happiness had already powdered Edmée. Thirty days of this accumulation of nothingness and new creams and lotions between Pierre and herself and she would no longer be the woman he loved. Indeed, that was what took away a part of the weight that she believed to be remorse concerning Pierre: she was already no longer the one he loved. All of her former self still felt affection, devotion, and love for Pierre. All of her new self rejected him. Besides, she was thinking about him less and less. She would have liked for Claudie not to imitate her in this, to remain connected to the family. . . . That would have made her silence, her insensitivity a little easier, for Claudie sometimes to have come to tell her, "I've written to Father, I have phoned Jacques." But Claudie didn't write, didn't telephone. . . . On the contrary, she even accentuated, one might have said willingly, one might have said implacably, that cruelty that her mother still wanted to think a game, a test. Out of what sort of cowardice would Edmée have been relieved to hear words from her daughter that she could no longer pronounce herself: for example, that she missed the family meals at home as they were entering the Seeds' long hall in the style of Louis XIV, or a tender allusion to her little bed as she regained the Elizabethan couch where she would sleep for eight hours with her child's snore without ever finding herself crosswise of the bed, or remarking that that Mr. Davis, who talked so pedantically about petroleum, really knew much less about it than her father—all this Edmée had trouble explaining herself.

But she suffered to see her cause so taken up by her daughter. That which for her was painful or a defense became for Claudie something ferocious and no longer allowed her not to see the situation in its true light. Above two children who adore each other, who wait for each other, who write and telephone each other, who are there to bring you back if you stray off the path, it is easy for a spouse to perform a few stunts up in the air. But with this Claudie, who never brought her father or her brother into her current life, Edmée felt like she was doing a trapeze act without a safety net. A good little girl, who for the time being might have wept the tears that she could no longer weep, and kind, who might have bestowed the caresses that she could no longer give, a little Claudie with a pen, who might have written the letters that she could no longer write—well, it wasn't out of the question that after the Seeds she might return to the others as she had after the park, where, in effect, Edmée had suddenly felt very high up, very far away. But Claudie remained a lump of intransigence and hardness. One might have said that she had heard, from the depth of her sleep, the complaints that her father one night had been unable to hold back, when he had called her selfish and coquettish. She did exactly what a woman does who has been accused of being selfish and coquettish: she was becoming that way. That's what she was. And the same thing also happened to her that was happening to Edmée. She began to blossom. She was becoming pretty to the point of distracting the senile Grandpa Seeds from his porridge at mealtime, he who had once recruited chorus girls for Ziegfeld. At times a feeling of desolation would fill Edmée at the thought that her home was split in two parts, one of which was all color—for nothing less than bright red would suit Claudie—and the other the shade of ashes, when it would have been so simple for the Creator to make do with a blend. . . .

Thus passed the first few weeks of silence, the two women beneath their projector, the two men at home beneath their little lamp. Sometimes one of the Mrs. Seeds would ask for news of Pierre. . . . He was doing very well, thank you. . . . But the Seeds knew how far to rely on a couple who give news of each other when they are no longer able to see, hear, or write each other, and don't even know if the other exists. Well, the Seeds knew he existed. One of them had run into Pierre sitting in Washington Park, the only site in all California where no one had ever seen a prospector for oil. . . . With his right hand on the back of the park bench, he seemed to be tapping out rhythms on a set of French drums. . . . His tie was poorly tied. . . . No, he wasn't doing very well. . . .

At times Edmée felt excused. If she was cut off from Pierre, it wasn't because of Pierre, but because of his *stylographe* (his fountain pen) or his telephone. It wasn't loving or adoring Pierre that was hard, it was approaching those insurmountable instruments with their Greek names. In order to make use of them you had to translate them, and, as they say, to translate is to betray — she was no longer up to it. She preferred not to touch that happiness, whose quality she couldn't explain, but which was without limits. She, whose life had been untroubled and never very busy, suddenly had a memory of a past without rest, without Sundays, without any vacation, without freedom. She had had, from morning to night, the major or minor pleasures of the human condition, an incredibly good family, music, a taste for theater, and a feeling for good food, yet she had the impression that now for the first time she was at ease, relaxed, satisfied, and well nourished.

Claudie, who saw everything, had her explanation all ready: her mother was at last living with those friends by day that formerly she could be with only by night, by way of her iron ladder, and who until now had been down on the ground only once before, that night at the Ambassadors Hotel. They were all here, with their horses, their dogs, their extraordinary automobiles, in this mixture of presidents, princesses, movie stars, and greyhounds who were the chamberlains of Claudie's sleep — in short, all those who used to receive Edmée up on top of the skyscraper while walking around on that slanting roof, and between Edmée and the rest there was a facility, a complicity that could really only be explained by their mutual intimacy with cornices and eaves. For Edmée the explanation was more severe: "Can I really be so insignificant?" she was thinking. "How is it that going from a middle-class life to a life of luxury should transform me, make me come to life! I look down on money, on wealth, but when they approach me I feel vitalized. I judge these people for what they are—futile, with nothing to do, and ignorant; yet being around them acts like a cure on me. It's as if there were some error of fate concerning me. I'm a happy woman burdened with playing the role of unhappy women. A woman who has everything she wants having to represent the unsatisfied woman. A magnetic woman having to play the woman who hates. My whole life long I have never known fatigue or pain, and here I am now with a mission to be the one to deal with sickness, anxiety, and death. . . ."

And she was no less surprised, after a day of silence and forgetting, that evening, at that brilliant hour of the Seeds when the dullest guests would sparkle like those insects that women used to wear in their hair and that they would pierce with a needle, to find that the only man she found at all attractive was precisely the guest who seemed the most worthy, the most modest, the one who seemed the most like Pierre. She liked him for his simple clothes, his dark tie, the perfect part in his hair—Pierre's sole conscious bit of adornment—his serious tone of voice, and that fervor which never let itself be distracted by either pleasantry or discussion, Pierre's kind of fervor. One can't say that she didn't see the others, for the freemasonry of guests at the Seeds' was based above all on a corporal fraternity, on a corporal intimacy that brought men and women to distances at their most reduced, and quite a few heads came, when one was listening to music and song, to rest themselves on the knees of Edmée. . . . It was the harvest of heads of which Frank's head had been the seed. . . . There were heavy ones, light ones, heads with blue eyes, one with a red eye, heads with wrinkles, and smooth heads; heads that were at ease right away, which as soon as they were in place would maneuver their eyes and mouth with dexterity, who would take the role of Adolph or Romeo, and others that were clumsy, who took the part of Holofernes or John the Baptist.

But it was the head of the false Pierre that Edmée had wanted to weigh in her balance. She invited him to sit down beside her. He didn't understand of course, or else he wouldn't have been Pierre. And so as to be considerate to this replica of Pierre, she dispelled her remorse at leaving the authentic Pierre without any news. The false Pierre let himself succumb to this friendliness and to confide in her. He let her know he was poor but that he was getting into gold mining in New Guinea, that he loved music, loved painting. Everything that Pierre had said, word for word, when he had first met her. One evening she understood that he had a project, another project, more ambitious than finding gold in clay rather than quartz: to rest his head on Edmée's knees. But the task was too much for him. Even though Edmée had prepared her knees and smoothed her skirt—he didn't make it, bumped into her, slipped off. He talked in a distracted way, like someone who has an idea in his head concerning that head itself. Just like Pierre. The innate clumsiness of Pierre for anything having to do with tenderness and its minute ways. . . . The false Pierre soon departed, moreover, to the great happiness of Claudie, who hated him. She had not noticed his resemblance to her father, but an instinct which was both the admiration and the despair of Edmée allowed Claudie to suspect what game of memory and the past it was that her mother had been playing with him. . . . She saw him disappear with joy, like a real father. . . .

All those who couldn't be fathers—the half-nude glories of the tennis court and the pool, movie stars in purple jackets, the centaurs—Claudie, on the other hand, was forever touting and talking up to Edmée. In that preliminary competition imposed on Edmée's admirers, which was the tribute they paid her daughter, Claudie eliminated mercilessly those who did not light up in the light of the Seeds, that is, in gold or luxury. She eliminated also the timid and the weak. Having the right to bring her back to her mother were only those who could carry her on their shoulders, on their heads, on outstretched arms, or behind them on horseback. Edmée's court consisted very soon and exclusively of those types who were the exact opposite of the figures with which Pierre had surrounded her life, from Wagner to Pasteur— he who could best saddle a reluctant horse, he who could stay underwater for two minutes, he who could lasso a flower from Claudie's mouth, a white flower so that there wasn't any confusion with her cheeks. They would come and sit, or stretch out around Edmée's chaise longue, with a familiarity that their nudity made seem like a kind of slavery, would rush to perform some service that admitted only mother-of-pearl, tortoiseshell, and platinum, replacing a human presence which had been for her until then only a presence of heads by a presence of their entire bodies from their hair down to their toes. They seemed to possess, moreover, less sense of sight, hearing, or even touch, and inspired much less concern in Edmée than the old busts she once had to deal with, and on which the senses were so closely and dreadfully united. The attention of these faceless bodies appealed to her without really moving her, and she took a sensuous pleasure in allowing the responsibilities and charms of her own face to become diluted inside her.

As a child she had often had the same nightmare while dreaming: the trees took on heads, the rocks and the eddies of rivers as well. Wasn't the nightmare of her waking hours of the same order? Wasn't it that humanity was taking on heads? Heads by which she was seen too much, heard too much, sniffed out too much, tasted too much, and following which the body dragged along only as the executor of deeds both high and low. The head would seduce you, poor woman that you were, and simply pass you on to some body, a body concealed and anonymous. Anonymity at the Seeds' was reserved for heads. Their features were not engraved but merely painted in harmless watercolor, and, in particular, these heads were pretty much lacking in the only weapon that Edmée was really afraid of, the weapon of speech. Faithful to Pierre without reservation, Edmée had nonetheless up to now not been all that sure of herself. Her theory of virtue was that men have a password which can get them any woman when they use it right. The word not usually being the same for all women, it happens that as a result of many a mix-up quite a few virtues remain intact; but all the accidents that happened to Edmée's friends, women who were well behaved, quite impervious, proved to Edmée that she was right. It was always words that had been their downfall, as they say (and as women don't say). It had never looked like an abduction, being taken by surprise, letting down their guard, or an attack of brute force. It was in his role as orator that man had won them all. Not one had given in to a man who stammered or couldn't speak. At the Seeds' the men were all silent.

But even more than this security in regard to men which gave her back the right to be beautiful, coquettish, and simple, Edmée was savoring, at this fair, on these terraces full of movie stars, a privilege that she didn't have with Pierre: she could escape the looks. Whose looks? It was a question she couldn't answer—not those of Pierre, obviously—but looks that were spying on her in her slightest moves, her slightest shift in mood. One couldn't say, moreover, that this dated from her marriage to Pierre. Already as a young girl she used to feel around her a sort of harassment, a kind of entreaty. It was the presence of someone who was the opposite of a thief. Of someone against whom she would open windows at night in the country, who kept her from bolting the door to her bedroom, someone who seemed to expect from her only a consent, a moment of weakness, a moment of solitude, in order to slip her some very precious gift. This sense of precaution, which was her principal rule in life, to touch life only lightly, to be a musician without talking of Mozart, to be a lover without appearing so, to be reverent yet discreet toward God to the point that one would have had to martyr her to get her to confess his name, to speak neither good nor ill of the weather, of the seasons, of Michelangelo—all this was the apprehension of an animal near the trap, her certainty that at the first word, the first gesture of passion, she was caught. It wasn't always easy. It wasn't like at boarding school, where she owed it to the always perfect Elisabeth Vandepotte never to be first place herself, to be second in drawing, second in religious instruction, to play only Elise in *Esther,* the doe in *Saint Geneviève,* and only the doe's head at that. There were quite a few occasions when the yellow of a piece of fabric in a painting at the museum or the sight of a dog about to go to sleep beneath a porch gave her the feeling that suddenly she had placed first on the brink of beauty or on the brink of anxiety. At these moments, the night stirred like a curtain and the sky was adorned with incomparable first prizes; she turned her glance away from that: the unknown breath was on her neck.

For a long time Pierre, through his enthusiasms, through the noise he made over great names, through his racket over masterpieces, had put in flight whatever they contained that was fatal. Edmée had often rejoiced at his cries, at his indignations, at his invocations of feelings and superhuman presences whose surest effect was to leave them to themselves, nice and bourgeois. A woman lives all day long with a series of beings whom the husband never really sees, presences she cannot denounce, who follow her and brush by her, presences inside her but from whom she is temporarily delivered if the husband gives a loud cry. No husband could make a greater outcry than Pierre when it came to human grandeurs, and as little Jacques himself, despite his tender age, was beginning to make his voice heard with the same effect, Edmée had for a time been able to believe herself safe. And all of a sudden, by that pressure, by that silence within silence, she had recognized the entreaty. The bait was simply different.

It was through that which is nothing, that which has no name, through that which flops or doesn't count that one was trying to reach Edmée. The world to be scorned picked up again there where the world that was splendid had failed. Now there had appeared before her at home a parade of all that was shop-worn, everyday, and scuffed, and, in the street, of all that had not tasted happiness. Perhaps, if Pierre had become Tolstoy and had given full vent to his pity on these occasions, he might have rendered them harmless too. This was not the case, and this intervention of the mediocre, of the vulgar and the banal, in order to keep Edmée attached to a life of escape was far tougher to deal with than chamber music or the school of Fontainebleau, and it was turning into blackmail. She felt remorse now, like the remorse of holding herself back, of not giving herself. To what she might be led, if she were weak enough one day to no longer contain this tacit consent—whether to sainthood or to wantonness, to virtue or to crime—was what nothing up to now had indicated, but it was beyond doubt, to judge by the anxiety that she felt every time she returned home, that Pierre and Jacques, through their innocence and their enthusiasms, had joined ranks with those defenseless and pitiful objects by which she was being baited. They sparkled with frailties, they glowed with nongenius. Not Claudie.

The days when Edmée flirted with this unknown pure love, when there was a sort of gaiety in her, as if what might be demanded of her would be innocuous or picturesque, would be to enter paradise with donkeys, would be to dance nude before the blind, those days gave way to others when she couldn't function. Not without risking tears and catastrophe, either about conjugal affection or maternal love. Here at least with the Seeds, if she felt like a deserter, desolate, she was at least calm. Arrayed in snobbery, in foolishness—without mentioning the dresses— she was here like Achilles dressed as a woman and surrounded by maidens. In this crowd of celebrated or extravagant characters, she felt removed from making a choice, from being chosen, and returned to that which lets you live in peace, to a fate of the second order. . . . That was what made returning to Pierre so painful: waiting for her there was a perfect husband, a child without fault, and a fate of the first order. . . . (But why insist today? I write these lines on board a ship off the island of Timor. On an atoll I see a very white Dutchman who has come to attention before what he believes to be a Dutch liner and which is really only a sentence in French.)

It was at the end of the fourth week that she received a letter from Pierre ordering her to return. *If you haven't returned by that date,* wrote Pierre, *I will have understood. . . .* Poor Pierre, who didn't understand, who would never understand, who addressed you as *vous* just at the moment when he should have found something ten times more intimate than the familiar *tu,* who was writing at the very time when her silence itself was beginning to speak clearly, both insistent and discreet. Of course she would return, since her husband ordered her to do so. What did it matter that the universe would be repopulated with heads! It would even be touching to redye and revive the old clothes in their wardrobes that she had tried to bury there on the eve of her departure. Then too, Pierre was so kind, so strong, so weak! Not to mention little Jacques, the mere sight of whom deserved a mother who would walk all the way from Santa Barbara to Los Angeles with her suitcases on her head, or with a cross on her shoulders and her knees bleeding! She would hold out her arms to Pierre on the platform at the station of course. One would embrace him to console him for the four weeks of absence. . . . One would listen to the lyrebird imitating a saw and anything else that Pierre might want it to imitate, a hammer or a file. . . . One would listen to the voice of Pierre saying "I order you to return. . . ." Why order? She was obedience itself. She got up. She went to pack her bags.

But once in her bedroom, she sat down and wrote:

*My dear Pierre, don't wait for me. I don't know where I am. Nor from where to start out, nor by what road to get back to you. I don't believe there is one that leads to me. . . . I'll find one that leads to Jacques. . . .*

"Should I put the letter in the mail?" asked Claudie.

"No, I don't have a stamp," said Edmée.

It was her last bit of resistance. . . . She hadn't counted on Claudie. Claudie had a stamp. Claudie's arsenal included all the equipment for execution that Edmée always found lacking. It would have included, for the right day, the nails, the spear, and the sponge with vinegar water. She had stolen a stamp from Jacques, six months ago, the day when he wanted to write his godmother. She carried it at the top of her kit bag. It was dried out; when you licked it, it had the taste of chocolate, but the glue was gone. It fell off the envelope somewhere en route. Pierre had to pay the postage due.

# 6

The specialist for angina pectoris was awfully sorry. One would have thought that the young woman was disappointed not to hear him reach a conclusion of angina. No, it was not angina pectoris.

"What is it then?"

"It is nothing."

"I'm suffering as if I were dying. For ten minutes now I've been suffering as if I were going to die."

"But you're not going to die. It's nothing at all."

She really would have been wrong to complain. There are scarcely more than two or three pains that indicate nothing, reveal nothing, or do not shout death to your face. This useless pain in this ravishing and healthy young woman was to Dr. Raszky only a show, a seduction. For he could see it. Some can see the flame of a rum omelet without the chandelier being put out. It had fallen to him to be able to see pains. At this moment he was contemplating, around a heart-shaped heart, one of those high flames that burn—though without consuming—within the breast of certain European nuns. Dr. Raszky's window was open: the flame was undulating, and would dart out at times. . . . What would it have been like in the night? Could such an anomaly perhaps be explained by an affinity with someone who was really sick, or because the Creator had sent the bill to the wrong person? It was worth investigating. Perhaps there was in fact somewhere a case of angina pectoris that was painless. One would still find it. By listening to the hearts of all the happy children, all the proud men, and all the satisfied mothers, the case would yet be found. . . .

"So much the better and so much the worse—it would have been so convenient!" Edmée said to herself, as she gave her place to another patient whose pain turned out to be a red-hot horseshoe stuck like a clip between the glottis and the pharynx, with half-caked blood in the little holes left by the nails. . . .

With angina pectoris everything could have been explained normally, cleared up normally: Claudie would have had a mother who suffered from angina. Quite a few girls are in this category. They look after their mothers' angina—first without knowing just what it is, although the mothers themselves know very well. They look after their mothers' angina later on, when they know what it is and the mothers have forgotten. At first what they think of as rheumatism brings to their faces worry and torment. Later on what they know to be angina puts a false varnish of smiles and blessings on the face they offer up to the patient. But at least the mind doesn't wander. During the whole time of the sickness, the torture, and the maternal agony, you know where you're going when you're inside a family. . . . Besides, Edmée wasn't really all that keen on the real angina—the false one would do quite well enough.

Dr. Raszky's pinpointing of the false angina had meant that the life led by Edmée and Claudie could continue, with a few added medications, just as it had been going on for the last four years, calm and happy. . . . Edmée was rich now, and one of the first ladies of Hollywood. It had all started, four years ago, like a movie. . . .

"Don't you think you might personify common sense?" one of the big studio heads had asked her one day at the Seeds'.

"Definitely not!" had replied Edmée. "I once fell in love with a public park."

"That's a pity. The Irish woman who represents common sense on our True-to-Life Board has begun to raise toucans. I would have given you her seat."

"Toucans surely have common sense," said Edmée. "That must even be extremely curious, the common sense of toucans."

"Perhaps, but my Irish friend doesn't care about that. She brings them to our meetings because of their noses, because they look like Kaledjian, my assistant director. She even paints them—to emphasize the resemblance—around the eyes in red and manages to make them dribble. He's going to be forced to recognize himself."

"But there's always a difference in that toucans don't talk."

"I know, they screech. But my assistant director doesn't talk either, he screeches too, and it's through him that I know the cry of the toucan. Besides, there's really no need to debate the basis of comparison. He's one of them. He eats sideways. His ties are tango-style. Around sidewalks he is led by his nose. . . . The Irish woman is going to leave. . . . Are you quite sure you don't personify common sense? . . . Did you embrace your park? Did you have any children by it? What did it say to you?"

"To paint my husband in bright red."

"In any case, you personify something. With you one feels in touch with a certain sureness, a certain truth. Come on my board, we'll find out which one it is. . . ."

They had soon seen that it was truth itself. The adviser on wild animals, who knew what time each one got up and had insisted on broad daylight for Siegfried's dragon, the adviser on Arabs, who kept an eye on cases of conjunctivitis among the extras, even the advisers on verisimilitude for documentary films—dealing with eclipses over Guatemala, smiles on lumberjacks, and diamond settings among the Borgias—they all had to quickly acknowledge that even in their own specialty Edmée was the most expert. From the first day that she replaced the Irish woman—it was quite true by the way that the assistant director was a toucan—that alliance between the puerile and knick-knacks, which was both the specialty and the horror of Hollywood, had at last given way. Edmée believed in feelings and not in local color, in Romeo and not in the balcony, in Desdemona and not in the handkerchief, in Judith and not in the head of Holophernes, carried by the hair, weeping and dripping blood.

In the first film submitted to her, which was *Mazeppa*, by the mere fact that she had suppressed manes and tails in the wind, kvass fizzing in the beakers, harness rings shining from the stallions' rumps, alder trees reflected in the Volga—in fact, everything that offended her—she had launched the fashion of a universe infinitely less garish and less aggressive than the universe was conceded to be until then. She hated anything that showed effort, whether it was ambition in men or the picturesque in nature. She didn't like types, or peculiarities that are translated by differences too obvious in age or face. So that, under her direction, a world of images was born where there was a gap of only a few years between the conscript and the centenarian, a few wrinkles' difference between the ugly and the beautiful, where the cosmetics of life obtained by accentuating old age or growth, vice or virtue, storms or moonlight, all became dissolved in a kind of resemblance and general ease of landscapes and beings. Even in documentaries, America lost its Grand Canyon, Africa its Zambezi, and from now on were only continents of valleys and flowers. In short, she had invented paradise. In this soft light, even if uncompromising, everything that was not true became comic or proved adulterated. The process of sorting things out operated by itself between the accessories of human happiness and those of human convention. The Eiffel Tower was of the first group, as well as the church of Arlington, and the peristyle of the door of the outer door of the antichamber of the chamber of the pavilion of the villa of Henry James, the brother of William James. . . . The pyramids, Niagara, and the turned-up noses of the virgins of Botticelli were of the second group.

Each spectator could savor whatever was most profound and most special to his delight in the midst of this world where everyone was similar. Humans rush toward whatever resembles that human house that they have been unable to find here on earth. The millions of Americans who besieged the films of Edmée were not going to the movies but rather at last to their homes, at last to their orchards, at last to their shores. There had of course been battles: Edmée had had to defend herself against the hotheads who wanted to take revenge on Christian Science by setting up, based on the principles of Edmée, an opposite religion. Since she savored less, in her new line of work, the powers of priestesses than the habits of typists, she shied away from all popularity. One morning she had refused a registered parcel which was nothing less than the solid gold bathtub presented by an Oklahoma flooring company to all women who were founders of new religions.

Claudie was sorry she turned it down. Claudie, who had just turned fifteen, believed in exactly two things, in gold and in the divinity of her mother. It hadn't been so long since Claudie had enjoyed really worshiping Edmée, with genuflections and a special pair of pajamas. She had found an enthusiastic ally in the enemy of the Irish woman, the old Armenian assistant director, who, from his stay in Erzurum, had retained a very particular understanding of the tastes of the gods, and would slip her special incense and soaps for special gods, wine used for mass in Urmia, and even chasubles. Edmée allowed Claudie everything, even to worship her, but she allowed it only to this daughter who knew all, who understood all, to the one she adored herself. Together, the two of them lived the life of an animal mother and daughter, side by side. Edmée would refuse every invitation for lunch because of a lunch that was urgent, the one she had every day with her daughter. Claudie would miss school because she had an invitation she couldn't turn down, the one she had every afternoon with her mother. They lived in a little house, surrounded by a yard that was scarcely any bigger, just a toy, like all the houses of Hollywood—Edmée wouldn't have accepted a house that could be taken seriously—that included neither cellars, nor storerooms, nor wardrobes, whose organism seemed to demand that one live from day to day the life of a blackbird, facilitated by the comings and goings of delivery vans. It was not only an innocuous and simple shelter. It was a house preserved from the sin of houses.

Whether it was her father's home, the properties of her aunts, or the apartment where she had lived with Pierre, Edmée had never had to deal with anything but houses laden with responsibilities, laden with the past, and which smacked of humanity, dead or alive. But in this one there had not been the slightest anger, the slightest illness, or even a single dead bird, though the birds in the cage were hummingbirds. The sleeping position had been taken there only by people who were still alive. It is sweet to live in the house of a child, and one that has not yet understood. . . . Why ever had Edmée agreed to preside over that banquet a month ago where her trouble had returned? . . . Since that day, everything was uncertain once more.

Edmée's distress stemmed still less from the pain, which was intense, than from her impression of being pursued, of being taken over by this stage character whose rights the advisers on verisimilitude, even if they were technicians, never dreamed of questioning, and which is your destiny. Dr. Raszky understood nothing about it. The main characteristic of Edmée's trouble was precisely that it wasn't an empty pain, the suffering of someone else misplaced on her, but rather a reminder, a sign that was meant only for her. When the anxiety had returned, she was given this jolt: she had been found again. For four years she had been able to conceal herself in this hiding place that was truth and renown, and suddenly the master singer, or perhaps simply the master, in the middle of the party, had spotted her, had touched her on the shoulder, had made himself known. . . . It was insulting at first: it was as if the headwaiter had dared pass her a letter. . . . But what irritated Edmée the most in this message was that Claudie was in no way involved. If Edmée had felt sure of anything, it was to have believed that from now on she could feel only maternal pains, that she could connect any suffering to Claudie, not only of the organs that had been particularly related to Claudie, of the womb that had borne her, of the breast that had fed her, but of all the others as well. One could always find the link: a whitlow or a rupture of the synovia were pains dedicated to Claudie, since Edmée's fingers had touched her, since Edmée's knees had bent down before her. . . . For a mother, to receive it from her daughter changes suffering into pleasure. If I bump my forehead, it's because I was thinking of my daughter. . . .

But this suffering, on the contrary, struck Edmée at every point in her that was not maternal, that is, nowhere in this body that was the body of the mother of Claudie, but at a heart in a different body, unknown to the other, and which had neither borne, nor given birth, nor nourished anyone. In vain did she try, every time the malaise appeared, to see in it some warning or apprehension concerning Claudie: but everything in her of either instinct or reason proved to her that Claudie was health itself, that no thief, no accident was in sight. The anxiety indeed concerned Edmée alone, a virginal Edmée, and pointed out cruelly—while Edmée had already passed on to her daughter, from one hand to the other, all her reasons to live—that nothing was settled yet in this sad world, and perhaps not in the world above either, as to what concerned her herself. It was too easy to believe that she was done with everything in preparing Claudie's future, in becoming Claudie's slave. Claudie was nothing, the anxiety was saying, Claudie didn't exist. Or at any rate, to each her turn. Edmée was the real question right now in the book of destinies. . . .

She had left Claudie reigning alone in the apartment, and it was a little girl who came to open the door for her, a little girl whose mother had been called back into the game by fate.

"I've come from seeing the doctor, Claudie. I thought I was ill. There's nothing wrong with me."

"Of course there's nothing wrong with you," exclaimed Claudie.

She pulled her mother to the couch, hugged her, and smothered her with kisses. If Edmée had had the slightest lesion, the slightest problem, it would have been revealed to her by this assault. It was her second auscultation of the day, the one that Dr. Raszky would have been able to bring off only by rolling Edmée on the floor, hurling himself against her with all his strength, butting his own head against that of Edmée without restraint, and rubbing his face very hard against the bosom, cheeks, and nose of his patient, and then too, suddenly, if while clutching her, Dr. Raszky had started sobbing his heart out while hitting her repeatedly with a door knocker. Yes, proof today had been given twice over. Edmée was a mother that her daughter couldn't run through by springing on her, who didn't bleed to the last drop when her daughter turned into a leech and stuck herself to her. Nothing was weak or sick or wounded in this maternal body. . . . Why couldn't one say the same of that other form of Edmée, who from the beginning had avoided the hugs and, sorrowfully, up above the two women lying there, was waiting with indifference for this emotional outburst to come to an end? . . .

"You will never suffer. . . . You will never die. I will protect you. . . ."

For a long time Edmée had believed in the protection of Claudie. Since she was born. Before that day she had had only herself to count on. She hadn't known her father any way but sick, her mother any way but consenting, her uncles any way but weak. . . . At home there had been only maids who were fainthearted or dogs who welcomed all, leaving her always face-to-face with the ogre or the beggar. Whence that exposed air that used to make Pierre say that she seemed offered up to everyone. She was indeed offered up to Pierre, and Pierre had not provided her any further protection. On her wedding night, while she awaited the protector of protectors to unfasten every hook of her bodice, to pull off each finger of her gloves, Pierre had left her to undress herself, and she had had the feeling that she was taking off her clothes for life itself and everyone in it. . . . Let engineering students take heed! A man should undress his wife himself on their wedding night or she may undress for everybody! . . . Nor had Jacques given her any more protection. He was born resigned his very first hour, he didn't complain, and he was smiling already. Let the sons of only one day take heed if they want to inspire their mothers with confidence: they ought to sound a firm protest against life. She had felt his birth as the arrival on earth of that which is weakest, of the most condemned. . . .

The day when Claudie was born, on the contrary, a certain repose and happiness were also born, whose name she had found that very evening, and which was security. This little creature whose eyes were not yet open, who raged not to be able to see, who choked not to be able to hear, was protecting her. The first minute of Claudie's life was for Edmée the first minute without oppression, without apprehension. Everything was asleep at last inside Edmée, aside from herself, for Claudie would bawl loudly. The first week of Claudie's life was the first week when Edmée knew a world without spiders, without banana peels, without a hairdresser whose curling iron was too hot. It was the week when a dirigible blew up near the house, when a famine in India, according to the papers, killed two million Hindus, but the death of others, now that Claudie had been born, no longer seemed to affect Edmée in her personal heart; though before this day she would have suffered terribly in her tenderhearted way, now there was nothing but peace.

With the years Claudie had become aware of her role. The child-talisman who protected Edmée from the great ills of the world would also protect her, by means of mallets, traps, or poisoned fruit, from the dangers that her first readings or the season indicated as the most fearsome—flies, Bengal tigers, or the sun. Sometimes to enter her room, Edmée had to step over stretched-out ribbons or trails of colored sand; this was protection against ants or pirates. Claudie also protected against accidents: before she went out she would give her mother an inspection that seemed to cover her powder, her rouge, or her belt, but which in fact was meant to render harmless the crowds and cars. She considered her from top to bottom, taking in everything with her glance, not forgetting her heels. Claudie protected against pests and bores. Before any intruder, she would cling to her mother, defying him with an arrogant head that went as high as Edmée's navel: to get to her mother, to kill her mother, to embrace her mother, this salesman, this friend, this mouse, this father would first have to get past her own body; above the navel, protection was of course less certain, and Claudie trembled with rage when her father, without seeming to see her, touched his lips to a brow that she had not thought of defending by a veil of iron or a crown of thorns. . . .

Claudie protected against God, for one couldn't call it anything else but complacency on the part of God that sort of irresponsibility, innocence, and feeling of childhood that Edmée experienced around her daughter. With the result that she had arrived at dividing the gifts of this world into two parts, keeping on her side all that was benign, incidental, and harmless, and heaping on Claudie's side all that was glorious, dangerous, and significant. Like a mother who little by little gives up her jewels and precious things to her daughter—and, indeed, she was doing that too—she was passing on to Claudie the items of high destiny—love, horseback riding, the sublime, their triumphs, delights, and catastrophes, and it extended as far as her memories. She renounced any sensation that was too vast, any effort to exist, to exist individually, as if she were giving her daughter life itself in the form of a dowry, and she must subtract nothing from this dowry. At times, on the point of filling her lungs full of air from the sea or, on the edge of sleep, of stretching her arms until they cracked, she would contain herself, she would take in oxygen timidly by the nose, she would keep her arms alongside the body: the movement of her breasts, the swelling of her belly, feeling her body being quartered through languor nipped away at Claudie's kingdom, the things that were rightfully Claudie's. . . . She would read the most beautiful books with the tips of her lips; she would watch the most beautiful spectacles with the most restrained glances, as if she might have worn out, through the slightest insistence, personages or landscapes that Claudie ought to receive intact, and as if by pressing against it she was taking away the color of the world. In this universe, astonishingly vigorous and virginal, that through her reserve she had managed to erect for Claudie, she too was now living, but as a hostess, as a dowager, but on tiptoes, given over completely to the idea of Claudie's royalty, to Claudie as a masterpiece of nature.

And here she was obliged, by the fact of this anxiety, to pass into a world of thoughts, of troubles—who knows, perhaps of joys too?—beyond the reach and the comprehension of Claudie. She had been tempted to tell her everything but dared not. It was precisely the nature of her problem in fact to leave the impression that none of this concerned Claudie, that it was a secret between itself and Edmée. It was as if Edmée had an adventure with some fate that completely disdained Claudie, an obstinate fate that nothing would influence in its choice, that liked grown-up women, with golden complexions, bodies asleep, and attached no importance, despite the intervention of the mothers, to girls of fifteen, with their tresses, their rosy cheeks, hearts, and beauty itself. She excused herself for keeping her secret under the pretext of not alarming Claudie. But in fact it was the apprehension that she would betray someone by speaking, and that it would be completely useless. That she would perhaps betray herself. For, through a selfishness that she reproached herself for bitterly, she had reached the point, because of this sign, of detaching her cause from that of Claudie. A sort of freedom was being born for her out of this secret, a freedom which was winning over even her body, which was giving back to her her legs, her hair, her bare arms. There were birds, corners of roofs, and waves that were detaching themselves from Claudie's universe, that flew away or lighted up or broke off for Edmée, traitors in short. . . .

Betrayal now reigned around Claudie; she no longer had her privileges; she was no longer omniscient; she no longer protected—Edmée even managed to sprain her arm. Nothing was more cruel than this fear of having to observe that Claudie was no longer the cure-all, the good-luck charm, the hope; and if from her bed, Edmée anxiously spied on Claudie, it wasn't only that she wanted to again see shining over her that phosphorus that once rendered her visible to Edmée even in the dark of night. It was that all hope was not yet lost that a sign might confirm that she had not fallen, that she was still everything. . . . But Claudie's hands remained without stigmata, and no sign of the cross, no bleeding, lidless eye was suddenly tattooed on her forehead.

The unknown accomplice was not the only one to seek to moderate Edmée's admiration for Claudie. There were also her grades from school. This miracle daughter who seemed to Edmée the very essence of intelligence and comprehension was near the bottom of her class. Edmée, in the parlor where she came to receive the honor of the world, found out from headmistresses and professors that this particular honor knew nothing, and that her behavior was bad. . . . That her divination might have failed to inform Claudie of a single one of the first names of General Lee, that her state of grace might not be concerned with cretaceous terrain—well, this one could still admit. But Claudie proved utterly hopeless in precisely those areas where Edmée believed her to be not a pupil but rather a kind of supernatural authority: in ethics, in politics, in religion. Whereas at home every one of her words allowed one to suppose in Claudie a technical knowledge of the world and every one of her attitudes a preestablished understanding with the most significant personages of our physical and metaphysical general staff, in class she had with them only the connections of a child. In her homework, the definitions of God, of sin, of wisdom were so childish that Edmée saw in them some dissimulation, and the naturalness with which Claudie resumed her omniscience and her omnipotence as soon as she had crossed the threshold of her school and left it confirmed her mother somewhat in this thought.

Edmée was above all comforted by that which baffled the teachers the most, by the sort of preeminence that Claudie held over her classmates, and which those overseeing matters couldn't quite define. Claudie was not really familiar. She would spend weeks indifferent about the games they played and would make conversations of only a general nature; then, one fine day, overtly, in the middle of recreation, she would go toward one of the other girls, with whom she wasn't particularly friendly, and between the two of them there would begin a debate, almost an argument. The two girls, who had talked only a little before, suddenly seemed to be fighting over a subject whose importance was capital for both of them—Claudie, impassioned, insistent, and voluble, the other girl standing firm in her own defense, bristling with objections. This would last for two or three recess periods, then they would leave each other smiling, and it was all over, until the day when Claudie would take aside another girl, and an argument would start from the very first exchange of words, quite virulent, but subsiding and coming to an end after a few sessions. None of this pleased the ladies and gentlemen of the day school.

That suddenly, out on the playground, out of the silence or the complicit racket of the other girls, should arise a debate whose interest seemed, to the exclusion of the class programs, the only important thing in life, with as much seriousness and determination as if these pupils were not arguing on their own behalf but rather as the delegates of two parties who were disputing the world and the whole school, this was an attack on their prestige that they could not accept, but despite their curiosity, not one of them had been able to find out what was in question. If it was always the same debate, if Claudie's friends were convinced or if they did the convincing, if it was the settling of personal matters, of hearts in conflict, they had not been able to learn. The pupils they tried to question were evasive, even their own daughters. It wasn't really a quarrel, for there were never any threats or brusque separations, but there were red faces and pale ones and tears as well, on the part of Claudie too, but more rarely. Nor was it a question of dubious conversations; the choice of schoolmates and the indifference of the opponents as to whether others were paying attention removed all suspicion. It was exactly, said the headmistress, as if these children were discussing things strangely true or strangely mad but terribly important. . . . They, the teachers, would not have attacked each other in this way except to settle some big debate over Nietzsche or over the new swimming pool. One had the impression that when one of the girls had been convinced, the result of it would be an immediate change in the souls and attitudes of the pupils. That they would suddenly all be arrogant or submissive, all debauched or all blushing, all passionate or all cold. No. The duel would come to an end. One was victorious, and nothing came of it, and the girls didn't suddenly grow up, and they didn't suddenly all give birth, and they didn't sacrifice one of their own before the Mayan god that embellished the central courtyard, and they didn't become sleepwalkers, any one of which would have seemed less strange to the teachers, and above all less irritating, than the ease with which these featherbrains passed underneath their noses in what the math tutor called their fourth dimension. Edmée alone was satisfied: Claudie came out of the adventure with more stature in her eyes, and all those zeros that came to swell and expire on the surface of her homework were for her only the signs of a profound and latent life, only bubbles of air. . . .

But she could not hide from herself that she, Edmée, on the other hand, was becoming a good student. Whatever the homework and lessons were, she didn't know, but the awareness of that maturation that awaits, before Virgil and Tacitus, those students who have understood Ovid and Sallust, she felt the same thing about a tree, an insect, or a human face. A land promotion, which she found disturbing, had turned the valley, through which morning and evening she traveled to the studios, into something wonderful. And yet she had chosen this route because of its very banality, in that spirit of economy that urged her not to partake of things of the world—so as to hold back Claudie's part—except for that which had been already used up. Yesterday it was still ground whose general layout she could clearly see, grass worn down, trees that had served their time, volcanic rock without hope. Although it never would have occurred to anyone to go to stretch out or to put together a meal on such terrain, one could see the traces, as in any second-rate desert, of a picnic organized every day by some invisible couple. And suddenly, without the disappearance of a single tin can, without the crew of makeup men—for spring here had no effect—having begun to paint the leaves and filter the brook, because of this land promotion, which was really only mental, everything had been changed.

It was the same spectacle, exactly the same, and yet, with each stroll, it rose higher in the hierarchy of spectacles. For the other people who walked past her or who accompanied her, painters, actors, novelists, it remained without value, common and vulgar, all the more common and vulgar the more gifted and farsighted they were themselves. But the fact that for Edmée the world had chosen its poorest and most banal point to reveal to her its riches, its dignity, even its good taste, became on its part more than a confidence, it was a show of trust. Sometimes also an appeal, for—and this was the most curious thing—nature was offering her a date. Those trees that were there, that sky that was there, and even though she was alone with them, they were making a date with her. The invitation was pressing, from objects of nature that do not move or may be found everywhere, from rocks, fir trees, or moon, an invitation to get to the secret place where Edmée would meet them at last, as if their presence here were only a false presence. That's what they were saying, those oaks and magnolias, even if Edmée touched them with her finger, as one touches in order to stop a runner leaping over hurdles: "We are not here. Meet us, you will see what we are!" And the river over which noon or twilight had placed a mirror, precisely because it seemed to be no longer flowing, was rushing along with all the cascades and currents of its immobility toward that point of the world where it was making a date with Edmée. . . . Was it near, was it far away? Would they show up in person if she went there? Would they delegate their rendezvous to other trees, to other species? "You will see what the wind is!" said the wind, and it was precisely these presences, which she was tasting in their plenitude and their authority, that were giving Edmée the most freedom, the most isolation, and, alas, the most promise.

Claudie also benefited from the way everything appeared embellished. But Edmée had no reason to rejoice over that. Because of this varnish, the way everything stood out in relief to her eyes, she felt for the first time separated from Claudie. Or rather, Claudie for the first time was outside of Edmée. Not once yet had Edmée imagined that her daughter did not live, sleep, and grow inside herself. The birth, the first birth of Claudie, had simply moved her from the womb where her mother didn't see her to a more ample maternity where Edmée did see her. She was still carrying her daughter, but outside herself. The sheath where Claudie had taken shape had merely been turned inside out, was the surface of Edmée's body, her face, all that space around them, and it was there that Claudie lived. She left only to go to the theater, to go to school. She invited her little friends into her mother's womb, she sang there, she danced there. The cry, the sight of Claudie swimming out there in the sea, gave Edmée the same shock as the stirring about inside her of a Claudie not yet born. Summer and spring had been until now no more than interior gardens, and suddenly it was over.

She now felt Claudie separated from herself, the tie was cut. Claudie didn't tug on her anymore as she left for school: it was just her daughter leaving the house. The comings and goings of her daughter that had been like caresses to her were now simple comings and goings. Her daughter no longer walked on her in order to walk, no longer lay down on her in order to sleep. The hugs and kisses of a Claudie glued to her mother did not by themselves replace the perfect assent of a Claudie gone for the weekend, of a Claudie alone at mass. . . . How she had gotten away, on what day this second and sad birth had taken place, Edmée saw very well that she herself was more responsible than was her daughter. This anxiety, this internal solicitude that followed, this intrigue that she had accepted in her daily walks with objects and creatures, that was what had made her let things go in her maternal body and had let her drop the child that she should have borne for as long as she lived. The wrong was irreparable, like any birth. In vain, when Claudie lay down beside her and hugged her, she would close her eyes, but she only felt all the more Claudie outside of her, and at night she, who yesterday was still inside her, was no more now than an infirmity, and the most painful spectacle was this—yesterday the sweetest, that of Claudie asleep—now giving herself over to a sleep that was no longer a fall to the deepest part of her mother, which was her sleep, but now only an obstinacy to cut the last link, the last look.

Nursed by an air, turned gold by a sun that was no longer Edmée, nourished by water, by toast, by salads that were no longer Edmée, Claudie was losing that resemblance of flesh and voice, and was taking on temper, taste, and smell, like those who have been born. Edmée was feeling the greatest pain of her life: learning to count two. To that excessive sense of security which led her to let Claudie go to sea alone and to go up in a plane followed a nagging concern. What runaway streetcar would spare Claudie, what swimming pool would not defile her, what oil lamp would not explode in her hands in this world where her mother was no longer water and fire? And there came an evening when Edmée noticed that, like all the rest, like everything that was not her, like the trees and the wind in her valley, Claudie too was making a date with her. When she was sitting at her table, even in front of her mother, her head in her notebooks, her whole being, her hands, her dress, were saying, "Mother, meet me. I'm making a date with you. . . ." With all her presence, she confessed an absence that would wring your heart. It was useless to go up to her, to take her head, to touch her hair. "Where are you?" asked Edmée. "In your arms," said Claudie; but that meant that she wasn't there, it was rather a call toward the region, toward the world where she would be. "I'm making a date with you," said the shadow, the silhouette, the silence of Claudie. . . . From all the other beings it was a promise, but from Claudie it was really as if Claudie weren't there, didn't exist! . . .

Edmée would make a date to meet her at some street corner, to take tea, so as to have the illusion of seeing her at last come up to her, so that, thanks to a small meeting, they might meet each other forever. She would arrive ahead of time, and her waiting, and her happiness, and her torment were like those of a mother who is at last going to meet a daughter who left a thousand years ago, but from the taxi, from its open door, she saw rushing forward, embracing her and assailing her, a Claudie in whom everything, gestures, laughter, and clothes, all offered her the real rendezvous, and, with her mouth right at her ear—with this one phrase, "How good I feel when I'm with you!"—was saying to her, "Meet me, meet me! You will see who the real Claudie is!"

"Should we leave? Should we leave Hollywood?"

"Oh yes, Mother!"

"Right away? Forever?"

"Oh yes, Mother!"

It was with words like these that Edmée found Claudie again, with her scorn for all the situations, the friendships, the habits. Of course her daughter would leave this existence and these friends without turning her head, just as she had left her home and her father. Edmée, who was all respect and submission, wondered why she felt nevertheless this cruelty and impassivity on the part of Claudie as if they were at the base of her own life and was inclined to obey—rather than her own impulses—these pitiless exclamations.

"You won't regret Hollywood?"

"Oh no, I won't regret Hollywood."

"You won't regret either Mr. Clark, or William, or Mr. Kaledjian?"

"Oh no. I won't regret either Mr. Clark, or William, or Mrs. Betty, or Bob, or Mrs. . . ."

"All right. All right."

She cut off Claudie's enumeration, for the list would have included everybody whose name Claudie knew. Claudie's phrase would have gone on: "I won't regret either the old gentleman with the long nose who keeps me stocked in candy, or my boyfriend, or the ugly woman who gave me my gold watch, or my little enemy, or the pretty woman who lends me her horse, or the horse itself. . . ." These were the litanies, the commandments of Claudie. "You will not regret your father, nor your brother, nor your first home, nor your second. Nor those whom you hate, nor those whom you love. You will not keep worn-out penholders. You will throw your dolls away if they have lost a finger. You will forget in a second those who are absent or dead. . . ." Edmée didn't know whether she was scandalized or fortified by Claudie's attitude about death. Claudie ignored it. When a neighbor or a friend died, she never spoke of it again. He had ceased to exist. The heart of Claudie was the first place in this sad world where the light and memory of the deceased were switched off. One can guess what history meant to her. Or the memory of her dead dogs.

"Unless," thought Edmée, when she had judged her daughter severely, "I am the guilty one. This insensitivity serves my purpose. I have near me a little god of indifference, of disdain, of oblivion. That's how I slip into pity and my attachments. All the more if he loves me, admires me, or thinks about me all the time."

"Where are we going?"

Wherever could they go? They were going to try to find the place of rendezvous where all those beings either absent or present were waiting for Edmée—the trees, the birds, her own daughter. Edmée's contract was up. She didn't renew it. She had enough funds to buy a house and live, and besides, work at the studio was becoming unbearable. Without counting the anxiety that attacked her at almost every reception, every party, she no longer felt qualified to supply common sense for the dramas of

Shakespeare, whose turn was now coming up. The director had to call back the Irish woman. A decision he didn't have cause to repent. *Hamlet* was a huge success: she had introduced a solitary ram, who, indifferent, came and went, doing the same promenades as Hamlet, giving the audience an animal lesson, letting himself be petted by Ophelia—she thought he was sweet, he was a merino—passing without any notice before the skull of a ram's head, and entering the actors' greenroom to butt with his horns a dog who had provoked him. It was the ram in the last shot, who, unexpectedly, had just been grazing on the roses that a reconciled Hamlet was offering to his future wife. . . . The audience cried. . . .

And the day of departure came. Edmée had to make a choice among her dresses, like the evening when they left for the Seeds', but this time it was easier, just the reverse. It was no longer a matter of discovering vermilion and gold in a modest wardrobe, but of putting aside the fabrics that had become too gilt or too rich and bringing back that black or gray or beige that she had once rejected. Of course they weren't the same ones; the neutral shades from her wardrobe were now of the best material, of marvelous design. She had at least gained that in this first metamorphosis: she was now a superior neutral. A more fastidious fate would have given her back the clothes left with Pierre, but everything is regulated by approximation in this sad world, even as regards providence or misfortune.

What had become of them anyway, what still remained of the leftovers that had marked her place in that single closet: dark dresses and cotton kimonos that had continued to touch every night Pierre's jackets? . . . No doubt they were now being worn by the poor. At the very most there might still be a hat up on the top shelf, one of those faded old hats that they put on scarecrows to protect the cherries. . . . The cherries were being protected in Pierre's bedroom. . . . The shoes, Pierre must have given them away. But the shoe trees? The shoe trees were all that were left to him of his real wife, since she hadn't left any adjustable hands to maintain the gloves. . . .

Claudie's bags were simpler still. Claudie, who never got dirty, who never wore anything out, left no residue either of old dresses, old toys, or old books. It all fit into a small suitcase, really not much bigger than the one used for the other departure.

They left one fine day without letting anyone know. All Hollywood first believed there had been some sort of accident and even made a search for the bodies. But that week, throughout America, washed up by the tide, dredged up from the depths, the bodies of mothers and the bodies of daughters turned out to be isolated, separated by miles and miles. . . . Thus it was learned that they weren't dead.

# 7

It was only in the third year of their stay in San Francisco that someone came to the rendezvous. It was Frank. Frank was buying some ties near the Saint Francis Hotel when he noticed through the shop window a girl who was indicating that he should drop the blue-and-white polka dot and choose the red tie instead. He was weak, he had obeyed. From the sidewalk, the girl had rewarded him by sending a kiss. He wasn't too surprised by this. Frank's adventures had always been notable for being unforeseen and for lasting only a moment. Of those that had lasted more than a moment he had little reason to be very satisfied; but, from one train to the next, inside the station, from a bus to a taxi stopped by the same traffic cop, from a boat going upstream to a boat going downstream, he had had a series of lightning-flash intrigues—including bedazzlement, consent, and good-bye—with the woman that some current of the world opposite to his own had fleetingly brought before him.

When a woman knows that the liaison, however complete, can last only a moment, she unconsciously summons all her kindness, her joy, her assent, her grace, and those kinds of angels that used to surrender to Frank from across the mirrors in a train car or through the barrier before the metro, all radiating devotion and constancy, all without name, without address, who love you selflessly, who leave you without a breakup, that race of women who pass you going the opposite direction, who are going up in the elevator when the elevator is taking you down, the only unobtainable woman, the only faithful one . . . all in all, this was the woman that Frank preferred. What beautiful children could come from those encounters! Frank was grateful for his habit of always having at hand some object or book; he was able in that way, beneath the hostile eyes of onlookers, to toss on the lover's lap a novel, a cigarette, sometimes a cigarette case. It was little, to be sure: one would have preferred to offer a cat, one's heart, one's life. But this time, through the shop window, his partner was more constant. She was going in the same direction. She had moved up like himself to the window where the socks were on display; she obliged him to abandon some grayish green socks in favor of a pair that were mauve. He resisted, for he hated mauve; she threatened him, she wouldn't love him anymore—and suddenly he recognized her, not from her features, but, as a painter, from her special colors, from a red, from a cream that he had seen only on that face, and he recalled a particular palette: he recognized Claudie. . . .

"Mother, I'm bringing you Frank."

For those were the words that Claudie used. She didn't say, "I ran into Frank," or "I caught sight of Frank." She said, "I'm bringing you Frank"! And in the days that followed, she said, "I found Frank for you, I risked my reputation in front of a shop window so that you wouldn't lose Frank. . . ." If a debate should arise someday, here below or up above, as to who was responsible for the horror that followed, Claudie couldn't deny a thing. She had brought Frank back as if life were no longer possible without him, as if her duty as a daughter had been to seek out Frank at any time and any place. There was nothing she said that didn't begin with "Now that Frank has been found. . . ."

If one were to believe Claudie, it was Frank that both of them had been looking for in Washington Park and on the terrace at the Seeds', Frank that they had been waiting for at the little house in Hollywood; it was to track down Frank that they had gotten a police dog, that they were subscribing to a magazine for painters. Edmée wasn't so sure about it: she could hardly find more than two objects in the apartment that might really have been waiting for Frank to come—a sketch of Claudie by a Czech artist and an Italian frame bought in a sale. These two came to life, these two simply shone since Frank had been found. They had recovered at the same time both their nationality and their reason for being. Prague and Rome were jubilant since Frank had corrected the sketch just a bit, since he had caressed the frame. Edmée had more doubt concerning her own enthusiasm. The court would bear witness: she never spoke a one of the words that were always coming from Claudie's mouth: *starting today, . . . finally, . . . from now on, . . .* those words of the traveler when he has crossed through the mountain pass and first catches sight of the plain below.

When she had seen Frank come in on Claudie's arm, Edmée had thought, on the contrary, that Claudie had found him for herself. This man that Claudie had brought back to her mother, she was taking over for herself: she went horseback riding with him, she went swimming with him, she was becoming a cook for him. Beneath that superior law that had dictated that Frank was there for Edmée, Frank and Claudie had become inseparable. An unwritten but implacable law silently decreed, starting at dawn, that his whole life long Frank had loved only Edmée, yet it was Frank and Claudie who were embracing. . . . Edmée was much more alone at home now that Frank had been found for her. . . . Moreover, there was nothing questionable about this intimacy—it was clear that neither Frank nor Claudie had the slightest amorous interest in each other. But on Claudie's side, it was no less evident that neither was it a matter of either friendship or camaraderie. . . . Edmée admitted it to herself with regret: it wasn't Frank that Claudie had brought back, it was paternity.

Claudie didn't suspect it, but every word of their conversation proved that this was a conversation between father and daughter. Claudie was learning from Frank what one learns only from a father—the scientific name of rhubarb, those devices designed to expose ballot boxes with false bottoms in elections, and the exact measurement of an inch, a foot, and an ell. With Frank, Claudie was catching up a bit every day on those girls favored with a father concerning the sharpening of pencils, making whistles from willow bark, the de-fleaing of a dog, and the significance of the swastika. She was learning how men walk—never known to orphan girls—learning card tricks, and beginning to be fond of the two masculine objects that she had hated until then, suspenders and bedroom slippers. Edmée couldn't really suspect a passion that in another time would have led Claudie to embroider a Turkish skullcap for Frank's name day.

What Edmée herself felt was neither jealousy nor fear, but rather disappointment. First of all, fatherhood brought out in Frank a host of lacks and trivial defects that were not apparent when he was a bachelor. But above all there was a sort of abdication in the conduct of Claudie. Edmée had deplored her daughter's aversion to her father, but deep down, she had to admit that it was perhaps the reason for her admiration of Claudie. Claudie was avenging her. It was a very special vengeance. She was avenging her on a husband whom she loved and for whom she was everything, was avenging her on men in general—uncles, cousins, and strangers, from whom she had received only smiles, gifts, and acts of kindness and for whom she felt, as a young woman who was kind and had everything, only affection or pity. It was out of the question to suppose that there was any reason to take revenge on her own father, who had died in her arms while sucking on a licorice twist with his tongue all black, or, for that matter, to take revenge on any father whatsoever, whether he was a gambler, a drunkard, brutalized his wife, or courted his daughter—but what else to call this instinct that urged her to support in Claudie a constant disavowal of all fatherhood, a certain insolence even before the fathers of her schoolmates, this conviction that she was born fatherless, indeed

the only girl born without a father. And now, out of her defer-
ence for Frank, out of her friendship with Frank, here she was
recognizing that she owed her life to men, owed her life to one
man. To tell the truth, Edmée had forgotten him. . . . Unless one
was to suppose that Claudie might love this father precisely because he was without wife and without children. . . .

Besides, Edmée could no longer conceal it from herself:
this precedence that her daughter had over other human beings,
this mission that she attributed to her, Claudie was really
abdicating little by little. Her health was less good: she was abdicating her immortality. Her speech was less clear, she had a
tendency to stammer, her steps less sure, her walk hesitant; she
was abdicating that so very pure sound that she emitted on earth.
She was becoming at once both slow and furtive. She turned
away if she spoke; she hid her face if she laughed: she was abdicating her face and her flash of lightning. She no longer asked
questions about her childhood; she was abdicating her young
salmon instinct of swimming upstream with her short life toward the sacred cool—she was going downstream. . . . Her lot of
feminine concerns, which she had been deprived of to an incredible extent, those concerns that were allotted to Eve the day she
understood she was nude—sweetness, politeness, respect for the
wishes of others—Claudie was now granted in full measure. To
this diminution in the order of archangels corresponded a promotion in the human order. She developed a taste for study. She
began to rank higher among her classmates. She had renounced
that ignorance which in the eyes of her mother constituted all
knowledge. She repositioned herself to take her rank among
mediocre humanity. She placed eleventh. . . .

"Everything is going much better," said her teachers. "We
didn't dare hope for this."

At the beginning, Edmée could have wept. It was all going
better! Claudie was chlorotic and was losing her phosphate.
Claudie would trip over her feet and had to give up high heels.
Claudie, because of this abdication of her body, won ten firsts in
gymnastics. . . . It went as far as the color of her eyes, which

began to darken and would stare, like those of fish pulled from
the water; if this kept going on, she would win a beauty contest. . . . Her former obstinacy to learn nothing was no more than
an obstinacy to admit nothing. . . . Now she would admit everything. Now she was consent itself. In the world of numbers she
would admit addition and multiplication, in the world of men,
logic and metaphysics. She granted the Civil War, granted the
assassination of Lincoln. Each teacher who would announce to
Edmée that Claudie understood logarithms, was taking to ana-
lytical grammar, and was beginning to spell well was really giving her notice that Claudie had renounced yet another of those
gifts that made her unique in this world.

"It's wonderful!" she heard. "Your daughter no longer
knows how to fly through the air! . . . It's all going to be all right!
Your daughter no longer knows how to say everything while remaining silent. You can be very proud! You have a daughter of
flesh and blood, a daughter interested in embroidery. Not like
the one doing petit point, who can crochet, but she'll be there in
a year. . . . You should be delighted! Your daughter no longer
lives off the morning dew, she's no longer as tall as a pine, she no
longer shines like a sun. She no longer stands out among the
girls. You're going to see her tonight when she comes home,
modest, clean—for she washes now. You will take her for another girl. . . . Congratulations!"

And it was true. Every evening brought back to the house
a Claudie more and more like her classmates, who now had to be
combed and brushed, whose glow was being lessened, who had
her first bad tooth, her first sty. She was going to suffer those ill-
nesses which as a result of her divine nature she had not had as a
child—measles, scarlet fever. There could be no doubt: was it in
her walks with Frank, was it at school, at the theater, was it in
her mother's own caresses? Claudie had touched a human at the
very moment when humanity was contagious.

Accustomed to seeing her always distinct and luminous in
the midst of her friends, distant even from those she was talking
to, Edmée was now obliged to discover her in groups, arm in

arm with another girlfriend, at times with many others. . . . She passed her on the street without seeing her. She didn't see her anymore. She recognized her as one recognizes strangers, by the color of her hat, by her raincoat. If one had presented to her Claudie's arm cut off, she would have recognized it by her ring. . . . There were now at home many arrivals and departures: Claudie no longer knew how to be there without being there, how to be absent while being present. Every gesture of Claudie at the apartment was now governed by demands that she didn't seem to admit before; to see clearly she would turn on the lights, to go out she would open the door. . . . Your daughter no longer reads without a light and without a book. Congratulations! . . . Edmée couldn't see the least of those specialists in that humanity to which Claudie now belonged without hearing these dismal compliments. The greengrocer who congratulated Claudie for no longer being the produce, the shoemaker who congratulated her for no longer being motion itself. Claudie now no longer left the gas on, she would now answer the telephone. Edmée was never surprised anymore when she came home by the smell of something burning or by one of those tiny fires involving the rug, the lampshade, or the wastepaper basket, which the mere presence of Claudie used to render incandescent. . . . Claudie was no longer fire. . . . Congratulations! . . .

Nor water either. The ceiling below the bath upstairs could now dry out without fear. Claudie knew her weight, knew her volume! She no longer had a craze for getting into a bathtub filled to the very top, as if she weren't going to take a bath but rather dissolve in it. . . . There could be no more doubt. . . . Claudie would follow the rest. She would take over from her three aunts, her four great-grandmothers, the billions and billions of girls who had gone before her, take over from her mother too, who was not to be fooled. There now began to creep into her acts toward others that attention, that pity, and that devotion which pass for being the signs of a moral flowering and which are only the putting in place of that egocentric net by which virgins prepare unconsciously but rapaciously the realization of their own happiness at the expense of others. Edmée knew from experience what to make of that tenderness concerning nature, those gifts of oneself to the seasons, that impulse toward beautiful causes, those failings concerning beauty, which lead girls to the crest of sentiment from which they descend again to men with their nerves, their certainty, and their domination.

These tears of Claudie, these debates, this conviction of being a rag and a plaything in the world, Edmée knew were the proof that Claudie would be strong, would be able to manage with marriage and a husband, would have an orderly widowhood, would bear without harm bereavements and human contacts. Perhaps she ought to be glad for Claudie: for the old Claudie, indomitable, impervious to sentimentality, harder to move than a stone, she foresaw a future of extremes, of sacrifices, of sorrows; with the new one there was less to fear. Claudie's pity for the poor, those sudden rushes of love for her girlfriends, those frantic dashes off to people seen one time, those outbursts of emotion at the theater or a concert—they all simply proved to Edmée that a whole series of acts both wonderful and awful which still came naturally to Claudie only yesterday were now forever eliminated: Claudie's suicide on the same day as the death of her mother, for example. Claudie was becoming sensitive: she would no longer kill herself over Edmée. . . . She was reading *Hamlet* with tears: on the evening of the death of her mother she would no longer stretch out in a white gown on the funeral bed, perfectly agile and lucid, for at least a dose of Veronal will take away your headache in the beginning. . . . And besides, why the Veronal? The old Claudie would have died, naturally, from the death of her mother. . . . Well, that was over. Edmée was living from now on with a daughter who would live after her. . . . Congratulations. . . .

This disappointment had its own revenge, that of every sort of decline—mediocrity. Sometimes Edmée in the evenings, with Frank winding up the phonograph and Claudie changing the records, would suddenly find herself again in the life that was her life before, in the time of Pierre and Jacques. The altitude was just a little lower. Pierre knew everything and Frank knew nothing. Jacques was first place and Claudie eleventh. That was what she had won by running away with a celestial fire: a second-rate home, where all the guests of the other were already announcing themselves—Beethoven or van Gogh. It was by these illustrious visits that Edmée recognized that everything was lacking. On the evening when she had seen a portrait of Whitman show up on the wall of Claudie's room, and where within the week Poe and Edison also appeared, she had understood what they were going to bring with them, here as in the other place: pure mediocrity. Soon they were everywhere. Nothing reproduces like the great men. Their portraits also served, hypocritically, to cover up on the walls all traces of the other Claudie—ink stains, the marks of objects thrown with all the force of an irritated arm, scorched spots left by the lamp, all the prints left by an indomitable creature, and some real prints too, from the time when Claudie didn't wash her hands very much. But at least time passed and the anxiety had disappeared. It seemed as if Claudie had paid the ransom for it.

And this completely changed her relations with Claudie, the idea that she had become a girl like other girls to pay off her mother's ransom. Everything that was the most displeasing, the most banal about her new nature turned into how she moved you the most, how she touched your heart. For Claudie to start humming *Song of India* or show a taste for maraschino cherries was like having the Lord decide to save you by the skin of your teeth or your toenails. Everything that was obnoxious about her girlfriends—their pretentiousness, their silly chatter, their red noses—now became adorable to Edmée. Claudie had freckles? She was paying off her mother's ransom to the sun; paying it off at night, for her teeth were not as white in the morning. And since the fear that Edmée had of suffering seemed to her like a consent to this sort of deformation and degeneration, the latter had become for her a constant source of humiliation and tenderness. Her daughter had been changed into a girl. Even so it was a lot better than having her changed into a parakeet or a cat.

In fact for the first time Edmée really felt that she had a daughter. From her own experience she knew what a daughter meant. It was to announce a life that Edmée could not admit, a life of marriages, of sons-in-law, of heads and bodies, of child-bearing. . . . It was in that impulse of aversion that she had had Claudie, who would have her own children without the help of a mate, just as Edmée in the end imagined having had Claudie. An illusion given the lie today. All you had to do was to look at poor Claudie, with pimples on her forehead and her skinny thighs, to have the certainty that she was born of a man, and, if paternity can be judged by resemblance, born of all men. It was Edmée's obsession in the street; in the primmest passerby or the most deceptively sprightly, in the humpback, in one with rickets, or in the corpulent, there was almost always some feature of Claudie. Rare were those she could disqualify. Even that Chinese man, who had her eyelid. . . . There had been a mass rape, where the masculine gender had rushed forth all together, the Chinese man included, for the procreation of Claudie. Just once, on a boating party, Edmée was seated beside a man who had nothing to do with it. He was tall and gentle, he was strong and able and let the others take action. He was intelligent, tender, and let the others talk with Edmée, let the others touch Edmée's arms lightly with their hands. . . . As she left him she understood who he was. He was, if there had been one, the father of the former Claudie.

Edmée, when she thought back later about this part of her life, realized the conspiracy that was then hatched around her, the unconscious plotting, more ingenious than Iago's, of the two beings who loved her more than anything in the world. But what could she do to avoid the trap to which modesty, renunciation, and tenderness were to lead her so inevitably? Claudie would be indignant to the point of killing herself if anyone told her that she had pushed her mother to accept so facile a solution: a daughter and a lover. Yet never had an intervention been more insistent, more pitiless than hers. One can't say that Edmée was mad for Frank. There was a reserve about him that gave one the impression that Edmée was the one in love and he was shying away. But Edmée wasn't fooled. She couldn't love Frank unless she gave up her destiny, which was clearly not to love Frank. And yet this was what the slightest gesture, the slightest word from Claudie demanded. Throughout the whole winter, she had resumed her childhood habits of complicity. She would leave her mother and Frank alone for the evening, would prepare cocktails, cushions, and divan, and would change the honest living room into a decor about whose virtue and membership the couple could be left in no doubt. Or, if the weather were beautiful, she would ask Frank—she herself had to work, had to make a name for herself in the world, had to become tenth—to drive her mother out to the bay. She knew what was exchanged, what was given away, and what was taken in the line of cars parked along the bay, but when Edmée returned later, Claudie was peacefully in her bed and embraced her in her sleep with the frenzy of those who approve you and console you.

There were also days when Claudie, suddenly nervous and dominating, seemed to blame her for her chilliness with Frank, as if she were refusing him, for her own life to come, some sort of permission or example, and also, thought Edmée, as if the virtue of her mother were weighing on her. She had a way of siding with those kings who prefer love over the crown, and this became an innuendo, a demand. Edmée was indeed thinking about her crown. . . . Frank seemed to be following a protocol of liaison knowingly measured out by Claudie. Now he was bringing flowers. He brought them with a great deal of precaution. He had learned his botany from the herbarium of spun glass at Harvard and had retained from those studies a fear of breaking flowers by touching them. Claudie had demanded that he do Edmée's portrait at his place; she sent them to the studio right after a lunch where she had made lavish use—Edmée wondered why—of celery and spices. On her name day, she demanded that Frank kiss Edmée. Her whole being called for a love from the others that she was too young to wish for herself. None of this, however, would have been enough. The truth was that Edmée sensed that love for Frank was giving her still more force to love her daughter. The kind of friendliness she felt for him, as soon as it became tenderness, increased tenfold the tenderness she had for Claudie. The modest attraction she felt for his kind eyes turned into attacks of love when it came to the face and body of Claudie. By the fact that a man loved her and lent so much importance to her touch, to her smile, that smile, those hands, and those eyes became more maternal and more ardent. It went as far as the notion of decline and error which would cast on her life with Claudie all the pathos and anguish of human failings. Her indifference to so many men, to so much masculine homage, had brought her nothing as far as Claudie was concerned, had provided her no new way of loving Claudie. She would give away nothing that belonged to Claudie, and Claudie would gain thereby. She foresaw already the turmoil with which, in the arms of Frank, she would think about her daughter. And was that not the only means of also acquiring the sort of equality with other mothers whose absence weighed on her relations with her daughter: mothers love, deceive, are deceived, and suffer. . . . She was frustrating Claudie by never having been any of that.

That was why, one evening she came home later. . . . Since her days at boarding school, the voice of her conscience at serious moments enjoyed speaking in elevated language, a recollection of *Esther* or *Polyeucte*. . . . She had been hearing it for some weeks now saying, "I understand your sighs. . . . I abide by your laws. . . ." That evening her conscience spoke with more dignity, more nobly still: "I fall at your feet. I accept your yoke. . . ." It was the feet of the Lord, the yoke of the Lord. . . . But only Frank was present. . . . And the experience was conclusive: everything was there, she was better loved, she was more gentle, more maternal. It had rained; the wet coat that she hung up on going back to the coatrack also brought her its sentimental homage: mothers must face water, snow, and hail. . . . There was even the remorse, for a second, for the tenth of a second, of having forgotten Claudie.

# 8

The following week Edmée went out again with Frank, but on returning home she didn't hear Claudie call to her from her room. It was the first time. Whether it was ten o'clock or midnight, Edmée was sure to see two arms emerge from the sheets and close around her in an embrace that grew more ample with every year. One night Claudie had murmured, "I hatch like a bird when you come in." And since then both of them used to call this awakening the hatching of Claudie. But tonight there was no hatching. Aside from the hair, the rest of the body was an egg that showed no movement. Edmée thought at first that she was asleep. But it wasn't Claudie's kind of sleep. One could recognize when Claudie was sleeping, not only from her little snore but also from her seeming to be dead. She didn't stretch out, she didn't snuggle up into a ball, her head wouldn't be resting on her arm: no, she would be lying there, arms hanging down or underneath her like those of the victims in an accident, one leg askew, forming an inhuman angle with the left leg remaining straight, and also sometimes with her eyes open and only the whites showing. Edmée would then arrange those scattered members, would close those eyes, would straighten out the clubfeet, in a sort of ritual toilet, a funereal overhaul, which would return both life and buoyancy to this cadaver of lead.

Tonight Claudie was living: her two legs were together and showed their full length under the sheet. If one saw only her hair, it was that she wished to show only her hair. It was that she wished to hide her mouth, her forehead, her nose, it was that her eyes required a veil beneath the eyelids. Edmée was afraid that she might be ill, but her hair was not moist, and underneath the hair her head was cool. Reassured, she wanted, as usual, to tend to the bed, to tuck in a Claudie already tucked in, but the bed didn't lend itself to this, for there was no disorder, and one would have said that Claudie had just gotten in bed that moment or that she might have gotten up again just to get into this rigid position.

It was when Edmée had gone on into her own room, feeling a little helpless, that it occurred to her that Claudie was perhaps feeling some kind of trouble. Her heart gave itself over to a selfish sort of kindness: yes, to have to console her daughter! Her daughter who had never complained, whom no burn or cut had ever brought to Edmée with a face in pain, this daughter would have to be consoled tonight because of some sort of pain, and Edmée would not fail to do so, since the opportunity presented itself, indeed, to console her for all the cuts in her life, for every one of her burns.

She paused in getting ready for bed tonight—she would need more preparation, even more time, for she had to appear as never before, appear as a mother of consolation. Never, for any night, had she so prepared herself to go sit down presently beside her daughter, to gently lift, as one withdraws a bandage from a wound, the sheet from those eyes where she might still find a few tears. The pajamas were from the night before; she took out a fresh pair of pajamas, of a color that would be pleasing to Claudie through her tears. She lingered in the bathroom, knowing that one of Claudie's special pleasures was to hear in her half sleep the sounds of her mother going to bed. She forced herself not to be silent. It was difficult tonight in this return that retained, in spite of herself, something guilty and clandestine. She let some small bottles hit against each other on purpose, put her bracelet down so that the platinum sounded, and let her rings drop, one by one, down onto the glass plate. Claudie was probably feeling very moved, there in her room, hearing all those things that were stone or unfeeling metal as they fell from her mother.

She hesitated at the moment of washing her face. By a sort of fidelity to Frank, really a refinement of her tender feelings for Claudie, she didn't wipe off her lipstick or the light mascara around her eyes. It was only fair to keep the face of both mistress and mother. . . . This charming girl of sixteen was becoming the daughter of that embrace at the beginning of the night. Just time enough to come home in the rain, and there she was born already. Edmée leaned over her, still disconcerted by her conception, moved to her depths by the idea of applying maternity so freshly on top of love. . . . Yes, there was the justification of her conduct, of those evenings spent with Frank: it all led up to the birth of this daughter. . . . Frank embraced her, and, on arriving in her room, out of that white lump there in the bed, she saw the hatching of this daughter. . . . A daughter whose eyes were full of tears. . . . She couldn't make up her mind to lift the sheet. . . . Where are tears any better off than right there in the eyes?

But the eyes were not weeping. The eyelids were pale, closed not from sleep but from the same obstinacy that closed her lips. And they had not wept. The cheeks were glossy and pure. That which held sway over Claudie's face was even the opposite of tears. The system of humors had given way to a system of strange dryness. Not that it was in any way hidden: it seemed even to display itself, under a cold sun. Edmée read on that face a sort of contempt, of defiance, of provocation. For the first time she saw the stranger, something far away on the features of her daughter. If her daughter had not been her daughter, she would have been just like this. The recollection of Frank was suddenly painful, unbearable to her, like a useless experiment, like some great effort that was wasted and vain, since Claudie, tonight, had not turned out to be its offspring. . . .

"No hatching tonight?"

She regretted having spoken. There was no response. One sensed that Claudie had heard. But only because there were no movable lids to close off the ears by will as there are for the eyes. And because there wasn't the same sort of thing for the nose, one guessed that this too was regrettable, for it was evident that Edmée's perfume was too strong for this face. One read on it, though without a single feature showing any change, that it suffered not to be able to protect itself further against the presence of Edmée. It did not see her, it did not touch her, but it heard her and it sensed her. It was protected against the taste, the savor of Edmée; it clenched its teeth as if to protect its tongue from them: but it could do nothing against her voice or her insolent fragrance. . . . At least that was what Edmée felt, suddenly in full flight, all her senses alert, faced with this callousness. . . . In one minute she had passed from happiness to panic. . . .

"Must I put earplugs in your ears, oh my daughter, so that you don't hear me? . . . Must I press your nostrils together with my fingers, my beloved daughter, so that you can't smell me? . . . She wanted to believe she was exaggerating, that she was mistaken. She bent over, kissed her forehead, and even left a red mark, which she didn't dare rub off with her handkerchief as she sometimes did, in spite of Claudie, who used to plead with her to leave it till morning. She pulled the sheet back up, not as far as her hair, but up to the cheeks. Her confidence was returning. Girls at that age may hate the whole world one fine evening, including their mothers. Tomorrow it would be a matter of getting her to hate the whole world, without including her mother.

Claudie had had a fuss with a friend, had read some unforeseen book that had put her at odds with everybody, starting with herself. It was perhaps herself she was sulking at, paying for this sulking at the highest price: refusing to kiss her mother. What a sweet task she could look forward to tomorrow, having to reconcile Claudie with Claudie. Besides, at her age it was good for a girl to have a bout of nerves. In fact, perfect to have a daughter who was not always your reflection, your mirror, your flesh. . . . This false happiness might have to be paid for later. Some evening later on, coming home, the mother might find her daughter not asleep, but with her eyes obstinately shut tight, her face full of defiance, mute. . . . Edmée shuddered to return thus to reality by way of this detour. . . . Suddenly she heard a sort of running in the hall. . . . What was going on? . . . She went back to Claudie's bed, bent over the body, bent over the face that hadn't moved. . . . Her heart sank. The red mark had disappeared.

She was trembling as she got into bed. She didn't take time to take off her makeup. She took refuge in the night and the shadows with her daytime face. Not to have found that fleeting imprint was suddenly more terrible to her than not to have found a mark branded with a red iron. For nothing remained of it. In two minutes Claudie had found a way to erase it, and now one saw nothing more on her skin than a little redness, a kind of shame. . . . She had rubbed hard. . . . She must have spat on her handkerchief, a handkerchief surely no longer under her pillow, but already thrown far from the bed. That was the meaning of that furtive running. . . . She got up and went to the hamper of clothes to be washed. A handkerchief was indeed already in the soiled linen, with red on it. She tried to think it wasn't possible, that it was one of her own handkerchiefs. She took it out of the dirty clothes. It was definitely one of Claudie's handkerchiefs, one of the twelve handkerchiefs she had given her on the feast day of her saint. Claudie hadn't needed to rub herself with all twelve, to throw away all twelve of them, just one had been enough. The eleven others would serve to wipe off kisses given the week before, the year before. . . . Edmée took it and carried it to her room, saved it from its fate as a rag, slipped it under her pillow, as if she had to save something from some end, from a death, as if she had to save her kiss. There it was safe. There

Claudie could do nothing against it, Claudie aided by laundry delivery women, by Chinese launderers!

What could it all mean? It was as sudden as those pains that appear one fine day, a really fine day; they quite particularly choose a really fine day to appear, and then turn out to be leprosy, arteriosclerosis, and cancer! There had to be something seriously wrong in any case since in less than a quarter of an hour Edmée had gotten used to it, in that contagion of bad luck that spreads even faster than death itself. Was it Claudie's indifference, her hatred? Claudie's responses were never incidental, never simply blunders. They were always, even in her second form, the most precise expression of her nature, and that part never changed. If she had loved and sought kisses of the type of the one on this handkerchief up to this very day, it was because nothing was dearer to her than Edmée. Her mother's mouth was dear to her, and her teeth and her breath, and, near or far, all that was part of that kiss—lips, tongue, her modest glottis, her saliva. It's because she thought of all of it with love. And if she loved to slip her arm around her mother's waist, it was because she loved that waist, and her stomach and her back; if she liked to sleep curled up against her mother in the car, it was because she loved her mother from her hair to her knees. It was even, when Edmée thought about it, the only assurance, the only consciousness that she perhaps had of her happiness: this approbation without end given by her daughter to everything that was her, body and soul, to all that assortment of organs or details that one is not particularly proud of—toes, kneecaps, membranes of the nose. Edmée felt that Claudie admitted everything, admired everything in her mother. From this she acquired a certain confidence, a certain grace. When in the city, she would take a certain kind of stride that her daughter loved; twice she had kissed Frank with lips that her daughter loved. The disgrace that she had inflicted on her for nine months, Claudie was making up for it by the way she had been changing her for sixteen years now into that mother of elegance and lightness so adored by her daughter. On this score Claudie had never shown any temporary stubbornness or whim. Not one single time since she had been born had she ever failed to smile at her mother, failed to beseech her kiss. Since she had become the new Claudie she was even more passionate in what she sought. Edmée sensed very well that this excess ardor was that which she couldn't yet give to love itself, but since love wasn't there, it was still a good thing to try. . . .

If tonight Claudie had this hardness, had put on this mask, Edmée wondered if it wasn't forever. . . . A mask she already knew, that she suddenly recognized. It was the face that Claudie reserved for her father, when Pierre would happen at night to bend over the bed of his daughter; and Edmée also recalled that often, when her father had kissed her, with lips that didn't leave a mark and were dry on purpose, Claudie, as soon as he had turned his back, would wipe off the kiss with her hands in haste and rage. . . . But it was because she hated her father, hated his mustache, his ears, the hair on his arms, his gnarled toes. It was because she would grit her teeth if she thought of his Adam's apple, his kneecaps, or his belly button. Was it going to be like that from now on for Edmée too? She hadn't even used her hands to wipe off the kiss, but a handkerchief instead. You can't throw hands in the dirty clothes. . . . And suddenly there came back to her a body humiliated, limbs not accepted, vile lips. . . . No, it wasn't possible! There was some misunderstanding. Claudie was sad, wanted to be sad, and maternal love was such a remedy against sadness that she had turned it down tonight. . . . Edmée was still lucky, however; some daughters begin this rebellious life at birth. . . . She would get used to it. Even if you thought that no sadness would ever lead your daughter to find herself sullied by your lips, even if you expected that the sad moods of your daughter would bring her to you more gentle, more admiring, and more loving, you have to tell yourself that you are there to help her and to cheer her up.

When you come down to it, it is infinitely more fair not to have to take pleasure in your daughter's sadness, to take no advantage from it, to take no inordinate comfort in her disappointments and her tears. Whatever slight benefit she might have gained by seeing Claudie sobbing in her arms and cursing life while covering her mother with kisses, Edmée would do without this. The two of them would suffer together. And the mother would be less selfish. . . . But what could she do all night long with this body, with this maternity that Claudie no longer accepted? . . . No doubt it was the moment to let noble phrases form themselves in her mouth, such as "Your path is so hard! Your ways are so cruel! . . ." Claudie had wiped off the red, and her mother was now nothing more than a mother degraded. She stretched out on a couch. On the makeshift camp bed that one concedes to the sister who has gone wrong and returns home, to the exile or the wife chased away by the husband, she stretched out the mother of Claudie. . . . It was just what she felt worthy of tonight in this house. . . .

For it amounted to no less than that. . . . If Edmée's life had been happy, if she had never repented having lived it this way, if she had passed over the despair of Pierre and the absence of Jacques, if the world had been for her a sanctuary, an honor, a place of ease, it was because she had had Claudie's agreement. She had placed her conscience inside that unconscious little head, her sensitivity into that insensitive little body. That very coldness and that distraction seemed to her surer guarantees than passion and reason ever could have been. Claudie had been surrounded by ice as magnets and compasses are surrounded by calm, as impervious as a device that indicates the presence of oil or water, and only Edmée knew how to read it. . . . With Claudie everything that resembled Claudie in this sad world supported her, everything that was young, strong, and incorruptible. With Claudie she had the consent of a series of beings and objects that were much more necessary to her than human approval. With Claudie she had the season of the year, the lands, and the waters. Claudie in peace beside her, at the seaside, Claudie smiling at her, out over the bay, and it seemed it was the Pacific itself that was devoted to her, that proved her right. From her slightest reading, her slightest excursion, Claudie would bring back a monster—submissive as well—or an ocean, or a mountain. Her peace with little Claudie was to have peace with everything that is not everyday, with everything that is great—mineral, vegetable, everything that lasts. Edmée didn't suspect that she had such a need of the approval of the stones on earth here below. . . . That friendship that she struck up only with millennial creatures—it was more secure, you spare yourself a lot of grief . . . moreover it was the only friendship she was allowed—Claudie was its seal, its pledge, and the sinister truth was beginning to glimmer in Edmée's eyes.

How could she have gone so far astray to imagine that Claudie was pushing her to love Frank? It really was about Frank, wasn't it, Claudie? You understood suddenly that I went over to Frank's place the other evening, didn't you, Claudie? I've become the opposite of what you thought me to be, of what I was, haven't I, Claudie? You will never talk to me about it, I will never talk to you about it; that bouquet of violets that I'm throwing in the fireplace, you won't ask me if Frank was the one who gave it to me a little while ago at his door; those pieces of torn-up photo in your wastebasket, I won't try to find out if they're what remains of your picture of Frank; tomorrow morning every object in the house that receives waste—wastebaskets, clothes hampers, the garbage pail—will contain a scrap of something from Frank, but we will never talk about it, will we, Claudie? The only thing I would like to know is, why were you embracing him, why were you always trying to make him look nice, running your fingers through his hair, pointing out the best brand of lavender, tying his ties? Did I know that you were pulling on the knot in his tie so that no one else could ever undo it? What mother could resist a man caressed, prepared, and anointed by her daughter? Think about that, Claudie!

She turned on the lights. This darkness was unbearable. She could accept not understanding, but in the light. It was good to see. It was at least something that the judgment of Claudie had not turned her blind. To see objects, portraits, and fabrics that knew nothing as yet, that were not yet aware of the denial, of the excommunication. In this bedroom, nothing was known of the disavowal of Claudie. The portrait of Claudie itself had guessed nothing. It was smiling. It was approving. It approved, like Claudie yesterday, the red on the lips, the departure from home, the liaison with Frank. One could of course already make out the disgust and indifference that it would show tomorrow, but it was difficult, you had to make a real effort, it took good eyes, eyes without tears. Claudie's gloves lay on the edge of the little round table—a Stevens, Pierre would have said—and they still had all the softness and affection of the night before, but for one good reason: because the hands of Claudie were no longer in them. Edmée shuddered at the idea that from now on everything that Claudie might leave behind would be without Claudie, that her feet would slip out of her shoes, her Richelieu shoes, out of her boots, out of her pumps, that her body would be gone from the dresses hanging in the closet. She had already removed Claudie from her portrait. . . . Every time she went out Claudie would take everything along, from her fingernails down to her ankles, and race back to try to find anything she might have left lying behind, maybe in her stockings or in her books. . . . Edmée would find herself in the middle of a nightmare—what a fury Claudie would be in, if returning unexpectedly, she were to find her mother sitting there with her head, her own head, Claudie's head, in her hands! . . .

She had to sleep. She wiped off her lips with care, taking a long time. Without thinking about it, she had wiped them with Claudie's handkerchief. She opened it and spread it out. Of course it wasn't Veronica's veil. But aside from the red, it was clean: one might have said that Claudie had had it ready, her action planned in advance. . . . A good thing she hadn't also had eraser gum and acid at hand. . . . Edmée got up and went to toss it into the dirty clothes. If by chance Claudie came back also to look for it, she would see what a lot of red there was in that kiss. Passing in front of the door to her daughter's room, she couldn't stop herself and went in. This time Claudie was sleeping, with that little snore that she pretended not to have, begging her mother to say in fact, even to herself, that she didn't snore.

She was snoring, gently, calmly. The snore that she denied, the snore that belonged to Edmée. She listened to it as a sort of language that deep inside Claudie had not denied her. Then she leaned over, and with lips now dry, gave her a kiss. Claudie stopped snoring. Claudie was preparing, once her mother had left, some new spurt of aversion. But she could rub all she wanted this time. Without opening her eyes, she murmured something, something spiteful.

"I thought you had a touch of cold," said Edmée. "You were snoring."

It was a modest bit of revenge. To say that she snores to the one who wants to ban you from life seems little enough, but to see Claudie's face turn suddenly red, one could guess that she resented it as an affront, as an equal exchange of blows.

Edmée went to bed toward morning. She had time to dream that if Claudie wasn't speaking, it was because she had become mute. And if she didn't open her eyes, it was because she had become blind. And if she grumbled in her sleep, it was because she had fallen victim to an illness called Claudie that made you grumble instead of saying "I love you." They were three terrible misfortunes. . . . But so light compared to the other misfortune that Edmée thanked heaven for them.

Usually the first one to get up would go to embrace the other. Edmée remained lying in bed, with a vague sense of hope; but from Claudie`s side all was equally quiet. For the first time Edmée felt herself lacking any power of divination concerning her daughter. Until this morning, she knew, without seeing her, without hearing her, what occupations Claudie was devoting herself to. She could tell whether Claudie was getting dressed, was reading, was at the window, or was in her bath. Both would sometimes laugh about it—for example, when Edmée was bringing the electric iron at the very moment that

Claudie was spreading out her chemisette to iron on the board, or bringing ink just as Claudie's pen was running out. . . . But her second sight was failing her today. She wouldn't even have been able to say if Claudie was still in her room or had gone out. For part of her motherhood to thus escape her, the situation had to be more serious yet than she had thought.

She tried to imagine if Claudie was dressed or lying down, if she was sewing or if she was working. She no longer found any reply in her head. This alone was already appalling. So it was going to be necessary now for Claudie to call out in order for her to respond, for Claudie to ring at the door in order for her to let her in. Her motherhood was turning into a second-rate motherhood, where mother and daughter are forced to talk in order to understand each other, to be present in order to see each other. It was she who had become deaf and blind. She got up, bumped into the wall, stumbled over the armchair. Deprived of her most noble sense, her sense of balance also seemed affected. . . . But above all there was this silence; she felt as empty as the apartment, bereft of the cries, of the ringing of the doorbell, of the presence of Claudie.

She got dressed. It was no small matter. How does a mother get dressed on the morning after the night when her daughter has denied her? What does she put on for that daughter? She mustn't wear the wrong dress, use the wrong face powder, the wrong lipstick or mascara. Appear with the wrong body either. And in the bathroom she had to confess that it was more the body meant for Frank than the body made for Claudie. But the bathrobe was still damp and the soap soft and wet. From these traces Edmée felt some relief. Claudie was not yet at the point of having her own bathrobe, her own bar of soap. Nor her own mouthwash, for the glass was still half full. . . . Edmée used the rest. She poured the mouthwash in her mouth as if it were the only liquor she still shared in common with Claudie. Strong liquor. . . . She was forever telling her daughter that she didn't add enough water. She stopped short of drinking it. In any case, getting ready that morning turned out a little better than she had imagined—the mouthwash used by her daughter and the same soap, the same nail clippers and cologne, and the hairbrush, on seeing which the most skeptical detective would have to agree, by the presence of three long blond hairs, that she had brushed Claudie's hair within the year, within the month, within the hour. . . .

She still had to fix her hair. . . . Yesterday's hairdo was not simple, and this was yesterday's. She would never do it that way again. She still had to put on lipstick. In that, she wouldn't give in. It was yesterday's. It would always be her lipstick. That was the red that would mark the cheek or forehead of Claudie on the evening of reconciliation. As there aren't any dresses intended for such mornings, Edmée put on the first suit she came across. Claudie hadn't liked it particularly up to yesterday. Claudie wasn't going to hate it particularly after today. Edmée had worn it the day before yesterday at the horticultural show, where Frank had wanted to buy a manual lawn mower for his small yard. How far away it already seemed! Frank's grass could grow all it wanted; she would never again push that little machine with the mother-of-pearl handles that she had picked out because it could be pushed like a baby carriage. . . . To push a baby carriage, even in that guise, even to make the earth bald, was something she could no longer allow herself to do with impunity. . . .

Suddenly, in a flash, her second sight was restored: she knew where Claudie was! She wasn't in her room. She hadn't taken a bath. Edmée recalled now that the bathtub was dry, without a one of those tiny rivulets and streams that seemed to emerge from all sides after her bath, after Claudie, goddess of fresh water. . . . She was at the swimming pool. She had used the bathrobe and the soap as if they were articles of slavery and had gone off to plunge into water that was her own. That belonged to ten thousand Americans, forty Swedes, two hundred Irish, twenty Chinese, but that didn't belong to her mother, that did belong to her. . . . She was diving in so that the maternal water was washed even from her face, was breathing in even with pleasure that scent of chlorine that she normally hated. . . .

Then the tableau faded away. . . . Once again darkness, utter silence. . . . It was at the very moment when she was sure that Claudie wouldn't come home for lunch that the door opened and Claudie came in—she had a key, but never used it just so her mother would come open the door for her—and this return was infinitely more dreadful than she herself could have expected.

Claudie's coldness, her hard countenance, all this she had foreseen. That Claudie would not embrace her, would not ask her how she was, that she would go immediately to her room, like the days when there was a visitor she found tiresome, that her mother might be such a visitor herself—Edmée had reached the point where she found this almost natural. And that Claudie at the table now should not ask for the salt because she would have had to ask her mother for it, or go around her, or reach in front of her, she who loved salt so much, well, this too was tolerable. That in this earthly lunch, face-to-face, where Claudie was discovering her teeth as weapons, where, for the first time, Edmée was seeing her daughter endowed with nails and jaws to tear and bite, that they should both feel all at once that animals who go off to eat alone are really right, even this was bearable.

But the worst was that Claudie had changed. It was there on her face, where suddenly Edmée no longer saw either the insolence of the first Claudie or the foolishness of the second, in her walk, which was no longer either provocative or spineless but supple and dignified, and in the tone of her voice, which was no longer insulting and no longer whining. A third daughter had been born of Edmée and Frank. . . . How had she not already noticed the change? It couldn't have taken place overnight! Claudie's eyes were no longer either hard or tearful. Below them appeared those rings that had never before come to take away their clear limit as birds of prey, yet they had nothing in common with the rings under the eyes of simpletons. . . . A girlfriend called her on the phone, a friend of no distinction, . . . but in answering her she showed a kindness, a sweetness, and a spirit that announced a devotion to girlfriends even of no distinction, a finesse to girlfriends even of no distinction. Edmée's heart was torn in two. So it wasn't because she had suddenly included her mother with all the others, with that mass of humanity for whom heretofore she had showed only defiance or fear that she had broken with her. . . . It was because she meant to single her out from them.

By the way she answered the maid and the mail carrier, which Edmée heard through the door—she could also see Claudie's smile through the door—one could guess that these people had become for her the way they appeared to the girl in whom has beaten one fine day that sort of heart full of pity and generosity that we all have to carry around for at least fifteen years. But it turned out that the only creature who might have been until this morning exempt from her hatred was from now on the sole object of it. There could be no doubt, Claudie was in love. Not with a boyfriend or some man. But with her neighbor, her human neighbor, her animal neighbor, her tree neighbor. She must have touched with her hands, not only on her way to the swimming pool but also on her way back, and without hope of washing them, the beggars, the children, and the handrails in the subway. . . . She was in love with everything. . . . Minus her mother.

Thus began this new life, of a Claudie such as her mother in her happiest moments would never have dared wish her, gentle and tender, and of that mother herself, whom Claudie could no longer bear. In a transaction whose terms Edmée was unable to make out, Claudie had exchanged her mother for the world. She had everything. She had received all at once, in exchange for one single human being, all the others, who became her fathers, her brothers, and her mothers, along with their attachments or their marvelous hybrids, which are the plants, the animals, the seasons, and the sky. By the sigh of relief that she gave in spite of herself out on the landing—it could be heard inside the apartment—one understood that it was enough for her to take one step outside the house for her to feel at home. At home in the street, at home in the rain, at home in a museum, at home in the swimming pool, at home with the French lion tamer who kept her from entering a cage with forty female lions, kept her from entering her home. All the minutes of the month that followed were for Edmée only so many revelations of the kindness, the affection, and the weakness that Claudie felt for the world, and, for herself, there was nothing but her hardness, her intransigence.

The two women, inside the cramped apartment, had adopted, without ever having spoken of it, habits of life and a way of moving about that never more put them face-to-face. Their tracks did not overlap, and if a hunter had followed them, he would never have seen their trails any way but separate and distinct. Happy collisions in the bathroom, at the wardrobes, at drawers or telephones were avoided by a timetable whose secret will never be known by any railway company. This no longer even stemmed, as in the first days of the estrangement, from the fact that each was on the lookout for what the other was doing: it was simply that a new physical rule was governing each of them which caused an alternation in their wishes, their time of waking up, their needs. They would come together only at mealtimes, when Claudie was there, for she was going out now every evening, when formerly, her mother being out, she used to dine alone. Edmée wasn't going out anymore and Claudie knew it. She knew that Frank was no longer coming to pick her mother up, neither in the afternoon nor evening, but she pretended to still believe in their walks and drives, in their dinners, and she would stretch her absence around dates that weren't taking place, with a disdain and scrupulousness that were nothing more than pretexts for leaving Edmée in solitude. And in truth it was almost a kind of rest for Edmée.

To find herself face-to-face with her daughter only for eating was becoming torture. Face-to-face with Claudie for reading, praying, suffering, or closing your eyes, that was still bearable. But this confrontation while chewing and swallowing was a challenge from Claudie. . . . And how useful all those little table instruments now appeared which at first sight seem so pointless! The mustard spoon is designed so that your mother doesn't have to serve it to you from the tip of her knife. The sugar tongs are there for taking the sugar so that your mother's fingers don't have to put the cubes in your cup. And napkin rings keep the napkins from ever getting mixed up. For Claudie was now folding her napkin. That napkin, which three times a day for eighteen years had remained after the meal on her chair, under the table, or which had to be found by means of some sixth sense—for Claudie would get up at every moment—as an object specially hidden for a mind reader, in the most unexpected and obscure corner of the house, when it wasn't simply on her plate where she was absorbing the remains of the cream or some currant sauce; but nowadays the napkin was an altar cloth, and Claudie, in order to fold it, had instantaneously discovered the recipe for folding napkins of her grandmother on her father's side, the most meticulous one.

Edmée, when she was alone one day, changed the rings. Claudie decided that day—formerly a day for Frank—to leave the house at one-thirty and to come back at nine: Edmée had the time to change the rings. Claudie didn't know that she was wiping her mouth with the napkin that had served her mother that morning. There was a spot that made Edmée's heart beat with concern, but Claudie luckily didn't see it. And the experiment was done. And since the hands that held that napkin didn't break out in blisters, since her lips didn't split open when she wiped her mouth, since her cheek remained pink when she patted it with the napkin, it was clear that the harm didn't come from Edmée, clear that this was the napkin of a woman who was wholesome, honest, and good, and that Claudie's imagination—which was expecting the dregs of the wine and putrefaction from it—was the only thing at fault. And the experiment would have been as conclusive if it had been carried out on Edmée's underclothes, also repudiated by Claudie, or on Edmée's books, which Claudie didn't read anymore, or on Edmée's kisses. But this last experiment was never carried out.

Three months went by. Already the clothes that Claudie wore were no longer those selected by Edmée. Colors would appear that Edmée had set aside up to then because she knew they weren't becoming to Claudie, like yellow and pink, and now they were becoming. Her daughter also took on a beauty that she hadn't foreseen, that wasn't the one she had foreseen. Her hair became curly. Her nose, which tended to be a bit long and turn red, was becoming straight and white. Every day brought a perfecting of light or appearance to Claudie that proved to Edmée that she had known nothing about the body of her daughter or what an unexpected prism she signified for colors. Edmée had not understood any more about her soul. Claudie, with one leap, had become at once all that could be desired, not by a mother but by a father: she was first in her class, champion of the breaststroke, and chosen to defend her school in the tournament of female debaters at Berkeley. She returned triumphant. Edmée learned nothing of the competition if not that the subject had *not* been "Explain why it is that from the time of your birth you have always held your mother in your arms. . . ." A fine subject, but the jury was of course obliged to take orphans into account, and Claudie had been able to profit from that. . . .

Claudie was becoming pious. She received a first also in religious instruction. All she had to do was to change one word in the commandments, one single word. "Thou shalt honor thy father and thy mother. . . . Thou shalt honor thy father and nothing else. . . . Thou shalt honor thy father and thy daughter. . . ." For Claudie, in that rage that had made her reject the paternity of Frank, must have come around to thinking about that other paternity, namely, that of Pierre. There was not yet any picture of her father in her room, but Edmée guessed that one day, obtained by she knew not what means, a photo of Pierre would appear. Already, as a result of an atavism that could no longer be challenged, the portraits of famous men in Claudie's room had become, in unrelenting promotion, the very same ones who adorned the office, work, and life of Pierre, the leaders of humanity. There was Pasteur leading his flock of great men. There was the same reign of leaders there had been with her husband and son. This daughter whom she had thought to be of her own faith, whom she had brought up to believe in what is easy, modest, and natural, hastened to regain her place in line for the sublime and the complicated. And Beethoven would soon be there, with every musical corner piled high in human sentimentality. And Lobachevsky would be there, whom Pierre was so mad about, with his four-dimensional geometry, entering the life of a Claudie who could only deal with one. . . .

That's what the little idiot was doing. It was herself she was exchanging, new and inexplicable, even if not acting alone, for a Claudie who would wear out in the same places, enjoy the same words, tremble at the same hours as all the other girls in the world. And Baudelaire would be there with his cats and his canals. And Longfellow with his maples and his bayous. . . . "Mon enfant, ma soeur!" That's what Claudie was becoming. . . . A pity. . . . "Oh my child, oh my daughter!"

Have it out with her? To what end? I wanted to preserve you in my image. I wanted to raise you to my level, above other women, other mothers, other daughters. I haven't been fooled by those poor pawns that great men are, nor by what they become once they're dead. I would have told you that all your tears over the Fourth Symphony and your joy over the scherzo were nothing compared to your stubborn little brow and your mouth without a thought. I would have found you a place between the doe and the elk, between the kite and the seagull. I would have given you a soul without wrinkles, without remorse, an astral body without humors. What is that shining so in the night, they would have asked, what is it that by its mere presence can make a bright day seem dull? . . . It's her, it's my daughter. . . . I would have found you a place between the liana and the beech tree, between the agate and the diamond. You would have known what has been my joy, what is the only joy, since I have lived alone with you, you would have known freedom. The only freedom, freedom from free men. . . . Submission to each season, each age, each hour: freedom. The sweet enslavement to meals, to baths, to sleep: freedom. . . .

You don't want it? Too bad! You give yourself to great thoughts, to great efforts, to everything that the other girls give themselves to, to restraint, to purity. You're a little whore. Too bad. . . . Whatever you're going to gain, the fact is, instead of ignoring them, I'm going to hate them. Those who took my daughter—I'm not going to leave them foolishly in their self-satisfied vanity and hypocrisy. If the eyes of your Pasteur are pierced with a needle, you have only yourself to blame. If you find your van Gogh with horns on, your Brahms record scratched, it's because they aren't all-powerful, it's because they can do nothing against a woman who hates them. They may bribe people, they may steal children. But if someone bashes his ears or puts out his eyes, what becomes of your musicians and your painters? If someone cuts off his hands, what can they do against him, your sculptors and writers? They can't get to him anymore, he is out of their reach, and if he kills himself, he escapes them completely, leaving them with long faces and in humiliation!

She hadn't seen Frank again. He had written, but she hadn't replied. He had come by, ringing the doorbell with the agreed signal, but now it kept him out. He had set times for her to meet him, which at least allowed Edmée to circulate downtown on those days without fear. She was in no way reluctant to elude him, nor did she feel any sorrow in losing him. Since she had no longer been able to have a daughter, her own daughter, at each of their meetings, the whole idea of them had become unbearable. What she had loved in Frank hadn't been much different from what she had loved in Pierre, the necessity of him: Pierre was the necessary partner for a bourgeois happiness, Frank the necessary partner for a bohemian happiness. This happiness was no more, and it would have required a different humor to find a partner for misfortune. That would no doubt come along in good time. . . . There were still a few apparitions, not of Frank himself, but of what remained of him in the apartment, some preserves and some cakes that he had given, some flowers that arrived one fine day, so splendid, so arrogant that Edmée thought they would wring her heart, since they seemed, from their entry, and although sent to Edmée, to side with Claudie. The worse for them. . . . She caught sight of Frank one last time, in a shop. Frank was looking at the display window where Claudie had first found him. And that was all.

The end of the month arrived. And with it, the day when Edmée used to give Claudie her pocket money. The transaction was handled this time like that for a maid. Edmée appeared to be paying her daughter for her services as a daughter, her presence as a daughter. Things hadn't been quite first rate this month, but it was true that the compensation was small. For fifty dollars you couldn't have a daughter who would take you in her arms every evening, who might weep just thinking about you. A daughter who lived with you, with a body in revolt, who ate with you, with her lips showing disgust—but that's all you could have for fifty dollars.

There was never any explanation. One sensed that Claudie wanted it and sought it. Often, in a biting tone, she tried to provoke a retort that would have started a whole scene. But Edmée would never go along. It was the only way in which she was still mistress: not to accept an argument. Moreover, it was to be believed that even if Claudie couldn't talk at home, she was still talking elsewhere. From the false air of friends that Edmée would encounter by chance, she understood that Claudie had told everything and had betrayed her. Had told what? . . . Claudie was also betraying by correspondence. She was writing letters and receiving them without the help of the mail carrier, perhaps through one of her girlfriends or general delivery. How was it that so much maternal love had wounded her one day, how had so much maternal sacrifice made her rebel one day, this was clearly the subject of the letters that she was writing at night, her door locked by key. Edmée heard the sound of the lock: that meant Claudie was starting her letter. . . . Then, at the end of an hour, another sound: that meant the letter was finished, that Claudie had been betraying for an hour. . . . At the beginning

Edmée had gone so far as to wish that Claudie might fall ill. She thought that everything perhaps might have been changed. Typhoid fever, preferably, which takes away the memory. . . . An illness that would have allowed her to save Claudie from death and to die herself. Or, if God were kind, for her to fall sick in turn and to be tended by a Claudie who had been saved. . . . And Claudie could have fallen ill again, if her folly reappeared once she was cured, and then Edmée too, all over again, and she accepted the idea of all of life passing by in this kind of alternation if there was really no longer any hope of their going out together, dining together, or smiling together without the presence of either fever or delirium.

And there was a beginning of this happy life. One afternoon Edmée received a call that Claudie was in the hospital. She had been carried there from the gymnasium. She had an attack of appendicitis and they feared complications. She should come with a suitcase and could sleep next to the patient. A sort of grace filled Edmée. She packed her bag for the duration of the illness so that she wouldn't have to go back home, wouldn't have to leave Claudie for a minute. She put in the bag everything needed for a mother in the way of simple dresses in drab colors for the operation and blood transfusion, and a nice little sweater for the day when the doctor would announce that the patient had been saved. Night was falling when she arrived, falling on an awful past, a past that was gone. Claudie had not betrayed her here: the woman at the front desk and all the nurses treated her as a mother who was loved, even adored; they hurried about and helped her find shortcuts and back elevators that got her to Claudie a few seconds sooner than the normal route, a few seconds, a few centuries.

A folding cot had been set up beside Claudie's bed. . . . But when she bent over her daughter, she saw that all hope was lost, all hope of saving her for herself. In her pallor and her sudden thinness, Claudie was the same Claudie of the first night of estrangement—mute and blind, but blazing with defiance. She leaned over. She kissed her. She had forgotten to wipe her lips and a bit of red remained on Claudie's brow. "I don't know what's wrong," said the nurse, "she was talking and laughing a little while ago. . . ." But Edmée knew. "Did she ask for me?" she said, in a final hope. "No, one of her friends gave us her address. . . ." Such was Claudie's last recourse not to have to talk to her mother—peritonitis. They were left alone. In the middle of the night Claudie was restless. Edmée got up and bent over her. The red, like the other time, had disappeared.

She picked up her suitcase. She went to ask the night nurse to watch over the patient. She gave her Pierre's address. She said she didn't feel well. "That often happens," the nurse said dryly. What was it that had happened? That mothers didn't love their daughters? . . . Fortunate mothers! . . . Or that mothers, when their daughters are suffering too much, quietly go back to their homes? Edmée wasn't going back to hers. She had by chance taken her checkbook. She never went back. That night she went to stay in a hotel. She departed the next day without leaving a forwarding address. That way it would be impossible to let her know even if Claudie did die—the other Claudie, the one who wasn't already dead. . . .

# 9

She had just returned. One of the taxis that take the regular smokers back home from the Chinese quarter for modest fares had left her as usual at the corner of the square. And as usual she had sat down there for a moment. The blooms of the night flowers were closing. The still creeping heliotrope was preparing for its fate. The complete spectacle of the dawn was unfolding in front of her, according to the rules, but she saw nothing of it. . . . An indifferent spectator was all the dawn needed today for it to create the right nuances in its ceremony, certain little refinements. As it happened, the dawn began to improvise as far as the heliotropes were concerned. Their bed of plants was flooded all at once by a gleam of light, by a false sun, just before the rise of the other one. The flowers didn't know what to do. . . . But Edmée saw nothing of this. . . . Her eyes were open, but all she saw, straight in front of her, were the flaming letters of a sign that would light up and then go out again. They spelled out the idiotic and immense names of Smith and Parker, but Edmée was sure that any minute they were going to spell out Claudie. . . .

The dawn also invented a horizontal cloud of purple and green. . . . Until then it was known that green was reserved for the twilight. It was that day that the dawn invented the horizontal cloud of purple and green, but Edmée didn't see it. . . . Edmée was thinking that it was going to be a miracle to see the word *Claudie* lighted up in letters over sixteen feet high above the city! . . . And the most miraculous thing of all was that a publicity agent—so known for their egos—had thought of playing this trick on Smith and Parker, and providing this surprise for Edmée. It took a complete knowledge of the world and of the human heart to imagine such thoughtfulness. It demanded of the publicity agent that he should know that for six months Edmée had wished herself deaf, blind, and mute to the name of Claudie, but that she could not bear this day if she didn't hear it or see it. . . . She would find a way not to bear it. . . .

For the publicity agent to have grasped the hour and day to this extent, he would have had to be in touch with everything concerning Edmée and Claudie; unknown to them, he would have been living with them, he would have seen Claudie's birth with his own eyes, he would have seen them leave for the Seeds', he would have seen what Edmée herself had only been able to guess at: Claudie wiping off the red mark. . . . Perhaps God might have been this publicity agent. . . . And indeed, suddenly the word *Claudie* flashed on. Not when the sign was lighted, but between the blinking off and on. You would read *Parker,* then you would close your eyes and you would read *Claudie.* . . . You would open your eyes and you would read *Smith.* . . . It wasn't that you heard the word *Claudie.* . . . The agent hadn't thought of adding a recording to the sign that would shout out *Claudie.* . . . One could do that oneself. . . . But Edmée didn't dare cry out, simply out of fear lest Claudie might respond, lest Claudie might appear. . . . For that she wasn't prepared. . . . The sun was rising, someone had called for the sun. . . . It wasn't her. . . . Then she went back to her hotel. . . . She was about to lie down on the bed with her clothes on when there was a knock at the door. . . .

She remained motionless, her arms stretched out toward the bed, with one leg raised. . . . A snapshot from the dance. . . .

Indeed the only dance she had danced for six months now, this feeling of petrifaction. . . . They knocked again. . . .

She had turned around now, facing the door. It wasn't that she was afraid. . . . Or rather, it wasn't the fear of a woman who comes home alone at dawn and all at once hears the knock of the tramp who has followed her. . . . That sort of fear she disdained. . . . But the knock had been gentle, humble. The one who wanted to enter this room was gentle and humble, or, if it wasn't human, it was some thing that was gentle and humble. Some woman next door, suddenly devoted. Some police officer bringing back a purse. . . . Or Kindness itself perhaps. The allegories themselves had been really going out of their way for Edmée for some time now. . . . Well, it wasn't Justice in any case— Edmée's life had nothing to do with Justice, and besides, one can't knock so discreetly, so calmly, with scales in one hand. . . .

They knocked again. . . . Of course they knew Edmée was there, they had seen her come in. . . . They knocked as if they knew that this tapping didn't count, that it was only to let Edmée know, that it was only to prepare her for the real knock on the door, the one that would follow without delay. . . . And in itself, it was good to hear someone knock who wanted to enter your room gently and with humility. And the room would have stood it very well. . . . This bed needed kindness, a bed she only made up in a hurry. That door, opened and closed by a hand that was cold and indifferent, had a need to let some human who was warm and kind come in; the door is an arch of triumph for humans and we forget it too often. And that coatrack had a need, not for a coat to be hung on it but for a coat to be entrusted to it. It was the first murmur, the first revolt of these objects, treated up to now without any regard, their wish for a visitor who might ennoble them in their own eyes. . . .

For Edmée alone, the entrance of kindness and tenderness in Edmée was an intrusion that she could not hope to bear. . . . A friendly glance in the street, sympathy from another rider on the streetcar, or of the streetcar itself, especially the handsome new streetcars on Broadway—this was already too much for her, it was an offer, an advance from a world that she could accept nothing from anymore. . . . She went up to the door, with that silent step the smokers have that no ear can make out. . . . Not to spy on the visitor, but in order to know what she might be able to feel, if it was really her, as she approached this famous tenderness, this famous kindness. . . . There now. . . . She was separated from kindness, from the concern of men, only by the door. . . . She had flattened herself against it, clinging to the frame in her fatigue, her arms spread apart. She risked nothing through the wood of the door, no more than would a china plate through an asbestos coaster. . . . And really, that was a good thing. . . . It warmed without burning. . . .

She waited for them to knock, for now she was the one who would receive the blow. . . . They would knock at chest level, just about where her heart was, if it were a visitor, either male or female, of average height. . . . They knocked. . . . She received a deep wound. . . . She hadn't expected anyone to drive a nail in her like that, right through her heart. . . . But the die was cast! . . . Too bad for the poor neighbor woman who wanted to bring her some fresh milk, too bad for the beggar who was bringing her purse back to her, for the dog who had followed her and was claiming her for his master. . . . She really wasn't up to giving a name to some dog that was found, and how could a dog live without a name? . . . And too bad for Frank, who knocked on doors with his head—the knock was low, and Frank was a giant, but he might be on his knees. . . . And too bad for Pierre, who knocked on doors with his elbow ever since he had rheumatism in his index finger. . . . And too bad for her father, who knocked on doors with his key. . . . Though it was quite something that a key could open doors like that, by intimidation and magic, without any need for the lock, . . . and there are those who have died who come to knock at the doors of their daughter. . . . No. . . . She would open up only for Claudie. . . .

"Is it you, Claudie?"

A voice answered:

"No, it's Jacques."

The door opened, without Edmée being able to say that it

hadn't opened by itself. It opened wide. . . . Jacques really was there. . . . Yes, it had opened by itself. . . . It was bolted and locked by key but it had opened all by itself. . . . And Jacques was there.

He looked at her, a little hesitant, with eyes she was amazed not to find more surprised. . . . Clearly, everything that can be done in a quarter of a second in order to change into a woman who has slept well, surprised in all the splendor and clearheadedness of getting up, who has slept peacefully three hundred and sixty-five days of every year, who has the face of a wife, of a mother, the face of happiness, who is in touch with the world through radio and film—all that, instead of a woman who has known nothing for six months, understands nothing, has slept only by day, spent her nights in insomnia, and later in opium, whose face is covered with a sordid dawn, her eyes starting out of her head—all that, Edmée had managed to assume at the sight of Jacques. But she knew how weak this transformation was, how different she was from the mother that Jacques had last seen as he left for school, his principles of geometry his only recourse, his only consolation, his only principles, . . . and if he really wasn't surprised, it was because he was expecting anything, it was because he knew everything. . . . And all that can be accomplished by thought alone in order to change a refuge into a real room—to get rid of flowers in a vase that were faded two weeks ago, a washbasin full of water, a night table left open, a two-dollar Buddha and a cheap dragon whose only purpose seemed to be to act as spies for real Buddhas and real dragons; to transform a spiderweb into a corner that was clean once more; to change a shriveled lemon into half a grapefruit—all this Edmée had done. But anyone other than she herself might not be sensitive to all these changes, and if Jacques looked at this room without surprise, it was because he expected anything, because he knew everything. . . .

But what exactly? And what was she really? With her eyes on Jacques, she sought eagerly to know what she was, and suddenly, when she had seen to the depths of herself, ready to find there only vanity and fault, and instead found beauty and kindness, proof a hundred times over of her innocence, of her truth, an outcry that she was right over the others, that God was on her side, that in her life there was only one fault, only one person hurt by her, wronged by her—this same Jacques who hadn't dared to say behind the door "It's me" for fear that she might not recognize his voice or that his voice might have changed—and that it was precisely Jacques who was there, humble, as if he were the one asking pardon—at that point she no longer felt any shame, neither for the Buddha, nor the unmade bed, nor the dirty water in the basin, and she led him into her palace. . . .

"So there you are at last!" he said. . . .

It was the only thing to say. . . . To say that he had waited for her every month, every hour, as if she were the one who had come back for him. . . . As if she were the one that nothing had been able to restrain from looking for her son. . . . That he was waiting for her. . . . That she had come. . . . It was the only thing to say. . . . It was the truth. But the difficulty began when it came to sitting down. The armchair wasn't clean. . . . The bed unmade.

"Have you had anything to eat?" she asked.

That too was the only thing to say. . . . It was like the song of the fellow who cuts off his mother's head and then slips on her blood. . . . And the head says to him, "Did you hurt yourself, my boy? . . ." She might well think—in this domain where no one ate anymore, where no one might ever eat anymore—to ask him if he had had anything to eat. . . . But the difficulty began when it had to be admitted that breakfast, in this house, was taken in the form of pills. . . .

"You know what I'm going to do?" he said. . . . "Because I'm very hungry, I'll go pick up my suitcase and come back later. I'll eat something down the street. . . ."

He left. He embraced her. Edmée sensed that he was embracing her in order to embrace the other mother, the one who was surprised, lost, numb, the one he would undoubtedly never see again, and he left.

Then Edmée set to work. She began with the room. In a quarter of an hour it was ready. Everything that wasn't right for

Jacques disappeared, thrown into the garbage. There was a garbage can full to the top, which she carried down herself, for the scavengers were due to pass by. There had always been a sort of understanding between her and the garbage collector. She would throw out things—never waiting for them to be worn out—only when they could serve as messages, as confidences to a world that was lower but devoted. The scavengers would know very well why that can was overflowing with silk, with gold, and with kimonos worn out at the back but still usable—it was because her son had come back. What a grand party tonight for the scavengers' wives when their husbands came home; they would only have to button up the kimonos with the front part behind, the wives getting dirty mainly in front. . . . The heart of a cleaning lady that blossoms within every woman who is maternal or in love was beating strong inside her. She recalled something her mother used to say: "I dismiss any cleaning women who don't put their heart in their work."

She killed a spider with her heart. She made the bathtub gleam with a sponge, washing soda, and her heart. And there presenting themselves were closets, various nooks and crannies, and a whole series of volunteers to replace the statuettes and incense burners that were thrown away: a writing desk, some books, and a complete set of Robert Louis Stevenson, bound in red and gold, that immediately found its place, and indeed, really set off the whole room. You opened the door and you saw Stevenson. Going toward the window, Stevenson was on the right and met your eye. The table now seemed out of place and so was the wardrobe. It was like those evenings on coming home from a ball when Edmée, alone and weak, would handle the heaviest pieces of furniture with the ease of a professional mover. It was even easier: today the furniture itself seemed eager to return to this bourgeois order. . . .

And when the room was done, it was herself that she had changed. . . . And there was almost nothing left to do. Look at herself in the mirror. Close her eyes and open them again. A bath and a facial massage, this was done out of meticulousness, to top things off. She had washed it all off, both from last night and the dozens of nights that had gone before. . . . She was young, just a tiny bit younger than needed to achieve complete accord between her body and herself. But this, as far as Jacques was concerned, was surely better than the reverse. She put on the only outfit that seemed worthy of waiting for Jacques, a traveling suit which gave to the room its own relativity, which turned it into a room for a trip. Stevenson was delighted.

As Jacques was late getting back, she polished her shoes and put a few stitches in the other suit that needed a little mending at the shoulder. She was divided between the fear of not seeing Jacques come back and the desire of finishing her sewing before his return. There were also two buttons to sew back on. She began to slow down toward the end. She didn't feel capable of waiting for Jacques once she had finished sewing. But he arrived just in time, with his suitcase and some flowers. She had heard something crash at the bottom of the stairs a moment earlier. He had no doubt bumped into and turned over the garbage can. With his hands he had put back in the odds and ends of curtains and kimonos. . . . But none of this showed on his face, and Edmée never knew that the thing swelling his pocket was the Buddha she had thrown out.

He looked at his mother and the room with tears in his eyes. He had never dreamed of such a complete change, and he too seemed transformed. He had taken off his old suit. He was almost elegant. He whom Edmée had always imagined dressed in the rough, colorless material that Pierre had a talent for discovering out of the piles of fabrics marked *miscellaneous* was now wearing a suit of gray homespun with red stitching. . . .

One day, ten years ago, Edmée had wanted Pierre to order a homespun with red stitching. She had even brought a sample. . . . Pierre, gone to pick out the homespun, had returned with a blackish serge with chevrons; but Edmée would have sworn that the suit Jacques had on now was the same as her sample. . . . Had he come across this bright square of material in the drab wardrobe she had left behind when she went off to visit the Seeds? Or had Jacques perhaps heard her talking about it to

Pierre? . . . Had he got the idea of having the suit made up special just to find his mother? . . . Had he been to the tailor, sample in hand as his only bait, giving him all sorts of instructions so that the cut and quality of the homespun might not harm in any way the hunt that he was about to undertake, the hunt for his mother? Had he, for ten years now, admired and envied, heart beating with excitement, his father's friends who were dressed in homespun? It was very much the way Jacques was. In any case he had been right. It was the right cloth to pick. Neither the velour of Genoa nor the woolen of Sedan would this morning have had the power of this homespun. It left Edmée without strength, without resistance, all the more since Jacques had his nails trimmed in the almond shape that she used to urge in vain on Pierre—who cut them almost square, nails being for him an example of animal survival to which he was reluctant to grant their clawlike nature. . . . But Jacques, off to hunt his mother, had pressed the manicurist to give him back his claws and to make them rosy. His teeth were dazzling white, a white that couldn't have been gained in one day, like the rosy nails: he who never wanted to brush his teeth, from the moment his mother left, must have brushed them twice a day, with violence and despair. . . . He would be thinking of his mother and go off, mouth and jaws clenched tight, to brush his teeth. He saw that his mother was looking at his mouth, looking at the faithfulness of the teeth, the love of those gums. He stopped smiling. . . . It wasn't possible to resist any longer! Both teeth and nails, the hunter was perfect. . . . More perfect than the tenderest game you might hunt. . . . It remained only to take his mother in his arms. And he did so.

"So there you are at last," he said.

He had already said it. But it wasn't yet true when he said it. The first time they had both seen each other under disguises that would have allowed them, had they judged it necessary, not to reveal themselves to each other. A Jacques without the homespun and gloves hiding his nails, an Edmée without strength and without honor. And now, with their masks of encounter cast off, they could face each other. Everything sounded right, everything

was true. It was true that she was there. And he wasn't a bit surprised to find her like this, young and fresh and in her room with
flowers—a room that only a little while before had been desti-
tute and ugly—as if he had guessed that she had taken on that
first aspect only out of convention and some filial rite. From the
bookshelves the set of Stevenson bestowed its own sort of grace.

"How did you find me?"

"Oh Mama! I always thought that you would go to San
Francisco. Do you recall? One day you said to Father, 'I would
love to live in San Francisco.'"

*San Francisco, homespun,* words dropped by chance and
which had revealed her trail. . . . Words that hadn't been completely sincere: she actually preferred men in tweed, and for her
dwelling, some unknown island. . . . But it was a lucky thing she
hadn't said so in front of Jacques. What would he have done?
Where would he be? And where is the unknown island?

"As soon as I could, I came here and looked for you. I've
been looking for you for four days."

He had had to look far and wide. And look for her not
among women of renown, nor among the queens of society or
professional women. He had had to eliminate drawing rooms,
hospitals, studios, and museums. Eliminate the parks, where she
no longer went, and the bay, where she no longer swam. . . .
There had remained the bars, the police stations, and the guides
to the Chinese quarter. But nothing on Jacques's face indicated
that he had followed anything less than a trail of glory.

"How is your father?"

"Well. Claudie is with him."

It was Jacques who had said her name.

"They get along very well. I'm at the university now. I live
in a dormitory."

He added, and, thought Edmée, may all women who are either happy or unhappy, who have everything or have nothing,
know a moment like that. . . .

"It was the only way I had of being with you."

Then it occurred to Edmée that this could also mean: One can't be with you while being with Claudie! . . . May all women who are either happy or unhappy, etc., etc., not ever have to tell themselves something like that.

They had lunch at home. Jacques didn't want to go out again. He was determined to turn this room that his mother had lived in for a few weeks into the place that she had lived in ever since she had left him. . . .

Finally she couldn't resist any longer. The moment came when she had to ask the question.

"What is Claudie doing?"

She was at once ashamed of her words. *Doing* or *making* didn't apply to Claudie. Claudie was the very antithesis of those obstinate and industrious verbs. Claudie herself had not been made. Jacques, to be sure, Edmée had had the impression of making. There had been the labor of her body, an enterprise, a collaboration; at the time one could read all this on Pierre's face and on her own: this married couple was making a child. They had the recipe, they were workers: they were making Jacques. But they had not made Claudie. What could be read on Pierre's face during the gestation of Claudie was: this man has not produced Claudie. He seemed absent, distracted; he was distracted while his daughter was being born out of nothing—his nondaughter. . . . And since the time of her birth, whatever Claudie tried to do—not to create or invent—but to do or make: her homework, her dresses, her tarts—it never came off right. . . . Maybe this one thing. . . . It was going to be interesting to find out whether her falling out with her mother had brought about any reconciliation with ink, needles, and flour. . . .

"You know, Mother," replied Jacques, who never replied except to himself, "I understood very well why you left Claudie that evening before the operation. Her delirium revealed all of it to us. Under the chloroform she cried out that every night you were burning her whole body with a red-hot iron. But you only had to see her body that was so white, that you had always cared for and whose skin didn't show a scratch. Do you recall how you never wanted her to put on shoulder straps, garters, or collars, or anything that might leave an imprint? She used to steal my rubber bands in order to use them on her legs. . . . And when she came out of the anesthetic, she was rambling and raving; she wanted to touch the scars with her fingers, saying, 'She kissed me there! . . .' It was jealousy, wasn't it?"

"Jealousy of what?"

"Just plain jealousy. She simply realized what she was, that next to you she was unfeeling, incapable of love."

Edmée wondered at first if she had understood rightly. But there could be no doubt. Jacques had clearly said what he meant to say. He meant that Claudie couldn't bear to see her mother in love. He meant that what had brought him back to his mother was that he saw her as a victim, like they say, a victim of love. . . . Dear Jacques! . . . Ah yes, there was no doubt that he had been made by his father! It was the same lack of instinct that had moved her so much in the past about Pierre when they were on their wedding cruise. On board ship when she would catch sight of some promontory, the voice of Pierre beside her would say, "How pretty it is, the mouth of that river!" And when she would see a river of turquoise blue emptying into the sea in cascades, she was sure that Pierre was about to say, "Why, one would swear that it's the Gironde!" And if he said at the zoo of some port of call, "Now that is the mammal they call the ochine," then it would turn out to be an egg-laying platypus. . . . And in the album of that woman with sandals, who was—all you had to do was look at her—affected, cheap, and treacherous, he had quite naturally written, "Unless I'm very much mistaken, friendship is going to flower wherever you go. . . ." Yes, he was indeed very much mistaken: there before Cape Matapan, they had found the lady of friendship nude at the door of the chief mechanic, who refused to give her back her dress.

The little Jacques he had made was surely made in his own image. Whereas Claudie at the age of six could discover avarice in someone extravagant and ugliness in a beautiful woman, Jacques, ahead of her in school, loved the liar for his frankness and the redhead for his looks. Claudie had never asked for any explanation as to why her mother had left home. She had hoisted herself on Edmée like the eaglet on the back of the eagle, ready to fly away on its natural migration. As for Pierre and Jacques, they had sought the reason why, and as they were made out of love and thought they were the very opposite of love, they had viewed love itself as the only thing able to tear this woman away from them, who, as it happened, was actually fleeing love. That was why he had come back, this poor Jacques who was love itself, but who was made for love the way a dog is made to be a bishop. And that is why he was here: it was his homage to love. That is why the sight of a deplorable mother in the light of this dawn had not surprised him; he had believed that she was returning after a night of love. . . . Dear Lord, how hard it is to get others to understand you, especially your children! There was Jacques, who seemed created for science and technology but who intended to take up love instead. . . .

What to tell him? Tell him, oh my dearest Jacques, haven't you looked at yourself? Look at yourself in the mirror: it's not that there's anything wrong with you, but you can see that you're a born victim, ready for the kill. And if you sacrifice the world of your problems and your logarithms for women, you are lost and you're going to suffer as no one has suffered. You have exactly the sort of face made for crying, face against the pillow, just the right chin and cheek to apply themselves to hands trembling with despair, the tall stature for waiting in the rain at street corners—without umbrella so as not to look foolish—and the breastbone of those who can sob without any recourse to tears, so very practical when they have none left. . . . You could seduce your mother with your homespun, but only because she's your mother, because for her that homespun is your flesh, your skin, with those little red stitches that are like the pimples you used to have, that you still have a bit, that love doesn't care for. . . .

But women won't give a damn about your homespun, or your pimples either, they will see through their peephole who you are, your heart so kind, so respectful, so ready to ache, and then, whether you cover yourself in wool, or cotton, or feathers, or hair, they will squeeze that heart in an instrument they have until you don't have a single drop of blood left. You've seen them, preparing cocktails and using a lemon squeezer; nothing is left, perhaps a bit of peel or rind, but this is nothing compared to their heart squeezer. I know them, the ones you will be drawn to. . . . It's not that they are particularly bad. They're neither clever, nor crafty, nor wicked, but that's the way they are. You arrive with a smile, roses in one arm, ringing the bell with your left hand like the nurses do, so as not to have to move the roses. Then they will take the roses, saying "Oh what beautiful roses!" and thinking that they don't have a vase for roses with stems that long, saying to themselves that as soon as you've left they'll have to cut the stems; and the heart squeezer will be applied, just a little bit, out of politeness, just to see.

And after fifteen bouquets of roses with stems too long, flattered deep down, they will embrace you, and be annoyed deep down that you don't bring the right vase to go with the flowers. And you will sacrifice your work to them, you will no longer sleep at night; at the flower shops you will try to find roses with longer and longer stems, they will be forced to buy pruning shears, and you will give them your very heart. Then you're going to see the heart squeezer! Using both hands and with all their might. And if there's only one woman in your life, you'll also get to see what the heart dilator is, and the heart hypodermic—their arsenal is inexhaustible. And if there are several, you will see that they have a way, when the heart has no more blood, of finding a false heart for you, a pretend heart that is no longer a heart, now that you know everything, now that you're no longer sensitive, now that you've surprised them cutting the stems off the roses, embracing the old gentleman who brings short-stemmed roses, and in a silver vase moreover, . . . but your false heart seems to feel and suffer and beat and struggle like a real heart in the suffering of sufferings. . . .

And if they don't do all that to you, it's because they lie to themselves or because they're idiots. . . . Oh, my darling Jacques, you who have left father and sister in order to come hear from me that women are going to embrace you, love you, adorn with flowers your life, your table, your body—that is what I have to tell you. . . . Besides, look at me, judge for yourself. . . . I am the first woman you ever loved, I am the one who will love you the most—and look what I have done!

"He's dead, isn't he?"

Who was dead? Frank? No, she had learned that Frank was alive. Jacques was talking no doubt of the one for whom he thought his mother had abandoned him. He was still wrapped up in his legend. Why destroy it, since Claudie had not approved, and since that legend was complete and, now, with the aid of death, over and done with? That Jacques might have believed her to be still in love, she could not have borne—she would have told him everything, but since the one who really never had been was dead, why pull some small truth out of the silence when it, like the larger truth, asked only to lie in peace. All the more so, she felt certain, since despite his admiration for love, Jacques was really relieved that there was no lover, that all that was now in the past. That there could be no contest between the love of his mother and the one that lay ahead for him. . . . It was an incomparable legacy that she was leaving him as a result of this catastrophe. . . . It was an abdication that opened up his whole career. . . .

Now there was a double reason to love her and take her in his arms. . . . Moreover, Edmée had been mistaken on this point: he knew how to take a woman in his arms. It felt right there. He also knew how to embrace. It was in fact in this assumed being that all those gestures of tenderness appeared natural. . . . He offered himself, he caressed, he gave of himself, tall and awkward as he was, pockets stuffed with notes and wallets, like an adolescent, perfect and nude. That oblong head became rounded to fit into her shoulder. His unkempt hair, both head and beard, became silky. . . . The flat planes of his face developed curves. Perhaps women after all would be responsive to this unconscious ability and authority that were turning into obedience, becoming slaves of love. It would be enough to close their eyes. It would be enough to be in love. Jacques didn't suspect that he was giving his mother, at this moment, through his embrace, the first experience of a love truly at ease that she had perhaps ever felt. Maybe after all there might be a woman who from birth would have a deep enough vase when he brought roses and a flat vase for when he brought violets. Maybe there would also be one who was destined to suffer because of him. Wherever she might be, may her parents care for her skin, see to it that she walks gracefully, dances well, and can swim! May all the forces of the day and night, the gods of gas taps and automobiles unite nonstop to watch over the one fated to torture this kind, tender, and harmless Jacques! . . .

So that was why Jacques had come then! . . . One is wrong to believe in chance, in the happiness of chance. People don't go out of their way in life except to bring you lessons, signs, or duties. Even your son. . . . When you run into your old tenant farmer in a train station, or Marshal Joffre sitting near you on a ferryboat, it isn't a chance encounter, it's that they are messengers. What they say through their voices is not at all what they say through their apparitions. "What a fine day," says Marshal Joffre. . . . "Get off the ferry when I do and follow me," says the apparition of Marshal Joffre, "and on the way you will find out the reason for your life. . . ." For beings that suddenly appear like this generally come to take you away. . . . The champion of the kidnappers is still God. . . .

And this was the case of Jacques. "Oh, Mother," Jacques was saying or about to say, "come back with me. You're unhappy. You have lost the one you love. Your room isn't exactly the palace of palaces. Come home. . . ." But the message of Jacques did not have this childlike logic and truth. That would really have been too simple. . . . "Oh, Mother," the message of Jacques was saying in fact, "you're happy, and this room is a wonderful place to stay. You've found the one who loved you. . . . But the time has come to leave him. Come. . . ."

"Oh, Mother," Jacques was saying, "since you don't have Claudie anymore, your life is so lonely. . . . Leave your unhappiness. . . . Come with me. . . . You're free to do as you wish. But I'm your son. . . ."

"Oh, Mother," the message was saying, "we know that the sacrifice of your daughter has opened up this domain that you were looking for when you left us. . . . Leave your happiness, come. . . . I'm only your son, but you can see that at this moment I am a sign. . . ." And it was not to Jacques, but to the messenger that she had to reply. . . .

The choice was hard. With her son once more in her arms, Edmée could recall even better that morning, after her flight from the hospital, when she had found herself for the first time deprived of Claudie. She had thought to wake up in desolation, and was surprised to find herself relieved. It was as if the amputation had taken place. . . . She had dragged around the inert member, paralyzed, like a stubborn virgin, and now it was over. . . . She was liberated, not only from the virgin, but from some sort of virginity: she was free. Claudie was no longer there, and everything was there. She had only to choose. . . .

Every scale of every nuance of every sort of heart and devotion seemed to present itself—the homespun of sacrifices and the tweed of voluptuous pleasures. Edmée, out of a sense of reserve that had never allowed her to engage directly in dialogue with the higher authorities of the world, that did not permit herself to say what the favorites of the Lord may exclaim, their wife turned into a pillar of salt, their son killed by some desert tribe, or their inheritance eaten up by the first banker to come along: "You gave me all, you have taken all away, so here I am to serve you. . . ." But she felt herself nonetheless at this same stage. . . . Someone had given her Claudie. . . . Then someone had disguised Claudie, then someone had taken Claudie away. . . . She said *someone* so as to designate this follower, this obstinate pursuer whose silent jubilation she could sense today. . . . His day had come, unless this game of Edmée, with a sort of grace always in flight and in promise, were not simply that instinctive coquetry of the most limited kind of life with the most sensitive kind of soul. . . . If he existed, the one who had prepared her like the fisherman's wife prepares the octopus, by flogging it against the stones of the quay, then let him announce himself, let him come in—it was really time for him to declare himself! . . .

She was waiting for it, she was invoking that state of high pleasure that had been promised her, asking only for a sign to indicate whether it was to come from renunciation, appetite, or devotion. She had opened her window, turned on the radio, and begun the newspaper, as if hands and voices and letters of fire were going to give her the secret, and that unknown address. . . . She had the free legs of a Judith, she was as naked as Job, as open to eyes and hands as Tobias. . . . And she had been disappointed at first, for nothing replied but silence. . . . No impulse, no vocation, no source from within her. . . . Yet heaven knows there is no lack of jobs that need to be done in this sad world. There was enough to do for ten Joan of Arcs, for twenty Charlotte Cordays. The whole world was calling for donors of blood, nurses for typhus, and dentists for cannibals in the South Seas. Much was needed to keep up the hospital for lepers, for which in fact there was an ad in the paper for nurses of good appearance who could play the harmonium. A direct allusion: she knew how to play the harmonium, she was of good appearance. People were needed to wash the feet of the miners of San Jose who had been hauled out after a month in the mines, to wipe the dribble from the mouths of the elderly in the nursing home in Olympia, to help get to sleep the victims of peritonitis, to hold down the arms of those with delirium tremens. . . . People were needed to give orders, people needed to follow them. . . . But Edmée had to admit that nothing in all this placement bureau was really for her. It was even as if her mission were to refuse missions. . . .

And little by little the veil had lifted and she had understood: this life without a goal of a woman without a man—there was her crown, there was her job. Solitary, anonymous, and pure, there she tasted the joy of the elect that other women find only in being surrounded, in being called on, and in physical pleasure. . . . That was the way the demanding master wanted her, for whom her modesty when faced with piety—in which neither Job nor Judith had shone very well—had never allowed her to give either form or name. . . .

That was what her destiny was: an intrigue without word and without gesture, but lasting, but intimate, with a presence that manifestly was not that of men; predilection on the fringe of official saintliness of a power only found here and there up to then, and which now let itself center on her, in warmth and attachment, like an enormous magnifying glass. The favorite of a king, that's what she felt herself to be, that's what she was. At times, saddened not to be able to give a name to this presence, to this preference, she used to say to herself that those women are really lucky who are satisfied with the conventional term of *Lord*. . . . It would all have been wonderfully explained in her own case. . . . One might have said that the one whom the others call the Lord, since it's a question of him, was tired of having various creatures in this sad world, outcasts or loved ones, and simply wanted to have a girlfriend. This was no doubt why Edmée's pity had never translated into trances or a vocation: God didn't want her for a legitimate spouse, he wanted her for a girlfriend. He wanted to experience the secret joys of a union not consecrated with the world of men. She was off to herself, at the back of the courtyard, but she was the girlfriend. Like *Back Street*.

Martyrdom, confession—they're really not worth that much: it's like declaring your own self a saint, it's wanting to approach God on your own, and it's all too human, far too human. One could understand that God might have need of a presence that wasn't altered by his own presence. . . . In that way one could explain the false situation she had with all men; God had put her outside the circuit—he had given her to a mining engineer so that she could be a woman, so that she could be a wife. And, at the right time—it was one of the least-difficult tasks he had set himself since the Creation, given the gentleness of Pierre—he had pushed the engineer aside and had led her up to his mezzanine. And this peace attained at last, this freedom within, it was God anonymous. That's what Jacques had found in his mother, a kept woman. The lover was never there. . . . The lover was always there. . . .

"Oh, Mother," Jacques was saying, "it's time for you to be happy. . . . Come back to us." "Oh, Mother," the message of Jacques was saying, "a woman has every advantage in breaking a secret liaison, even a happy one, even with a lover who is above men. . . . But come back to the world of men. . . ."

Such was the visit of Jacques. It wasn't what Edmée had thought at first, a visit between two trains, between two worlds, and it wasn't that the world of Jacques had passed so near her own that he had had time to get off. No. . . . Jacques was that Russian countess from the engraving in the drawing room of Edmée's grandfather, the one who in riding boots and with whip enters the dining room of the inn, enters the *traktir*, according to the text, where her daughter-in-law was having tea, *tchai* said the text, with the music master who had abducted her: Abalstitiel, said the text.

But why? By what right? The countess had to defend the honor of the Menchikovs by putting Abalstitiel, the music master, back in his place. . . . Not Jacques. . . . In the name of the need for a mother in the family? But the very sight of Jacques proved the falseness of this axiom. He whom she had left so weak and defenseless, how strong he had become without her! Edmée recalled her life with him up to the point when she had left him, having on her lips, in her arms, in her legs, all the words and gestures of service to a child of twelve, but now they were useless. There was no longer any need to wipe Jacques's mouth, to fold his napkin, to separate with both hands his two knees that he used to cross so obstinately. In the absence of his mother, everything that would have required a mother to combat or exorcise had either vanished or taken care of itself. A lack of need for mothers was proved by those handsome index fingers of Jacques, which, on the eve of her departure, Edmée had been forced to cover with aloe dressings so that he wouldn't suck on them and turn them into stumps. This Jacques, who without her devotion and constant attention seemed doomed to appendicitis, to being crushed, to being scalded with bouillon that was too hot, who would disfigure himself by mashing his nose against the windowpane—this same Jacques, one had to believe, as soon as his mother was no longer there, had become the perfection of perfections.

This didn't surprise Edmée. She had always had the impression that the very absence of his mother was his safeguard, was a panacea. . . . While she couldn't be with him for a minute without looking at him and keeping an eye on him, checking his water, his sleep, armed with probes and thermometers—for the presence of his mother carried the danger to the depths of his flesh—as soon as she wasn't there her worry ceased: he was cured, cured of life, cured of his mother. And right now, from the fact that he was in her sight and in her arms, nothing protected him any further, neither immanent justice, nor the law of numbers, nor statistics of age and sex, against the danger that mothers create around their sons and for which they are the sole antidote. No, the more she thought about it, the more she was convinced that Jacques wasn't using this kind of blackmail! She had not betrayed Jacques and Pierre. She had always felt an absolute security concerning them. She had entrusted them to whoever guards, whoever watches over, whoever alleviates, whoever dispenses. . . . Why say his name? He has none. . . .

There were of course some weak links in the management. The one who guards had not guarded Jacques from the barber who cut the beginning of his sideburns at a bevel. The one who alleviates had given him a slight stoop. The one who watches over had let a spot get on his jacket. The supreme dry cleaner hadn't been paying attention. But the evidence was clear: the usefulness of mothers remains an open question. . . . In fact, what concerned her about the truth of all this, the thing that disturbed her terribly, was that Jacques, in order to come back to her, had renounced his strength, his invulnerability. . . . And looking at him brought back her old anxiety of the week when the membrane of his skull had reopened. . . . No. She checked to make sure. . . . The skin had healed completely. . . . No, Jacques

dear, you'll have to try something else, you'll need to find some
argument other than the usefulness of mothers.

He did try something else. During the night she heard him call
to her. She got up in haste, the very same haste she used to have
running to his bed before she had gone to the Seeds', the haste of
the mother called by her child. It was toward the child Jacques
that she was running, and toward all the ills that she feared for
him then, a race toward meningitis, toward diphtheria. And it
was the little Jacques who was there. He took up the whole bed,
but he was very much the child she had left years before, and all
the flaws were reappearing that had been erased last night—his
forefinger almost deformed, his nails less kempt, his nose not
right. One day with her had been enough. He put his arms
around her, but this time clumsily. He was sobbing.

"Why did you leave me? Why did you leave me?"

He let her embrace him and became calmer. He asked her
pardon for having waked her up that way. Then the sobbing broke
out again. It was like a crisis. As if he were suddenly attacked by
some trouble that had been hiding for weeks and that had broken
out. Yes, it was his crisis. The crisis of Jacques was, in the middle
of the night, to think about his mother's leaving and to sob his
heart out. The pain used to hide behind his work, his cheerfulness;
a month, two months would go by and it was forgotten. And
suddenly, always at the wrong time, coming back from a banquet
at the university or in the middle of a dance at the Ambassadors,
he would feel the symptoms coming on, that wrenching of the
heart, his forefinger turned wrong, his nose out of shape, and the
crisis was there. . . . But why did it have to happen today? It was
unfair to his mother that it should show up today!

Edmée held him, cradled him, all trembling, held tight
against her this tall body once more covered with the white skin
of the body of little Jacques, overwhelmed when faced with this
pain over which she had even less power than she had over all

the others. For the proof was there: it was incurable. The crisis tonight meant that Edmée's presence was no longer a remedy, that she, the mother, could do no more against the desolation of not having had a mother, no more than the first woman to come along, that with all the kisses, embraces, words, advice, and caresses that she might lavish on him tonight, the vast amount of those that she had failed to give him was not reduced by a single one. If Jacques had thought by finding his mother to wipe out the years when she wasn't there, to heal the wound, he was now informed. Yet it was that desire to be healed that had drawn him here, and never had the means of access been so difficult. All the anguish of the patient who thought himself delivered of his sickness and finds that the sickness has returned was in his eyes. . . . Life has no remedy. . . .

The crisis passed. Once more he smiled at Edmée, was joking, embraced her, and pushed his confidence as far as to fall asleep in her arms. She held him against her as long as she could. At first it was easy, he was so light. . . . The dawn arrived. Then he became heavy and she released him limb by limb. She would have liked to be able to hold on to his hand, but it was the head that remained last. The head had about the same weight as little Jacques had had at birth. Finally she laid it down. The scavengers down in the street were shaking the garbage cans, disappointed to find them without any treasures today. . . . Edmée went to bed. For a moment she thought she heard Jacques sobbing. . . . But it was just a momentary return of the crisis. Perhaps he hadn't even noticed it himself. It lasted for a second.

He slept late. Edmée didn't wake him. It was her last dawn of freedom, since Jacques's first words would be to ask her to go back there, to what they also call the hearth in countries and houses with central heating. Understood. It was settled. Jacques had vanquished Abalstitiel. She would follow him. He would take her in his arms presently, when he knew that the suitcases were all packed. This time it didn't take Edmée long. Every year found her a little more detached from human furniture. She could die without any suitcase. . . .

# 10

Two hands covered her eyes.

"Guess," said the voice of Jacques. . . .

Even for a game, Edmée could not answer with a false name. In all the world she couldn't imagine anyone other than Jacques who might come up from behind and cover her eyes with his hands. Abalstitiel himself was incapable of this. Back when little Claudie liked to surprise her two or three times a day this way, cupping those little hands over her eyes, as if total darkness alone could keep her mother from seeing behind her, Edmée was able to come up with a few other names. Why, it was Pierre. . . . It was Frank. . . . She used to invent some too. It was the president of the United States. . . . Claudie would laugh. . . . It was Fatty—Fatty Arbuckle was still famous at the time. . . . Claudie could no longer contain herself. . . . It was Jacques. . . . Then Claudie would release her band, provoked. . . . No, it wasn't Jacques.

But this was Jacques, coming back from his visit to the new bridges, the one over the bay and the Golden Gate. He had inherited from his father this passion for constructions of iron and just for them had abandoned Edmée for an hour. She was by no means offended. A son who goes looking for his mother and who is in love with bridges deserves to find her there at the place where the two greatest arches in the world have been erected. . . .

Really, he didn't look so bad: a sort of halo seemed to envelop him, very bright, very pure, the sort of halo one can see around statues and in portraits; it was as if he had taken on some veil of beauty that was lying about. It wasn't made to measure but it was very sensitive. It pleased Edmée, not that her son but that the messenger should be handsome. . . .

And there he was, beginning to speak:

"Mother, wouldn't you really like to see her?"

It was a good thing he didn't see the start he had given her, that he couldn't see that she no longer saw him, that he no longer counted at all.

"Of course I would, my dear."

"When?"

"Whenever you wish. When you leave, I'll go with you."

"You don't have to leave. She's in San Francisco. She should have arrived this morning. I reserved a room for her at the hotel. . . ."

So Claudie was here! . . . Her first feeling was one of distress. . . . It seemed to her beyond her strength to replace by way of Claudie herself, by way of that Claudie so terribly defined and exclusive, the species of Claudie redistributed to the elements which chance alone sometimes gave her signs of. . . . The signs were in code to be sure, but signs nevertheless. . . . Another woman wouldn't have picked them up, but they would have to do for the time being. . . . All last week as a matter of fact, the newspaper that Edmée read had as its headline some big phrase or another with the word *Claude* in it. This wasn't exactly *Claudie*, it was really only *Claude*. But the sign was a clear one, and besides, headlines were very much Claudie's sort of thing: "Claude Has Conquered the Seas. . . ." "Claude Has Spoken Plainly to the Cuban Government. . . ." "Claude Has Never Given Up. . . ." It was a question, not of Claudie, but of the

French scientist who wanted to make use of the tides; still, to make the seas work for humanity was also very much along Claudie's line. . . . Claudie no longer approached her except through words related to her own name, through faces or clothes related to her own, or through birds, like a girl who had died. Now here she was, coming back to life, and a distressed Edmée wondered how she could endure a daughter suddenly reconstituted in a world so suddenly deprived of her. . . .

"Why didn't she come yesterday?"

"I wanted to have a day alone with you. I wanted to talk to you about her. For you to get to know her a bit before you see her."

Edmée was invaded by another fear.

"Who are you talking about, Jacques dear?"

"Why, who do you suppose? About my fiancée, Mother. About Marie-Rose."

"You're only twenty-one and you're engaged?"

"Oh, Mother! It's not possible that you haven't guessed this since yesterday? That someone like you didn't guess once?"

"No, you're not engaged, you can't be engaged!"

"We're prepared to wait as long as necessary. What is it? What's the matter?"

It was a lesson she really deserved. That was one she had surely asked for, as Claudie used to say. She had believed it was natural to abandon your son and not have your son abandon you, to prefer your daughter to your son and still have that son prefer you over all others, male or female. . . . The disillusionment was cruel. If the gentle, the tender, and the weak, those you love less, those you've wronged in every way, if they begin to betray you, to love you less, and to be in the wrong, then life is truly hopeless. The only thing to hang onto in life is the security of those we deceive, the admiration of those we tolerate, the kin to us by blood, and the flesh of those we're attached to only by convention and habit. How can you find anything lasting when the sacrificial victims will no longer sacrifice themselves? For the first time Edmée felt that the world was unfair. . . . So it wasn't a son she had watched over last night, but rather a fiancé. She hadn't hugged the body of a son, but that of a fiancé. Poor dear Jacques had come to seek the last maternal embrace before the first conjugal embrace. Beneath the shell of a suffering son was a happy fiancé. The god of the future lay asleep in his wrappings. Jacques had come for her to undo them, for her to deliver him. If he had had his crisis last night, it was because he had seen that this was not possible, that she could do nothing about it, that indeed, by her very presence, she did just the opposite. . . . He was going to have to drag his old body along with the new one. Unless he meant to try out the idea of absence, in a new way and seriously.

For the first time she felt herself in revolt. The only right that his fate allowed Jacques was to answer abandonment by love, to answer absence by faithfulness—or else somebody should have let her know: then she would have been the one to remain faithful. To have such a beautiful career as a son left behind by his mother, sacrificed to his mother, and to end like this! She was cruel, she felt herself to be cruel, but everything in her was repeating that the only ones who owed her anything were those whose life she had spoiled. That was her own logic. Was there then a riot of the weak in this sad world? Was Pierre also getting married? Was he getting along without her, shaving himself, eating his beef bourguignonne, grumbling about for his shoe trees, without thinking of her? Never had it been clearer to her that the nobility of her flight, her high flight, was tied to the obstinate love of those two creatures, and that if they let her go, it was her downfall. Our only nobility—didn't they know it?—was the nobility of others. The nobility of Edmée—was a man and an unhappy child. A man and a young man who persisted in living with an absent woman, in taking their meals, their joy, their work with an absent woman. Two men who disdained everything—she could never have imagined them dancing the tango, playing the lottery—except with a wife and mother who had betrayed them. . . . But now they were betraying her. It was appalling. It was. . . . It was like the opposite! It was like humility on Claudie. It was as if Claudie had come back repentant, demanding that her mother kiss her on every part of her face, bearing openly all the red marks, consenting to wash in the morning only if her mother were there ready to kiss her and mark her anew. Edmée simply refused. To lavish with kisses a Claudie who was fallen no longer had any meaning. . . . But what was she thinking about? Where was she? Jacques was the important thing.

"When will we see her, my dear? . . . Do you want her to have lunch with us?"

"Here?"

"If you wish. Or at that Mexican restaurant down by the bay."

He took her in his arms and hugged her. She combed his hair and brushed him off. He left. He promised to be careful about the streetcars. At the door he turned around:

"Her name is Marie-Rose. She'll talk to you about Claudie, because I'm pretty sure Claudie is also engaged."

Claudie was engaged? She really didn't care at all.

She was a charming little creature, with a light voice, a fine nose, and beautiful lips. Nothing more. She had a lovely bust, a slender neck, and hands that were graceful and ever alert. Yet she had nothing. To describe her, you would need adjectives. There wasn't any noun that seemed to fit. She didn't fall under any sort of repose, any kind of concern or desire. Nor, above all, since it was a question of love, did any of the nouns in the Bible really fit. She wasn't a hill, a grape harvest, a brook, an acacia. . . . It's true that Jacques wasn't a plane tree, a buffalo, or a golden obelisk. . . . Neither was she what you could call a real dear. . . . Jacques at any rate was a real dear. You sensed it in his curly hair, in his fine veins. . . . But she did seem sweet and had become the fiancée to an incredible degree. She had not yet taken possession of Jacques: she didn't brush his clothes, didn't even brush against him. One sensed that she must have touched him only with the mouth and by way of the mouth. She was inaugurating the gestures of her future marriage with a singular innocence. She served a virginal tea with virginal cakes, that was all. . . . The freeness, the innocence, the capriciousness that Jacques managed to find in her laugh, her walk, and her words were very much on a par, Edmée was thinking, with the gestures of an ant. . . . Her future seemed planned out for every single minute, right up to her death. Edmée could see in advance her whole day—getting up in the morning following Jacques's kiss, the water in the bath, reading the newspaper, the young wife's cookbook, the rest of the day, and Jacques's kiss before sleep. The human lot: they weren't the only ones engaged or even the only ones in love on this terrace. There was a fairly large number of couples made up of men with bow ties and women with crimson lips and stylish blouses, couples in love, in short. . . . O dear Lord, isn't it true that you created only the sun and that all the other creatures created themselves?

In truth, it was just as well that way. Jacques would never know his whole life long what a woman is. A real woman is rare. Most men marry a mediocre counterfeit of men, a little more crafty, a little more supple, a little more beautiful—they marry themselves. They see themselves passing in the street with a little more bust, a little more hip, the whole thing wrapped up in silk jersey for their use, then they run after themselves, embrace, and marry themselves. It's less cold after all than marrying a mirror. Woman is strong: she can step over floods, she can overturn thrones, she can stop the years. Her skin is marble. When you find a real one, she is the impasse of the world. . . . Where do the rivers go, the clouds, the solitary birds? They hurl themselves into woman. . . . But she is rare. . . . You must run away when you see her, for if she loves, if she hates, she is unrelenting. Her compassion is unrelenting. . . . But she is rare. . . . Besides, why was she talking about woman—poor Edmée, who hadn't been able to do a thing, either with her body or with her life? So rare that she hadn't even seen one. Except perhaps while bending over Claudie as she pretended to be asleep. . . .

"They're all looking at you, Mother. . . ."

Everyone was looking at Edmée, and she could guess why. She hadn't told Jacques. The fact was that everything that Marie-Rose was, everything that she seemed to have, simply made Edmée stand out instead. Until now Edmée's beauty had always clashed a bit with the hour, with those around her. She threw you off guard by her distraction, by her absence. . . . But here at last Jacques had found the remedy, and it was Marie-Rose. Marie-Rose would be talking, and the silence of Edmée was heartrending. She would be serving tea, and the immobility of Edmée could link you to the centuries. She would be laughing, and the smile of Edmée was enough to make you weep. The secretary of the founder of Christian Science must have had that kind of modesty, that pleasant way of setting off her mistress when they entered a restaurant. Yes, it was as a priestess that Marie-Rose treated her, and Edmée could easily guess for which religion. Jacques had talked. For Marie-Rose also, she was love itself, she who had sacrificed her son for love, for someone whose name no one had ever been able to learn. . . . "Me neither," thought Edmée. . . .

And the two of them, just as they would have shown a famous jeweler their bargain engagement diamond, were coming to have the great expert admire their love. "Oh dear Lord," Edmée was thinking now, "why always this same misunderstanding? These children want to make me say that their tiny love is the real thing. These men who are looking at me, these women who envy me—what they see in me is love. Naturally. . . . The only thing one personifies well is that which one is not. But why don't they consult me there where I'm a specialist? . . . Yes, I have an awl in my hands, I know how to use it, and I handle it well, but it serves only to distinguish what is true from what is false. . . . It's a tool for peace, for supreme peace. . . . It's true that I'm qualified to apply it to both objects and beings. Let someone show me this forehead or that landscape, this park or that night, and I can pronounce it Supreme Peace or not Supreme Peace.

"I'm afraid you're not Supreme Peace, my darling Jacques, with your heart that gets so excited it could burst when Marie-Rose butters you up, with your eyes that used to weep into your bath when you thought of your mother who was gone. Definitely not Supreme Peace, anyone who cries in his bath. Anyone who gives himself body and soul to the little body and little soul of a Marie-Rose. No sign of Supreme Peace, moreover, at this party, not on the brow of that man over there, even though elderly, even though touched by the moon. Nor on the moon itself—indeed, there seems to be some concern up there tonight. . . . Nor on Marie-Rose, who is no palm tree on fire, but who really is nice, who is no Sahara, but who really is sweet. . . . Unless it might be in the depths of that eddy, at the very center of that whirlpool that is my heart today. . . .

"No, you are the opposite of Supreme Peace, Jacques darling, you who are going to push your exams ahead by two years, bolt your meals, and skip sleep, all just to head for that little bed where you will bury yourself one evening with Marie-Rose. . . . But if it can give the two of you any pleasure for me to stamp Love on your childish nuptial game, very well, all right. . . . Not all the money minted is the real thing. . . . I will take the hand of Marie-Rose as soon as she is free of her little cakes, free of her teaspoons and her dessert forks, turn up the collar of her fur if it's cold out and pat her hair. . . . I will smile at Jacques whenever he smiles, laugh whenever he makes a joke. I will flatter with my hand and caress with my voice two poor little mortals who are obeying the same law as eels and mongooses. . . . A moment of silence, please. There is, however, over there, on the horizon, between the nose of the gentleman touched by the moon and the paunch of the maitre d', a small undivided space between the sky and the sea that I might stamp Supreme Peace. . . . At least I could have before your betrayal. . . ."

Marie-Rose was talking about Claudie, but Edmée was barely listening. It was as if one were telling her about the capture of an animal that one knows to be free. . . . Claudie was marrying a student from Berkeley next month, but this marriage so close at hand had no effect on Edmée. The fiancé was intelligent, rich, and very fast. At the four-hundred-meter dash he was even the fastest man in the world. "He won't catch up with Claudie," was Edmée's only thought. . . . He was handsome, he was in love, he could throw the discus fifty meters. "He won't reach Claudie," thought Edmée. . . . He was a serious worker, he was modest, he liked to improvise as he sang, and he always kept film in his briefcase—for inspired moments—that was "virginally" unexposed. "He won't have Claudie's virginity," thought Edmée. She knew Claudie's flesh too well, Claudie's mind, to see in her marriage anything other than a matter of convention in which her inner being was not affected. She would also take a lover when the time came. She lived in the world of men, she adopted their customs—it was the only way to make them invisible.

But Pierre, but Jacques, they didn't live among men. They indeed were the men. Everything that had no meaning as far as Claudie was concerned—fidelity, purity—regained its value with them, and, as Edmée saw more and more clearly, the basis of her own freedom was, in fact, their servitude. She came back to it again. . . . This adventure she had embarked upon, so long an enigma to herself, lost all sense if there were not, back in some quiet house, a child and a man who were resolutely firm and faithful. And now they were beginning to stir about. Jacques had taken the steps that lead to the cozy corner, to the scarf maker, the milliner, in a word, to a heart. And what was Pierre doing? If he was moving toward the bust of some aunt of Marie-Rose, toward some bosom very knowingly fortified, toward some knee he had caught sight of, in a word, toward a heart, did he suspect the denial that he was inflicting on Edmée? And it was not a wound to her self-esteem, the sorrow that a feminine presence might prevail over her memory—it was really that she had counted on them, that her whole life had been no less than an homage to a certain kind of honor that they personified, and that was constancy. . . .

"Does your father go out much?"

"Morning and afternoon."

"Yes, to the office. And in the evening?"

"He has his radio. He smokes his Châteauroux cigars."

All that went very well with the word *constancy*. And Châteauroux cigars went with it very well indeed.

"Do you have any aunts, Marie-Rose?"

"No. Seven uncles."

Edmée recalled the day when a feeling of uneasiness had once carried her back to Los Angeles and when she had paid a visit to Pierre. The sort of visit appropriate to make to constancy, without showing oneself. From the square that faced the apartment building, on a bench among the bamboos, she had spied on him. At noon he had arrived from the factory. He had gotten out of the car, which was large and quite new. He played the swell a bit as he locked the car doors, greeted by the staff at the entrance. "Look at me," he seemed to say. "Here you have a man who has succeeded. . . . Who is director and associate of the best petroleum company. Held in highest esteem by the potentates of the oil business. . . ." Then, this radiant moment having passed, outside the glamour of the car, his glow began to fade. The head hung down a little. His eye clouded over. "Look, look again," he seemed to say now. "Look at a man who has not succeeded. He had a wife and he had oil. Now he has only oil. He had love and an administrative council. He has the administrative council, but love is gone. . . ."

Then he had approached a man selling papers. "Look," he seemed to say. "Here's a man who understands newspapers, who judges them at their value, who judges them. . . ." He had bought the paper. "Look at me," he said then. "Here's a man who buys the paper and who is unable to read the names in it. He reads them all with the same name: Edmée. Roosevelt: he reads it as Edmée. . . . Hitler, a German form of Edmée. Crimes and revolutions and special cushions with an embroidered portrait of Robert Taylor for starstruck women, he reads it all as Edmée. . . ." A shoeshine boy nabbed him, got him to let him shine his shoes. "Yes, shine them," Pierre seemed to say. "You're about to give a shoeshine to a man whose shoes are worth the sun. . . ." And in fact he related to the little black boy how his slippers were of very special leather, the gift of one of the biggest ranch owners, a personal friend of his. . . . And the shoeshine boy left him, his feet shining, and his head losing more and more of its glow. . . . And he was heading toward the elevator, his eyes lost in the gold of his feet; on the tiles of blue glass he appeared to be walking on the sky, but his body was bent and he seemed to say, "It's not the sky I'm walking on and those who think so are very much mistaken. . . ." Then he suddenly went back: a child was writing with his finger on the dusty fender of the car; he had a talk with him, addressing him like a teacher. The child was frightened. "Let those write who know how to write," Pierre seemed to say. "I too was possessed of the urge in my administrative councils to inscribe the name of my adored wife on the mahogany. For the table wasn't simple veneer. It was the sort of massive mahogany that crude petroleum can offer. But I restrained myself and wrote it only with my finger—my breath on the wood made it visible—for the name of Edmée can be written with the finger without ever seeming to write, since it requires neither downstroke nor circumflex accent. . . . Look, I'll write it on this fender. . . ." The child left, confused, and Pierre couldn't make up his mind to go back in.

With that look that for three years had thought to see Edmée in every shadow, in every silhouette, the look that would run after her—it was always her, Edmée was false, but the shadow of Edmée was true—he was looking at those passing by without seeing them, and he was seeing Edmée without seeing her. . . . One could guess why he was lingering about like this: it was so as not to go back to the only place in the world where he was sure she wouldn't be. . . .

"Draw your strength out of that strength," had murmured Abalstitiel. . . . She had been strong. She had left again.

At the station, as she was putting Jacques on the train, she dared to ask her question. . . .

"Your father isn't getting married either?"

"Father? Are you kidding?"

"Good-bye."

On the wings of constancy—Pierre's, that is—the spirit of flight was already taking off again.

It wasn't the first time since he had run his placement office, the best in Santa Barbara, that Mr. Gonzales Martinez had seen a female client like this seek a position with a woman or older man. Sometimes it was a game. It was he who had placed the star of stars as housekeeper to a paralytic—a fake paralytic, by the way—because she wanted to know what a real housewife was like. . . . But the present client didn't seem concerned about some particular theatrical experience. . . .

"Unhappy? Any worries?"

"No."

"A nonexistent husband? Children running away?"

It was the way of Mr. Martinez. He guessed everything, a rough estimate perhaps, but everything.

"No."

"You're not forced to tell me. No love in your life, maybe?"

"No."

"You've probably never before in your life said no so often. You're more likely the sort of woman who says yes?"

"Yes."

"You would like to serve? It's in style. Are you looking for work, or is it perhaps servitude? Salary means little, right?"

"Oh no, it's important."

"No, I think not. . . . You don't know how to do anything?"

"Cook a cutlet."

"Anyway, there's no need for any sort of talent for the post I have in mind for you."

It was an odd route for a housekeeper about to take her position. He took the most beautiful road, then the most beautiful
drive, then it was as if he chose the most beautiful scenery, the
most beautiful trees. The choices were incomparable, but he always took the most beautiful. They arrived thus at the most
beautiful point on the coast. . . . More beautiful still for being
hidden.

"There it is."

An elderly Chinese servant came to open the door of the
car. Two Great Danes accompanied him. A bit later there was a
cat, of no particular breed, but not without breeding. . . . And so
fat you could have rolled her like a ball.

"There!" said Martinez. "You've seen everything."

"Seen what? Seen whom?"

"All those you will never see in the house."

"And the mistress?"

"There isn't one. It's a foundation. The mistress was my
oldest client. She died over twenty years ago."

"What must I do?"

"Keep the house ready for a return. My client lost her sister in 1858, a sister eighteen years old. She went on an ocean
voyage and didn't return. My client was never willing to admit
that she is probably dead. This property is pledged to her. . . ."

"Who was your client? A crazy eccentric?"

"No. Simply a sensitive woman."

They were in the library. Cabinets with latticework were
secured by rusty padlocks. . . .

"Very sensitive. . . . Look. She had these cabinets closed
and never opened a single book since the day when she was reading Dickens and came upon a passage where a junk man, in order
to silence his wife, told her to shut the grate on her sink. She
canceled subscriptions to all the newspapers."

Edmée smiled. . . . She had had a friend like that, who
would always put off her marriage till next year because the man
she loved would use some vulgar expression from time to time,
and this would affect her for a whole year. The first year he had

used the phrase "to chow down," and the second year he called someone "fat as a pig." Was she going to join a man in matrimony who in a year might say "He laughed till he peed," and in two years "It's no skin off my nose"? Any final hesitation left her on the evening of Bastille Day, when apropos of the rockets being fired he had used the verb vulgarly applied to the explosion of a firecracker. She remained an old maid.

"If I understand you rightly, I am to keep the house ready for the return of . . . of whom?"

"Of Hermine. Her name is Hermine. The Chinese man will take care of the gardens, and the woman who keeps house will tend to the lodge and outer buildings. I had a woman from Provence, very faithful, but the house reeked of garlic. The real thing: the house seemed ready for the return of Petrarch or Laura. . . . Not for Hermine. The woman left."

Edmée said nothing. Martinez guessed why naturally.

"You find this a little artificial. You would have preferred to be a real housekeeper. No need to hurry. Any woman who is young and pretty has a fine career as a housewife still ahead of her. . . ."

They went in. Clearly nothing was ready for the return of Hermine. Sheets over the furniture were like shrouds. Spiders were running about.

"On her deathbed she had a few doubts. But she changed nothing. After all, she must have thought, it comes down to the same thing. The house has to be ready in case of the resurrection."

Nothing was ready for the resurrection either. A bad housekeeper. All the watercolors in Hermine's room were hanging crooked. Unless it were Hermine herself who. . . .

"If she returns," said Edmée, "how shall I recognize her?"

"She will ring that Chinese bell near the entrance. She always used to ring it."

He added, sensing that this quaint detail somehow displeased Edmée, "Just look after the house, that's all. You can forget the rest."

"Very well. . . . I will."

"Only three people have a right to enter the gardens. An old friend of hers, Mr. Blanks, who was a shipbuilder in 1880, who comes to see the new ships pass by, and a Swiss couple. The wife is a professor of literature and he, of gymnastics. She reads while he performs dangerous jumps. However, for some time now he has gotten her to do her reading in a sweat suit. . . . Well, that's all. . . . You can see that it's ideal!"

It was only a garden, with the sky and the sea, but some rocks shot through the grass here and there, rocks of a quartz very close to crystal, and the heart of the globe was flowered with their glowing. . . .

It would be all right here, along with Abalstitiel. . . . It would be the honeymoon! . . .

Everything is ready for the return of Hermine. If she comes back an old woman there is even a room where one can light a fire. If she comes back young there's a little cape hanging on the coat-rack. The doorknobs shine and all the fans are working. The sheets are changed every week. It's lovely to change white linen. And fresh flowers. And pure water. Edmée felt muddy and stained beside Hermine. Sometimes she let the fountains run all night. Hermine loved the fountains. . . . Claudie too. . . . There might be a mix-up someday in the train-switching system of the Lord, and Claudie might arrive instead of Hermine. . . . They would manage. . . . There are thirty good years left to wait for them. . . . The birds since 1858 have been pecking around, rats have been eating eggs, dogs running after squirrels, and mongooses nosing about, just so the garden of Hermine might have the same number of lives, of games, of gestures. . . . The cat has had seven kittens. She carries them around one after another by the neck, in a perpetual change of house. With her teeth, by the nape of the neck. They suckle all together, except for one, that she tries to interest in the world while waiting for one of his brothers to pass him her udder. She licks them, when need be, one after another. Yes, motherhood is beautiful. . . . In two years it will be the centenary of Hermine, and Claudie will be twenty. There really is a very good chance that one might see them that year. . . . Edmée, so as not to get a shock, removed the clapper from the little bell. . . .

The day comes. The night goes. . . . Edmée forgets at last which of the two has begun. . . . From the world, not a bit of news. . . . Claudie's champion husband thinks he has caught up with Claudie, thinks he has embraced Claudie. He thinks that kisses without lipstick can take effect on Claudie's cheeks. He thinks that when a trembling Claudie shows the whites of her eyes, passes out, and comes to, that it's Claudie who is giving herself. . . .

From the one who sees to the upkeep of it all, great approval, great messages of calm. From time to time he passes on to Edmée, not the surveillance of the house, but the duty of keeping watch over that corner of the world where she lives. It was very beautiful already, but Edmée has purified the sky. She has tamed the sea. The Swiss couple is at rest; the husband sprained his ankle while trying, in order to seduce Edmée, to do a triple version of the risky jump. He succeeded only in the two-and-a-half risky jump. The palm trees greet Edmée, but they're not the only ones. Mr. Blanks comes every Saturday, the day when ships depart for China. From far off he watches the vessels, notes their names, gauges their tonnage, and lays odds as to their speed. Then when the sun goes down, he peers at it with dark field glasses and catches sight of Edmée at a distance, a great distance because he is farsighted. He bows very low to greet her. That's the official rate. . . . One bow from Mr. Blanks, a hundred bows from the palm trees. . . .

# 11

It was a letter from Mr. Kaledjian, the old assistant director from Hollywood with the toucan nose, the same one who, to court the adored Edmée, used to slip Claudie those priestly rarities saved from the pillaging of Erzurum. "Dear Madame," wrote Mr. Kaledjian,

> From Mr. Martinez I have learned of your retreat on the coast. Can I do nothing for you? "I will call you one day for sure," you once promised me. . . . I am touched to see that you believe me immortal. But as it happens this is not the case. The truth is that you ought to avail yourself of me pretty soon. Figures in blood pressure mean nothing, you used to tell me in the old days, but mine now stays around twenty-six. . . . The difference between the two figures is everything, you used to say, what's important is the width of the interval. . . . But I'm now between twenty-five and a half and twenty-six. Phlebitis is not so serious, you would add, and you liked to assure me that my blood pressure posed no problem for phlebitis. And you will also tell me that in matters of health, heredity is the only thing that counts, but I

*may now confess to you that, at the very least, my father was al-*
*coholic. It is for that reason that I don't drink. When I take a*
*glass, I am drunk from all that my father drank, plus the one I'm*
*having. My liver is not in good shape, but if I feared for my liver,*
*I might as well fear for my pylorus, which according to my doc-*
*tors is quite worn out. Besides, it's really all worn out as far as I'm*
*concerned. The doctors tell me that it's my overall picture that*
*keeps me going. They might as well have said it's the clothes I*
*wear. On Sunday, when I'm dressed up for mass, I'm in fairly*
*good shape. . . . What they fear is that my overall picture will one*
*fine morning keep me from waking up, getting up, being able to*
*breathe, and above all, from putting my clothes on. . . . So, it's all*
*falling apart. . . . With whatever is left, please get in touch soon.*

Edmée was moved. If Pierre had found out where she was,
she would have held it against him. But not Mr. Kaledjian. She had
always had much more faith in episodic characters than in heroes.
A succession of old men with picturesque names and souls, of dubious morals, of noble spirit, a bit eccentric, a little disreputable,
had always turned up around her just at the right time ever since
she was a child, turned up at those train switches of destiny where
for others angels with flaming sword are posted. For her husband
it had taken an encounter with Vincent d'Indy to get him into
music, and with the string quartet as mediator. Whereas the one
who brought Edmée to Bach was Monsieur Bouvringot, the
bankrupt former notary public, who had taught her the recorder.
And at all the crossroads of enthusiasm, of doubt, or of death,
where Pascal, Marshal Foch, and Beethoven were waiting for
Pierre with the exact face and pout that might have served to cast
a veritable mold of suffering or lucidity, Monsieur Têtepied, Mr.
Gonzales Martinez, and Mr. Kaledjian—generally speaking,
deformed, stammering, and unsure of themselves—grabbed hold
of the beautiful Edmée and directed her, with the foresight and
generosity of baggage porters, toward the indifferent side of suffering or the calm side of delirium. . . . It wasn't surprising that Mr.
Kaledjian should give some sign of life. . . . Edmée was aware that
for some time now there had been brewing, inside the house or
within herself, a number of events. . . . At this very moment, for

example, while reading this letter, she had an impression that she couldn't explain at first, which all at once became clear: she didn't feel herself to be alone.

She listened. For some time now she had been listening a lot. . . . But there was no sound other than the comings and goings of the guard and the animals. Nor was it Hermine making her return. . . . The bell, even without ringing, would have found a way to sound for Hermine. . . . The little cape hanging on the coatrack would have moved. . . . Nor was it a visitor—the two dogs would bark at the least approach. Suddenly Edmée understood. She was sitting down opposite an engraving, a portrait. Her eyes must have settled on the face, which itself was looking straight at her, and this exchange of looks had broken her solitary mood. . . . With her hand she made a sign to the portrait and returned to her reading.

But it was as if by this sign she had accepted the fiction, she had given the portrait right of presence. Moreover, she said to herself, it was the first sign she had ever made to a portrait. Or to any picture. Or to a bust. She didn't kiss photographs, she didn't caress statues, she didn't call after echoes. None of those notices posted in public parks or hanging in museums that forbid one to touch the Annunciation Angel of Bologna or Tanagra statuettes ever concerned her. She didn't talk to them either. While Pierre flirted with knickknacks, would steal a kiss every night from the portrait of Edmée—the head was always moist— would hold dialogue with them and, while reciting, liked to apply as his own the poem where Victor Hugo charges a flower picked at the seaside to go off and "expire over a human heart, abyss more profound," Edmée held herself vis-à-vis the inanimate universe with the sort of reserve that is expressed in society by the phrase *I do not speak to them.* . . . She did not speak to the glass that broke in her hand, to the gas that had been left on, and human effigies themselves had always appeared to her the way they appear to the eyes of animals: as nonhuman effigies. Today was the very first time that she was breaking with this restraint: when dealing with things you simply have to call them by their names. What was coming over her? Still absorbed in her reading, with her hand she made a second sign to the portrait. "Well, what is it then? Whatever is it you want?"

The portrait replied immediately. This was a portrait that knew what it wanted.

"Come see me."

It was the portrait of a man. She had just used *tu* to the portrait of a man. His name was at the bottom. It was Spontini. Spontini in dress clothes, with black eyes, and she knew not what carnal vanity in the lips and nose, and—but perhaps because Edmée had never really looked at portraits up to now—it seemed alive to an incredible degree.

"Let us hope that your music is as alive as you are," she was thinking. But Spontini seemed to be quite unconcerned about his music. He wasn't there as a musician, he was there by the right that any celebrated human has to preside over ordinary human acts, and the pleasure that Edmée felt on seeing him suddenly loom forth from the walls was like the pleasure of seeing your relief guard arrive. For some weeks there had been certain fault lines, things that were lacking in her life. She might not have admitted them to herself. But owing to the fact that a century ago, at an opera where Stendhal perhaps had a seat in the back of the house, an enthusiastic audience had applauded *La Vestale,* Spontini had earned the right to intervene eternally in human disputes and consciences. And the most extraordinary thing, thought Edmée, is that I accept it and that the sight of him comes as a relief. Indeed Spontini is my refuge in this sad world. . . . Not the only one, since I suddenly caught sight, in that other panel, as if a second window were opening, of Donizetti there smiling at me. A bit less plump. The collar less well kept. Another kind of refuge. . . . Thank you for the visit.

But in the evening, Spontini and Donizetti were already no longer alone. All day long there had been a hatching of famous men in the house. Wherever Edmée's glance fell with any directness, it would cause a painter or writer to rise up. Longfellow was in the salon, as a child—no doubt his first photograph.

Emerson was in the bedroom, shown as he was dying—no doubt his last. From the walls she was looking at, from the books she opened, a celebrated face was born, and even the busts of Washington and Franklin became visible to her. A sort of administrative council of her life was setting itself up around her; Chopin and Livingston were members of it as well. In this dwelling where she awaited only a woman who was dead, there was the intrusion of those against whom she had so carefully guarded herself until now, and she suddenly understood that it was the great men themselves.

"There they are," she said to herself. . . . "I'm at the point that Claudie was when they began to appear in her bedroom. They must be part of the plot."

To be sure, a plot had formed against Edmée, an understanding between the Chinese servant, the animals, the house, and the weather. The plot consisted in replacing the blissful Edmée who ordered them all about by an Edmée who was nervous, on guard, and susceptible. It was nothing less than a substitution of one Edmée for the other. . . . Edmée had to admit it to herself: the problems that she scorned the most once upon a time were the ones confronting her now. For example, that of the personnel. Edmée had never had any problems with maids. The servants in her home could persist in their failings as well as the qualities that went with them, she had nothing to say, no special conscience that applied to the servants, and yet the other evening, because of a little carelessness, although habitual, on the part of the old Chinese man, she felt herself overcome with a kind of crazy fit that she had never experienced, the wrath of a mistress against a slave that she had no doubt inherited from her mother and her grandmothers. The Chinese man had steered clear of her, and she, who had never been anything but justice itself and respectfulness for others, had been seized with the desire, as if from a contagion, to read the letters of a maid, to search through the bottoms of trunks, to double-check the weight of a pound of fruit.

The sacred divination of housewives had led her straight to an old dough trough from the former stable, to the third drawer below the trough, and inside the drawer to a pile of linen from which she had unwound in successive layers the rags of the Chinese servant, until she found finally at the center one of his pink shifts, three pairs of his stockings, and, at the very core, his tinderbox for lighting fires. The whole thing without a false step, any hesitation, any groping about. And this notion of the personnel, starting with the Chinese servant, had reached the laundress and the iceman, and had gone as far as the gardener who sold her honey. She had just discovered in her turn, as had her mother before, the conspiracy of suppliers, the chronic betrayal of domestics, and the holy war of mistresses and managers had enrolled her among its cohorts. Her suspicions only just stopped at the linen, the water, and the bees. She had tried to laugh at herself, to tell herself that she really hadn't fallen that low, and she had called back the old Chinese in order to prove to herself that she was calm and clearheaded, but at the very first lie her eyes had clouded over and her blood had started to boil. . . . She was indeed a vassal in the army, in the army that was anticook, antifly, and antidisorder. . . .

The plot of the animals was no less well conceived. The animals worked along the lines of affection, along the lines of sentimentality. They would lick what Edmée least liked having licked, her feet and her ears, and she was putting up with it. They would come to sleep in the one spot in the world where Edmée most wanted to be alone, in her bed. There was a cat whose paw had to be held, like a hand, while he slept. Edmée held it. The plot here was just the opposite of the plot of the men. It was a question of revealing everything to Edmée; the dog led her to the body of the rat he had killed, the parrot led her to the gold spoon he had hidden in the zinc lining of his goblet for sunflower seeds, the mother cats led her to their illegitimate litters. To the revelation of insubordination, selfishness, and anarchy that govern the human world corresponded that of love and of confidence from the animal world. But the harm was no less, since there was the same effort to distract her from the world of Edmée. All in all the plot ended up by returning to her those senses she had never felt, as she did today, so demanding, promising, or fulfilling. Her whole body ached like her breasts did when she was pregnant. Her daily walk, the walk where every tree and flower, every breeze used to offer her a rendezvous and was really only an absence, an infinite promise of a tree, a flower, or a breeze, now became the passing in review of a world both polished and complete. That flight of nature ever before her had stopped. A sense of modesty had turned into a dubious offer. It was all offering itself, all giving itself, turning shades of blue or bright red. It bordered on a bazaar or paradise. The gala shows of suns rising or setting, of moons full or waning, boats of Hawaiians singing in the trough of a wave, all hastened forth in servile compliance to sea and sky. One might have said that the whole universe had received a mission to distract her.

But distract her from what? Or from whom? She was turning into a gourmand, she was becoming a coquette. . . . For whom? . . . All the ways it took to distract Hannibal, or Caesar, or Saint Anthony—the means don't really vary—the purity of the hour, nude forms off in the distance, were tried on her and they worked. Such a host of ardent moments and hummingbirds brought her hypocritically to a modest condition that she had never known till now. Every week saw some gigantic deployment of nature organize itself, the result of which was to return to her one of the more mediocre prerogatives of the human condition. On the night of the cyclone, she was surprised to find herself embroidering. On the night of the sharks, she couldn't keep herself from hemming the curtains. "An earthquake," she said to herself, "would surely find me doing the cross-stitch again. . . ." She had days of doing the washing that were incomparable, nights of mending and darning that were dazzling. From throughout the South Pacific, rainbows, breezes, pelicans, shipwrecks, or whole islands themselves came flowing in, all just to give her a taste for wardrobes, lavender, and drawers in perfect order. This mix of autumn and the Pacific, of equinoxes and solstices, seemed to have no purpose other than to prepare her for some sort of reasonable marriage, for some solid middle-class fiancé. . . . For Pierre, thought Edmée.

Nor were the great men wasting their time. There they were now, craning their heads, Spontini the donkey, Donizetti the ox, just to witness the birth of the new Edmée. Since their first squad had occupied the house it had been a game among them to substitute their faces and lives for their works themselves. And now reading and music were becoming for Edmée what they were for Pierre, not the approach of an anonymous world, of anonymous passions, but that of human beings with names and faces that were terribly particular. That quartet *Death and the Maiden,* that *Circus,* or that *Guermantes Way* lost their purity as works not conceived, not planned; they abdicated their miracle, were no longer the sudden transformation of the day itself and all its events. On the contrary, they were now no more than a secret, the secret of the man who had written or painted them, and everything that had been until now for Edmée simply the most impersonal and most imperceptible atmosphere of her life suddenly became a confidence, a joy, or a complaint from the lives of others. Now when she was playing the piano or reading, she had to look up the biography and portrait of the author in the *Encyclopaedia Britannica.* She learned that Spontini had a bad disposition and took it out on the cuffs of his shirts, that Donizetti in 1842 indulged his pleasures to excess and was punished from 1843 on. Humanity for her was beginning to take on its faces.

These sonatas, these pictures and poems, in which she was once able to sense only a certain resonance, a sort of radiation of herself, now acted on her only as the publicity for a special kind of human joy or suffering. From the music of Schubert—birth unforeseen—Schubert was born, from the music of Mozart, Mozart. She read their life stories. Symphonies, operas, and songs were no more than an accompaniment, the accompaniment to their excursions, to their love affairs. The great men carried out their job, which was to furnish the many moments of life for the little men. They helped to infuse in Edmée a taste for intimacy, for rest, for quiet outings. It was as if someone, seeing her incapable of regaining her everyday life in a commonplace way, had charged Schubert and Mozart with teaching her the joy of a ride on a donkey, the virtue of arbors, the problem of cold fingers. And it succeeded. By mouth and by hand, as if feeding a little bird, they transmitted to her the taste of a lamp lighted at twilight, of a waltz, of marmalade, of breaded cutlets, and even, unknown to them, of the radio. The happy activity of these great men in the midst of their finery, their instruments, and their utensils, won her over little by little; she would wake up at night thinking that her apples were not on a bed of straw. Very much the way Mozart might wake up. . . . She had some traps set out in the garden to control parasites: it was easy to see Schubert helping her, with a hoe in one hand. . . . Who were they leading her to? Who to? . . . To Pierre, thought Edmée. . . . And the one they were pulling her away from, that she was also beginning to learn.

A note from Mr. Kaledjian, whom she had written to ask to send her a portrait of Mozart, no longer left her in the slightest doubt.

Mr. Kaledjian had arrived the very next day, with his portrait of Mozart. He had looked in the mirror before leaving. In truth, he much preferred to give that portrait rather than his own. "All the more so as one sees the hands," he was thinking. "With mine the index finger is deformed by gout and my habit of putting on my shoes without the aid of a shoehorn, and under the nail of the ring finger there's a red puffiness that looks curiously like eczema. Well, it is really. Why shouldn't it look like it? . . . Mozart's hands are incomparably more beautiful. The difference is that Mozart is dead and I'm alive, and I can listen to Mozart—it doesn't even cost me anything since I have a pass— and he can't. It's even unfair when you think about it. It's a dirty shame! It's a disgrace!"

The sight of Edmée gave him a shock.

"What a splendid woman!" he said to himself. "But she's completely changed."

It wasn't in Mr. Kaledjian's nature to be surprised at the changes in people. The nature of the occupations he had held since his departure from Erzurum allowed him on the contrary to find old friends again in the most diverse conditions without any surprise and to accept without discussion every sort of human transformation. In the photos of dictators, of peeresses, and of those condemned to death, he had on occasion recognized his typist, his telegraphist, or his librettist for the pantomimes of the Lilliputians whose troupe of players he had a few times directed, and this resemblance to companions now gone that seemed to surface in the portraits of kings of some ancient dynasty or of victorious generals no longer surprised him. He knew from experience that the only steadfast creature in this sad world is the dwarf. An assembly of dwarfs is an assembly of refusals to win wars, to direct the stock exchange, to be president of the republic. . . . He might have found it natural if Edmée had become ugly, put on weight, tinted her hair violet, or given herself a Korean name. But the change he saw in her was precisely what he would never have foreseen. Edmée was in the house that he would have imagined for her, in a part of the country that was her very own landscape, she was even more beautiful than she had been four years ago, her voice and gestures were more noble, and yet—Mr. Kaledjian found the word repugnant—there was over her a sort of veil that he had noticed only over certain actors after talking pictures had begun: a kind of decline. . . .

She showed him her domain, her house, her room. Every glance proved to Mr. Kaledjian that she was living here without any sort of eccentricity, without anything in any way base. They chatted. He learned that her health was perfect, that the famous attacks had never returned. The instinct that had made him the best agent for actresses on Broadway told him that not a tooth was missing, that her hair was not dyed. To use a metaphor that was dear to his heart, her eyebrows were still the arc of the Lord, her nails were supple, her mammary glands discreet and tender, her ligaments pliant. She had not shrunk by that quarter or third of a centimeter by which the least-susceptible star is affected after a flop. . . . The love he had for Edmée in the other compartment of his soul left him in no doubt either as to this point: she had not learned to lie, to deceive, to lie to herself, or to deceive herself. . . . Why then that sense of disappointment, the same that he had felt when he went back to see the little

Assyrian-Chaldean saint, the one who had seen Saint Thomas, whom Saint Thomas used to visit out of the curiosity of a former doubter, but whose appearance, speech, and obtuse face cried out to her that day — Saint Thomas doesn't see me, I am the one who will never be seen again by Saint Thomas.

"There she is, the perfect woman," Mr. Kaledjian was saying to himself as he ate his toast. "There she is, the perfect wife. But as to the perfect Edmée, there is no longer any question."

What Mr. Kaledjian didn't know was that not for nothing was he from the East, nor that Edmée could see his disappointment. His attitude, without his suspecting so himself, was always commanded not by his will but by the nature of the objects or the people who surrounded him. The attitude of Mr. Kaledjian, invited to dinner by friends, was completely different concerning the dessert spoons, as to whether they were sterling or plate, that is, his attitude was determined finally by the spoons themselves. At a rug merchant's it was enough to look at Mr. Kaledjian in order to know if a rug was genuine or not, even if the seller was a member of his family and the buyer an enemy. There were false starts to the springtime and false racehorses, where the attitude of Mr. Kaledjian would instantaneously give away the deception or the doctoring. The result of which at this moment was that his reverence for her could not quite conceal from Edmée a kind of superiority, a kind of liberty. . . . He bowed as low as formerly. His eyes, his heart were filled with the same voluptuousness and the same flutter of his glottis at the sight of Edmée, but he had a casual air and a slight rise in his voice which gave his gestures and words a humiliating tone of flattery. He lost it for a moment when he took Edmée's hand, just before leaving, to kiss it. "But it's not because of my hand," Edmée was saying to herself, "it's because of the stone in my ring. That simply means that the stone is real. I'm no longer real myself. . . . How kind he is! What a lot of trouble he takes to hide from me his disappointment! Never has Mr. Kaledjian been so considerate and polite before a piece of bronze coated with gilt!"

It was Mr. Kaledjian who found the right word for the enigma, as he said to her, already in his limousine:

"My dear Edmée, you can count on me. I'll find a way out of the problem. You can't go on living abandoned like this."

Abandoned! She suspected as much. If she had not dared say so to herself, it was precisely because she wasn't going to be the one to abandon another, it was in order to remain faithful. That presence inside her, all around her, that had never allowed her to have a moment of solitude, there was no further point in hiding it from herself, she no longer felt it, it was no longer there! It was all clear. That glow to the world, that shine on its objects, came from the fact that inside her the light had gone out. Abalstitiel wasn't there anymore, he was betraying her. So this was what it had brought Edmée, to have accepted him under his unofficial form, not to have chosen him, like the others, under his name as Devotion, as Piety or Sacrifice, not to have wanted to be nurse, nun, or heroine: under this form he betrayed you. Just because an official commitment wasn't asked of him, a vow, or a uniform, he took advantage of it, he betrayed you. Not bound by a contract, the divine presence was more fickle than a lover. He had left without warning, without leaving a thing! The nights of insomnia that were just a few weeks ago still nights of an unlimited confidence had suddenly become nights of headaches, nights of wrinkles in the sheets. The solitary walks no longer led to any rendezvous. . . . Solitude itself was no longer a rendezvous. . . . To be sure, Edmée knew that she wasn't the only woman in the world to have known this ease, this predilection, nor the first to be betrayed, but she deserved more consideration. No woman in the world had been so responsive in love for a simple presence. None had sensed better that disguise in the air, in light, in warmth, and then been abandoned to this degree.

None, in an affair where others rave, lose weight, and become emaciated, had remained so completely reason itself, so utterly a woman, nor had better sensed the value of her own kisses or of her human warmth with regard to this confidence without face and without name.

Had he then realized nothing? Had he then not understood what Edmée was, the kind of virginity that she had retained concerning men, the modesty with which she had traveled the circle of the elect? From this sort of affair, from which others would leave arrayed in finery and rich for life, she was leaving empty handed; she had gained nothing from the situation. This sovereignty of the world that had been granted her for a few years, she had used it to veil herself, to not know herself, to hide herself. . . . A more able favorite of the court would have left with amorous adventures, with memories—at least her letters. . . . But nothing remained for her but a heart renovated for the bourgeois life, the heart of a servant, fit for setting rattraps, for reading novels. . . . They were giving her back her luggage, everything she had checked when still a child, at the very beginning of this predilection: the great men, music, nature. . . . They were giving her back Pierre and Jacques. . . . They were giving them back to her in bad faith, with the sort of reasons that are alleged in breakups of the basest kind—"You belonged to another first, you were the mother of a family!" They were even giving back to her that which had not been taken from her, confusing her with some other favorite less perfect: she was becoming sour and spiteful. . . . And as if it had been above all a question of her body in this unreal affair (that they really had hidden from her), they were giving her back a body where she suddenly felt duties and demands ruling over her. Her fingers were so terribly fingers, her breasts so terribly breasts, her toes, her nostrils, so terribly toes and nostrils. . . . The other one, to place her more easily, was changing her into a woman, into what he thought was a woman. . . . Abandoned! Of course that was why she was trying in vain to regain that state of calm, of grace, of secret voluptuousness for which she had sacrificed everything, for which she was still ready to sacrifice everything. . . . She had lost it, and it was that which annoyed her the most—and it was natural that she should be annoyed, she who never was, since she was no longer herself—without her ever having been unworthy, ever having cheated. . . .

"But where are you then?" she wanted to cry out. "Where are you hiding?"

He was nowhere, but she had a huge appetite in the morning. He was nowhere, but her war continued with the old Chinese. He was nowhere, but there were wasps and mosquitoes and praying mantises. The universe was swarming over the absence of Abalstitiel. You could see what the universe really was, the signature of a front man, an out-and-out lie. That eternity could be fickle was simply incomprehensible!

One morning she woke up with the wrath of gentle women whose lives have been ruined, eager for revenge. If the other one thought that she was simply going to accept this malfeasance and return to the husband who was waiting for her back there, he really didn't know her; truly that would have been far too simple. "I took you in honor," he was saying, "and I leave you in honor. . . ." A fat lot woman cares about honor. . . . She would get her vengeance. She got out of bed, transformed by an implacable rancor; this disgusting blackmailer had to be humiliated. By what means? Women have only one. But a good one. They know how to humiliate their fellowman only through their own shame. Besides, didn't she have to liquidate now and forever all that secret pride? She surely wouldn't be any worse off for it. And if she did find herself worse off, what luck!

That afternoon, as it happened, the Swiss gym teacher was exercising all alone on the beach. There he was, handsome, intact, sprouting up next to the problem the way you find a curative plant growing next to hemlock. Beside your destiny there's always an antidote destiny. It was the antidote destiny that had dispatched Moravaz with his diploma in athletics from La

Chaux-de-Fonds all the way to California, and for eleven months now had brought him every afternoon to this beach. He engaged in—if men may be said to resemble those grouse cocks that dance, stretch, and shake their necks and strut about so as to seduce the grouse hens—all the exercises by which a woman can be seduced: the dangerous double jump (he no longer risked the triple), jumping over a sheep without the sheep, shadow boxing, the English oak stance, and the splits. He raised his head and stood there motionless. Edmée was coming toward him. This inaccessible woman was coming toward him. She was even headed straight at him, cutting across lawns and borders instead of following the pathways, the way you have to go to catch the dog. If you had stretched a cord from the garden gate to the gym teacher, the line wouldn't have been any straighter. He had his knee on the ground, for he was practicing for a sprint. . . . He remained on his knees. He took the hands of Edmée. From up above, God was watching it all, exceedingly vexed!

"What solitude!" he said.

"The very word," said she.

On the way back she looked Spontini and Mozart right in the face just to confront them. . . . They're all alike, dead or alive. It was as if they thought that by letting herself be embraced on the beach by a Swiss athlete she had cheated on Spontini and Mozart.

It really was Claudie. Mr. Kaledjian got out of the car, waved from far off, and looked around for a moment, as if to assure himself, in his legendary meticulous way, that they really were the mother and daughter in question. . . . To bring back Iphigenia to Hecuba, Polyxena to Jocasta, and a real Claudie to a false Edmée, or the reverse, would have been a truly futile occupation, and the feat of someone very absentminded. It really was

Edmée. He made a sign that no one should pay any attention at all to him. He remained at the distance that best suited his beauty and for which his coiffeur and masseur had prepared him, that is, some fifteen yards away. At fifteen yards, the Kaledjian overall picture was still very presentable. He hoped so at any rate, for the greatest distance away from his wardrobe mirror that he could get was some eight yards. . . . He himself, alas, would never again see an acceptable Kaledjian.

"Don't come over here!" he shouted. . . . "I don't want to see you!"

The two women smiled at him from afar. The overall picture held up magnificently until the moment when Mr. Kaledjian had to get back into the car. Then it became more difficult; the overall picture made it awfully hard for the knees to bend. . . .

Taking Claudie's hand, Edmée managed to bruise her own: it proved to be an enormous ring. On embracing her, she managed to scratch herself: it was the enormous earrings.

"My husband likes for me to wear jewelry," said Claudie. "Look. I have bracelets around my ankles."

As she hugged Claudie tightly, Edmée bumped into something. There was a bulge in Claudie's belly.

"That, now, is a girl," said Claudie. "We're going to have a daughter, an Edmée. . . . If you're willing. . . ."

She hugged her mother in her arms as she closed her eyes. It was really too much to have in her grasp tonight both her mother and her daughter.

"I love you," she said.

For that was the advantage of Monsieur Bouvringot, Monsieur Têtepied, or Mr. Kaledjian over providence and over God. When they arranged a human affair, it was one completely. No recriminations. No attempts to set the record straight. The angel Gabriel would have demanded an explanation between Edmée and Claudie. . . . There was only that touch of ill humor over the ring and the earrings, and that gentle defense of the baby. Moïse Kaledjian had simply restored them to the attitude they were in just before the quarrel. In any case it was one of those operations that Edmée had always thought Claudie capable of: erase the past, wipe out destiny. . . . No more than the reason for her hatred, Claudie would never tell the reason for her return. And she didn't excuse herself for her hatred, she excused herself for her return.

"You understand everything," she was saying.

Edmée understood only too well.

"And it will always be this way," she was thinking. "It's all backward. When I'm ready to receive Claudie, it's Jacques who arrives. Now when I'm the ideal mother for Jacques, it's Claudie who turns up. . . . I'm going to have to start going in disguise. . . . I'll have to make myself false. . . ."

Claudie held her in her arms, the little Edmée between them, the future little Claudie already preconceived inside the little Edmée. . . . Edmée could have cried: the fact of having clasped a man in her arms, of having kissed cheeks and hair and a man's lips had in no way modified her daughter, had not supplied her with other arms, other eyes! The passion of Claudie for her mother, the special body of Claudie reserved for her mother emerged miraculously intact from the conjugal embraces and the conjugal bed. Jacques had only embraced Marie-Rose a dozen times, and he no longer embraced his mother except as a Marie-Rose who was at once both more familiar and more distant. Claudie, for six months now, had spent at least a third of her days and nights embedded in the sleep and awakenings of Harold, and yet she was able to find for Edmée, lips, hands, and a belly that had never touched her husband. . . . Too late. . . . This return of the real Claudie, in her intransigence, in her virulence—Edmée was no longer up to it, would never again be ready for it. This alternation without any cure that, since the birth of Claudie, alternated between them without ever affecting both at the same time: this integrity and freedom, this being of the elect—she played at it once again, but this time, thought Edmée, to her detriment, and now forever more. . . . There she was facing a Claudie who thirsted for a wordless explanation, a passion without vows, but she no longer felt anything more than the usual mother, curious to know how her son-in-law was doing, about their apartment, and when the little Edmée would be born. . . .

"Your husband," she began. . . .

But Claudie wasn't thinking about her husband at all. . . . She had taken her mother by the arm and was drawing her toward the garden. Not to see the garden, or to look at the house from the garden, or to approach the sea from the garden. But because the garden had its pathways and she could follow them around with her mother on her arm, without any of those commentaries made by the flowers, the grass, the mountain, or the waves. They walked along in this way, in that sort of cloister or trail that they had once been able to reconstitute inside any room, no matter how crowded with furniture and objects. "I counted three times again yesterday the silver place settings," Edmée was thinking.

"How is your husband?"

"My husband? Harold? Fine. He's fine."

It was what Edmée used to say of Pierre. He was the best, the hardest worker, the most loving. . . . He was fine. . . . Claudie added, to close the subject:

"He gets along wonderfully with Father."

"Where do you live?"

This time, Claudie hesitated. As a rule *where* and *how* hadn't been accepted by them formerly. They used to avoid questions of place, of age, of cause and effect. . . .

"Around here," replied Claudie. "Not far. It's very nice."

It was all very nice, just as it had once been for Edmée.

"Mother," Claudie went on, "do you remember?"

And she talked about a day that Edmée's memory could no longer recall. And Edmée knew why she was talking about it, it was that she had the sort of nature that Edmée had once found indispensable in her intimates, a need for things to be without purpose, a kind of insensibility. Here was the day that Claudie was talking about: they had woken up at sunrise, no one had come by, not even the iceman; they must have gone without breakfast, had drunk something lukewarm, had not gotten dressed, and had gone to bed with the sun. . . . A day when they could have lived without clothes, when the soul wore no clothes. . . .

The most terrible thing, thought Edmée, is this past that is changing inside me, this memory that is becoming another memory. What I believe to be the most lucid part, the most innocuous, is transformed into an enigma, a wound. Bitterness, regret, and astonishment well up out of events and words that I thought to be sensible and calm. . . . Pain too. . . . Voices that didn't reach me at the speed of sound some twenty years ago are now catching up with me, they now reach me at the speed of light. . . . Poor Claudie, who thinks I'm listening to her. . . . Since this morning the only thing I've had ringing in my ears is that phrase of Madame Viénard, when she cried out to us, "They've killed my Georges. . . ." Why?

Madame Viénard had screamed "They've killed my Georges" all of twenty-two years ago, one night at midnight. It surely was time that her phrase should reach Edmée. She had scarcely noticed it then. Someone had beat on the shutters, Edmée's mother had opened them up, and Madame Viénard from down below had screamed out, "They've killed my Georges!" Edmée had gone down to let her in. Madame Viénard was a friend of her mother, the widow of a brewer who carried on her husband's business; she was a giant, built like a man, red in the face, and had three sons who were in the war, the one who tended to the hops, the one who tended to the barley, and the one who directed the bottling. . . . Edmée's mother, who was a little hard of hearing, had asked again what the matter was, and Madame Viénard had repeated, "They've killed my Georges!"

And for Edmée that had been only one sorrow among the other sorrows. Quite a few other sons whose first names she knew, whom she called by their first names, had been killed from the neighborhood. And she thought that over all those bereavements inside her, time had placed one single uniform tombstone. Her memory until these last days was of a trench of very solid earth from which extended neither clenched hands nor feet wearing boots. And Madame Viénard had come back twice to knock at the window, for the second son, then for the youngest. The hops, the barley, and the corks had no longer held much interest for Madame Viénard. She would come about the same time. You might suppose that the town hall wanted to put off the announcement of death all day long and could make up its mind to do so only at midnight. It was a habit to get used to: Madame Viénard would get dressed hurriedly in the dark, fasten her Italian mosaic brooch in the dark with its yellow basket against a black background, and come knocking at Edmée's house. . . . And these later visits should have been etched more sharply in Edmée's memory. And most likely Madame Viénard must have answered on those nights from the sidewalk, "They've killed my Alain, they've killed my Bernard. . . ."

No. Since this morning, "They've killed my Georges" alone seemed to resonate; and it was becoming more than a cry, it was becoming a motto that rang out, whose words were time honored and ruled the day. Edmée recalled now having heard the neighbor from the second floor who had opened her shutters a little and, being alerted, on closing them said after herself, "It's Madame Viénard. They've killed her Georges. . . ." And the following morning, during her early shopping at the Economiques Stéphanois, the *patronne* had said to one of her clients, "You know, it's just the end for Madame Viénard. They've killed her Georges. . . ." It was an expression adopted by the whole town. . . . "She's lost weight since they killed her Georges." They would say it to Madame Viénard herself. "That's the year they killed your Georges. . . ." Who were "they"? Edmée wondered. Who were the anonymous "they" that Madame Viénard, in her kindness, didn't dare designate further. "They" didn't have any name. She hadn't said, "The Boche killed my Georges." They were neither the Germans nor the French. They were that mix of gods, of men, of metals, and of currents that assemble young men on the battlefields and begin by killing a Georges. . . . Edmée was so obsessed by it that she had to resist not saying to

Claudie, "Have I ever told you about Madame Viénard? They killed her Georges. . . ." And Madame Viénard wasn't alone. From all parts of Edmée's past, similar chasms were opening up, mounting in appeals and in signs, phrases and faces insignificant in days gone by, and, under the disguise of Madame Viénard, or the man who sold newspapers and tobacco, or Father Voie, the priest, Edmée was forced to recognize that now, after a life of detachment, she was being given back her share of the angels of pleasure or of death.

"Mother," Claudie was saying, as her light limbs strode through the realm where no one suffers, "I ran across the yellow cardboard box yesterday."

It was in the yellow cardboard box that Claudie used to place the objects of Edmée's cult: the chasuble from Ourmiah, the wooden cruet from the Ark, and incense of the true gods, articles that Mr. Kaledjian used to give her. "But they're marvelous!" Edmée had exclaimed at the time. "I really want to give them to her," he had said. . . . "It's still what serves us best in life, the things we can worship."

"I even found," Claudie went on, "the canticle that Mr. Kaledjian told me was a translation of a hymn to the Black Virgin of Oulfa from the Caucasus. I'm convinced that he composed it himself, that it's his own work and was written for you. . . . It's utterly you in any case.

> You are youth without age
> and the ship that never wrecks,
> the ark of purity and the
> bastion of tranquillity.
> When they want to name their true love,
> the world and my heart both say
> Edmée.

Mr. Kaledjian had his talents. That was exactly what she then was. It was exactly what she was no longer.

"Mother," Claudie continued, "yesterday I went back to our park in Los Angeles. You remember when we ran away, it will soon be twelve years ago. I told Mr. Kaledjian about it. He congratulated me. He interpreted it as an excursion to the lost paradise. A legend of Oulfa has it that the first inhabitants of paradise were not Adam and Eve, but rather Eve and her daughter.

> *She took her daughter by the hand,*
> *dressed in simple cloth, and*
> *wandered off to Washington Park.*
> *Of the Lord her eyebrow is the arch —*
> *at the gate the angel*
> *raises the ticket window*
> *and lowers the sword.*

All this is really not appropriate, Edmée was thinking. I'm not going to spend the rest of my life lying in front of Claudie, trying to camouflage myself. It's the last sacrifice that I owe her — not to lie to her. . . . Perhaps I can make up for it one day, if the alternation is in effect.

"When is the baptism, Claudie? I'm going to be there. . . ."

"What's that? How wonderful! You will stay at our place."

"No, Claudie. I believe I'm going to return home."

"To Father?"

"I'm thinking about it."

Claudie looked at her; she was pale.

"If you're doing it for us you don't need to force yourself. Jacques isn't there anymore either.

"No. It's for me. . . . Talk to him. . . . Ask him when you have an opportunity."

"We don't need to ask. You know men! . . ."

She didn't hurry her departure. She stayed until evening. But there was now on her face a sort of glow, and a distraction that had never been there, and that Edmée knew well from having felt it so often herself; it was that for the last few minutes, Claudie had been all alone in the world.

> *Alone with all, alone with nothing.*
> *The great absence and all is well.*
> *A heart empty of default*

> *crowning the great presence. . . .*
> *Meanwhile the swallow skims*
> *the bell towers of Oulfa*
> *in the Caucasus. . . .*

It was the end of the alleged Armenian Canticle.

> *In Los Angeles so well named*
> *this is the mother, this is Edmée.*

But Claudie had stopped talking.

Pierre presided at the table. The whole family was there for the baptism dinner. These six people who had formed with their own carousel so many ties, connections, and circles in love, admiration, and devotion, and who for twelve years had successfully handled the interlude where they mimed and expressed the major sentiments of nostalgia, domination, heart, and freedom, they had tonight reformed a modest family with its pawns: the father and mother, the son with his fiancée, the daughter and the son-in-law, without counting the baptized baby, who on the sofa in the living room was wailing her head off from a throat provoked for the first time by the salt of the earth.

Rivers of light had flowed, upper school trapezes had hung themselves from the top of the skies, citadels of hate and love had been taken and retaken, the universe had put on, lost, and put on again its robes, its humors, its dizzy spells, and they were having dinner while talking about the weather, like acrobats after doing their number. They were dining slowly, there was no party today: tonight Edmée would not run away, tonight Claudie would not spit in her father's face, tonight Pierre would not go look at himself in the mirror in order to at last get a close look at the face of misfortune. . . . One really can't recognize acrobats who dine after performances, unless perhaps by a certain agility of the spoons, an invulnerability of the plates, an immortality of the carafes. . . . But for those seated here it was rather by an ennoblement of what they were serving, by what they were eating. . . . In that lay the benefit for this quadruple human adventure, the turkey was ennobled, including the chestnuts that had corrupted them, the minced liver was ennobled. One wasn't too sure what the guests themselves were beneath their festive appearance, lives wasted, gone astray, and worn out perhaps, but the bread was ennobled, and the wine. . . . The Passion, a Passion. . . . And perhaps ennobled also the means they used to taste their food: their hands, their mouths, their eyes, their senses. The act of swallowing was ennobled, and its corporeal cousins, and the act of speech, and the act of procreation, and the act of conception. . . . As to their souls, one could say nothing, except that the only thing that lay before them now in this sad universe was a road of nobility, and of compromise. . . .

Pierre was slicing this holy turkey, pouring this wine of Cana and tasting it: it was excellent, no taste of cork. Pierre was more than content, the wine of Cana hadn't the slightest taste of cork! . . . He sat facing Edmée, with his legs pulled back under his chair, for fear lest they might inadvertently touch the legs of Edmée. Since she had returned, that seemed to be his main concern, his main devotion—not to touch Edmée. He left her plenty of room and didn't linger to press her hand unless she was wearing gloves; had there been an opaque veil over Edmée's face, he might have felt at ease. . . . Between the Edmée that wasn't there and the Edmée that was there, perhaps what was needed at times was an intermediary Edmée, present but invisible. It wasn't that she hadn't returned to Pierre's life—she was sleeping in Claudie's empty room, she had resumed her old habits, when she slept and when she woke up, but for fear of offending her, of losing her again, it was Pierre who had departed from his own way of life. . . . It was a matter of not setting foot back in it, and he felt like a legless cripple when sitting opposite her, as he felt one armed standing beside her and fell silent as soon as she started talking. That was the most painful. It takes adventures like these ever to doubt that human beings all talk at the same time and that each word they utter has to bite down on the word of another. Pierre spoke now only when he could bite down on the silence of Edmée. When Edmée's voice had stopped for a moment, Pierre dared speak. Around every phrase there was a moat where silence was eager to cross over. He spoke more easily by himself, and he didn't suspect it, but Edmée heard him from her room. He said nothing of interest. It was a decidedly external monologue.

Jacques had had to insist mightily to get Pierre to remain in the apartment the day Edmée had returned. He knew very well that he wasn't the one she had fled, but he wasn't sure that he was the one she had come back to. He would have preferred to return in the evening, a few hours after she did, as if he were the one coming back, just as he had, on the morning she had left for the Seeds', played the role of the one who was going away. Viewed this way, Edmée might appear never to have left. Jacques had struggled hard to convince him. He had gotten the apartment ready for Edmée, that is, he had removed from the closets and tables all the mementos and cast-off clothes of Edmée and had carried them down to the basement in a trunk. It wasn't the yellow cardboard box. It was the black trunk. Thus the objects of worship of Edmée were stored away, one batch to the basement, the other to the attic, definitively.

She had arrived at the stated hour, just a minute late. But one minute no longer concerned Pierre. She had crossed the threshold, she had made that movement that consists in placing one leg before the other that we call walking, more precisely, stepping over; she had stepped over the threshold. The threshold had seen above it the scissorslike movement of the legs of the returning spouse, the stockings, the drawers of the fugitive spouse. . . . Pierre had not asked her a single question, not even about the last part of her journey, even about what it wouldn't have been indiscreet to find out, about the entrance bell or the functioning of the house elevator. Edmée felt, moreover, that he would never ask another. Not that he had understood. . . .

But he, whose instinct in life was to question and understand, accepted henceforth to live in the presence of a secret that would never be revealed to him. He had not given up the least bit of curiosity as to his specialty, the capillarity of petroleum or the weight of naphtha, and he kept up a correspondence worthy of the Inquisition about the methods of shipment of semirefined oils and the welding of pipelines; if a lime tree along the street bloomed before the others, he would study the compost and the site; if a magazine published a color photo, he would write the editorial staff to find out the details of the process. But he didn't ask any more questions about the world of men. Men belonged to a group that it was useless to try to understand.

He no longer asked for the addresses of drunkards or the badge numbers of police officers who were rude. Humanity has no address, one number is as good as another. Such was the result of that struggle that he had undertaken at the age of twelve to elucidate the world: he was living with the two billion secrets that were human beings. . . . And the dearest and most inaccessible was very near him. . . . A little special attention from destiny. It was always that.

In Jacques's room he had adopted the objects of his son, going as far as his habits, and, thought Edmée, who sometimes looked in to wish him good night, as far as his gestures as well. . . . She had resisted the urge to feel if his head was hot, to tuck him in. . . . It wouldn't have consoled him to learn that she had come back in order to be his mother. He was finishing some old pencil sketches, some old drawings of Jacques. He was lodging, for want of a man's existence, in whatever remained of a child's existence. Such was the first lesson as Pierre saw things: in the world of men and women the guardian must be more strong, more slender, and more in bloom than the tree. And this was the second: that happiness is not to be had by even the most average sort of person unless that person, endowed with all beauty, kindness, and knowledge, attaches himself and devotes himself to it every minute of his life. But let no one despair. That still leaves room for a bit of happiness in this sad world. . . .

Jacques was less to be pitied. Jacques believed in everything that life had taught him to be full of lies and obsolete—in the family, in the future, in rewards. All the dark corners that had shrouded his adolescence he would explain by a notion of lights: the flight of his mother was explained by love, his neglected childhood by work, his little conjugal liaison with Marie-Rose by passion, the cheap little name of Marie-Rose by the two radiant names of Marie and Rose. Edmée didn't worry too much about Jacques—the number of bereavements, renunciations, enigmas, and ugly moments that he would run into in life would surely be great enough to bring him near the very qualities of clarity, generosity, and beauty themselves.

With Claudie things were of another order. The former intimacy was not resumed. For her part it was not a matter of disdain or scorn. It partook of both admiration and embarrassment: she really didn't believe Edmée. This return of Edmée to Pierre, dictated by everything in her nature, Claudie continued to believe was a sacrifice. She would talk to her as to someone one knows to be lying. She accepted the fiction not only with regard to Edmée, but also with regard to her father, with whom she again became often indifferent or hard. Poor Pierre, who knew that he would never have both of these women at the same time, decided to content himself with the alternation. Sometimes, convinced of Edmée's lie, Claudie couldn't keep from wrapping her arms around her and embracing her. She seemed to be saying to her mother, "We're not going to talk about anything that really concerns you, we won't even talk about what doesn't concern you, but it is understood that in the course of this silence you won't lie to me!" And during this silence indeed, by means of a supreme lie, Edmée played the role of the Edmée of the old days. As in the old days, she would pass in front of statues without trying to learn their names, although alone, she would have stopped. Like the old days, she would pass in front of the shops of dressmakers or florists without wanting to give them a thought: they were on her mind anyway. . . . That's where frankness will lead you in life: to have a different lie for your husband, for your son, and for your daughter. You're lucky if you don't have a different one for yourself. But what good would it have done to tell them there is only one truth: a woman doesn't return home unless she's been deserted by the seducer? . . . It would have served Claudie least of all! The thing that Edmée could have borne least from Claudie was compassion.

That Claudie might feel sorry for Abalstitiel Edmée preferred to seeing her pity her mother. . . . The sentiments that
Edmée felt for her daughter, moreover, did not allow any confidence: there was a sort of jealousy and a great fear. . . . She feared
lest Claudie's fate turn out to be the same as her own. She had
every reason to fear this. It was clear that there was in Claudie's
existence an anomaly: all the luster that her marriage gave her,
the affection of the young couple, and the arrival of their daughter—this profit went not to the couple itself but to Claudie
alone. The great beauty that had come over her for some time
now, it seemed to Edmée, did not benefit the young husband,
nor did her serenity, nor her devotion. Claudie was, now that she
thought about it, being raised for beauty, fidelity, and kindness
as Edmée herself had been to a lesser degree in the perfect household with Pierre. If Abalstitiel had meant to reserve Claudie too
for some future affair, this is how he would have anointed and
prepared her. At every moment she caught sight of some of the
signs about her daughter by which she herself had been obliged
to recognize, fifteen years before, that her earthly happiness
was one of those coops whereby the fowl is fattened for the sacrifice. . . . The ways of heaven are not varied. The nonexistent
lover doesn't have any devices different from those of real
lovers. . . . The fortune, urbanity, and love of Claudie's husband
seemed to have been lent him by a third party, who was thus
maintaining the family in perfection and reserving the right to
intervene when his time had come. . . . This wasn't fair to
Harold, but neither had it been so for Pierre. . . .

Everybody knows that in this sad world it is precisely the
most successful and sensitive people who are the straw men of
destiny and its brutality. The very history of Claudie's marriage
left little doubt about its future: she had married her husband the
way Edmée had married hers—he was the first to come along.
He was the best, the most esteemed, the most estimable, but he
was like Pierre, he was the first to come along. Claudie, like
Edmée, and precisely from the lack of a strong attraction to men,
had given in to the first to come along. All Abalstitiel had done
was to arrange things so that in France the first to appear was a

top engineer and, in America, a millionaire. Simply because he had never supposed that Claudie would marry a dullard, nor Edmée a failure.

And now Claudie had gotten up from the table. Once it was Edmée who would interrupt her meal without the slightest pretext and wander off to the pantry or the windows. Claudie disappeared into the rooms at the back as Edmée used to do. It was that hour when Claudie, trying not to go to sleep, used to see Edmée, by way of the fire escape and the cornices, go off to join those magnificent dancers who would waltz with her up above the night. . . . Edmée wouldn't dance tonight. In fact that was exactly what she felt: a complete inability to perform the waltz above the world of men. . . . But at this moment Claudie was occupying her place up there. You could see it when she came back down, a good while later, out of breath, her hair a little ruffled. The hands of strangers had touched her. Exaltation and detachment were still with her. . . . Pierre didn't take in the scene. Jacques explained it as the joy of becoming a mother. Only Harold suffered, with the miraculous prescience of husbands that changes into miraculous blindness as soon as the wrong is consummated.

"Where have you been?"

"Where do you expect her to have been, Harold?" said Pierre. "The apartment doesn't have a secret passage."

It was true. When Edmée used to go off, she must have taken the stairs.

"You shouldn't be gone so long, Claudie. . . ."

"Oh?"

She sat back down. She turned her eyes to her mother, not to turn them to her mother but to turn them away from her husband, from her father, from her daughter, from the others. . . . Truly, Abalstitiel wasn't wasting any time. . . . Edmée felt a stab in her heart. She couldn't hold back the awful words: the mother has given him a taste, now it's the daughter's turn. Claudie's eyes were full of tears.

There it was. . . . He was starting in on Claudie.

# SELECTED WORKS OF JEAN GIRAUDOUX

This list includes the main novels and plays but does not include stories, film scenarios, or any work published posthumously. Giraudoux continued to write novels well after his success as a playwright; *Choice of the Elect* appeared after some of his finest work in the theater and thus represents his mature thought as a novelist.

## NOVELS

1911   *L'Ecole des Indifférents*
1918   *Simon le Pathétique*
1921   *Suzanne et le Pacifique*
1922   *Siegfried et le Limousin*
1924   *Juliette au Pays des Hommes*
1926   *Bella*
1927   *Eglantine*

1930   *Aventures de Jérome Bardini*
1934   *Combat avec l'Ange*
1939   *Choix des Elues*

**PLAYS**

1928   *Siegfried*
1931   *Judith*
1932   *Amphitryon 38*
1933   *Intermezzo*
1935   *La Guerre de Troie n'aura pas lieu*
       [*The Trojan War Will Not Take Place* or
       *Tiger at the Gates*]
1937   *Electra*
1939   *Ondine*
1943   *Sodome et Gomorrhe*
1945   *La Folle de Chaillot*
       [*The Madwoman of Chaillot*, produced
       after his death]

# TRANSLATOR'S NOTES

I have added some notes to clarify historical allusions that may mean little or nothing to today's reader or to the reader not of French background. They are arranged by chapter and page on which they appear. There are no numbered references in the text itself because I feel that one should be able to read a novel free of any notes. I have also added some literary comment where I thought it might be of help. Editions used for this translation were the Gallimard (Pléiade) and the Grasset (Livre de Poche), both from 1994; both offer the excellent notes of their editors, Jacques Body and Jules Brody (Pléiade) and Jacques Robichez (Grasset). I am indebted to them, particularly for the historical material. I am always indebted to the wonderful back section of my Larousse.

Finally, a word of special appreciation to those who were ever willing to discuss a point of translation or rescue me from some problem with the word processor; to my friends and colleagues Dorette, Françoise, Nancy, Tom, Silviu, Layli, Charlot, Maureen, and Tiphaine, I thank you all.

## CHAPTER 1

3

**the true Gordian knot**
Gordius, the king of Phrygia, had tied a knot that could be un-
done only by the man who was to rule all of Asia; Alexander the
Great cut it with his sword and fulfilled the prophecy.

## CHAPTER 2

19

**La Païva**
Thérèse, Marchioness of Païva (1819–84), a woman of intrigue and
later thought to have been an agent of Bismarck; in my translation
I added the word *spy* to this sentence to give the reader some indication of this background.

21

**Madame de la Boigne**
Charlotte-Louise, Countess of Boigne (1781–1866).

24

**André Siegfried (1875–1959)**
His *Les Etats-Unis d'aujourd'hui* was popular in the 1920s and
1930s.

26

**Charlotte Corday (1768–93)**
Stabbed the revolutionary leader Marat in his bath.

26

**Louise Labé (1526–65)**
Notable poet and a liberated woman in any age; the frank sensual-
ity of some of her verse might surprise today's reader.

26

**Madame du Châtelet**
Emilie, Marquise du Châtelet (1706–49), also a friend of Voltaire
and his hostess at her Château de Cirey.

27

**Marshal Foch (1851–1929)**
Field marshal of France, famous as a general in World War I.

27
**Georges Clemenceau (1841–1929)**
Notable orator and statesman.

32
**Otto Meyer . . . of Regensburg**
Apparently an invention of the author, a good example of Giraudoux having fun.

## CHAPTER 3

41
**Builtmore**
"Builtmore" instead of "Biltmore"—mistake or intentional satirical touch?

42
**A great lookout mast . . . to interior sailboats**
A line that suggests the magic that Edmée finds in Washington Park; "a beacon only to interior sailboats" also speaks to the primacy of the interior drama that is true of Giraudoux's entire work.

46
**the Chevalier Bayard**
Pierre Bayard (1476–1524), soldier and knight; "le Chevalier sans peur et sans reproche."

## CHAPTER 4

57
**vacation**
With this word the author announces a favorite theme: Edmée's flight from Pierre and home will turn into her vacation from the everyday world (see also Mr. Kaledjian's view on page 225 in chapter 11).

59
**Agincourt, Malplaquet, Trafalgar, or Sedan**
Four of the greatest defeats in French history: Agincourt (1415), by Henry V of England; Malplaquet (1709), by English and Dutch forces; Trafalgar (1805), by Nelson and the British navy; Sedan (1870), during the Franco-Prussian War.

59
**Blücher**
Leader of the Prussian forces, who joined with Wellington, the leader of the British forces, against Napoleon at the battle of Waterloo (1815).

59
**Sidi-Brahim**
Algerian village where a small French contingent held out against large native forces (1845).

59
**Metz**
French city won by the Prussians in 1870 that remained German until 1918.

59
**Austerlitz**
Moravia; where Napoleon fought the Austrians and Russians (1805).

59
**the Marne**
Area where Joffre led the French and prevailed against Moltke and the Germans in 1914; Foch won a second victory in this area in 1918.

62
**a pack bed**
Jacques Robichez in his notes to the Livre de Poche edition suggests that this unusual term is best understood in analogy to the idea of a packhorse, that is, an animal used for carrying heavy burdens; the pack bed, "grown stale from custom," would then be the opposite of the untamed or undomesticated bed (*lit sauvage*) that the author mentions in contrast.

70
**Mon enfant, ma soeur**
"My child, my sister"; the opening words of Baudelaire's poem "L'Invitation au voyage."

75
**Mr. Joshua Hall**
Probably another fictional invention of the author.


## CHAPTER 5

80
**The world continued to be for Pierre a book, not the world**
Giraudoux's pithy suggestion that intellectuality and its abstractions can lead to our divorce from the authenticity of direct experience, from real life.

81
**in a world where she felt that some all-powerful voices had called out her name**
Further indication of Edmée's election.

102
**Adolph or Romeo**
Presumably the hero of Benjamin Constant's penetrating psychological novel *Adolphe* (1816), a touching study of an obsessive passion.

105
*Esther*
Drama by Racine (1689).

105
*Saint Geneviève*
Saint Geneviève was a legendary medieval heroine and the subject of numerous plays in the seventeenth and eighteenth centuries.

107
**But why insist today? . . . a sentence in French**
A peculiar and playful intervention of the author himself in the middle of his story (which further removes it from any sort of literary realism); I have taken the liberty of setting the passage off in parentheses, although Giraudoux does not.

## CHAPTER 6

113

**Erzurum . . . Urmia**
Erzurum is in northeast Turkey; Urmia is a salt lake and city in
Iran. Mr. Kaledjian, who is Armenian, has known both, presumably through exile or the persecution of his people, and thus the
ironic understatement of his "very particular understanding of the
tastes of the gods."

## CHAPTER 7

134

**this precedence that her daughter had . . . her rank among
mediocre humanity**
This passage describes Claudie's transition from the ideal to the
human, between the different levels of life that Giraudoux is so
fond of depicting. The two levels are exemplified in the present
work first of all by the differences between Edmée and Pierre (and
between Claudie and Jacques). And "mediocre humanity" may itself be, in a sense, idealized, may itself be viewed as a beautiful and
necessary stage for our development, less rarefied than mystical
exaltation, to be sure, but equally essential to the human voyage.

## CHAPTER 8

160

**Mon enfant, ma soeur**
Again the first words of Baudelaire's "L'Invitation au voyage,"
which Giraudoux adroitly relates to Edmée and Claudie with his
shift to "Oh my child, oh my daughter!"

160

**I wanted to raise you to my level . . . an astral body without
humors**
Edmée is still lamenting Claudie's defection and return to the
human level. Note that women are placed first here, are presumably more natural and instinctive than men, and that even the great
men are no more than poor pawns, great men being satirized repeatedly in the novel.

## CHAPTER 9

182

**And little by little the veil had lifted . . . the demanding master wanted her**
One of the most direct references to Edmée's being chosen, of the elect.

183

**That was what her destiny was . . . *Back Street***
The key passage continues with further poetic comparisons and language in an effort to express the singular mystical role of Edmée and her special election. *Back Street,* a popular novel of the 1930s by Fanny Hurst, made into a film with Irene Dunn, the old story of a married man in love with a kept woman.

  The phrase I have translated as "this sad world" is used over and over by Giraudoux in this work as well as others and deserves a comment. The original is *ce bas monde,* and though "low" is closer to the meaning than "sad," I have opted for the proverbial ring of "this sad world." "Low" perhaps better expresses the author's melancholy refrain on how we are ever caught in the human condition, but repeated so often, "this low world" seems to me unsatisfactory.

184

**Oh, Mother . . . back to the world of men**
Claudie has made a return to the human level (for the time being), and Jacques—though unaware of Claudie's transition—senses that this is what his mother really needs to do.

184

**Jacques was that Russian countess . . . Abalstitiel, said the text**
That the strange story of Edmée should find its poetic meaning finally in an old Russian engraving may be unexpected, but seems somehow curiously appropriate.

  A word about translation is again in order: *l'Abalstitiel* means "the seducer"; we have been assured of this by the French editors and by the author himself in an interview. Giraudoux uses an article with *Abalstitiel,* that is, *l'Abalstitiel* (*the* seducer), but to write "the Abalstitiel" every time seems too awkward and heavy in English, and besides, Russian itself uses no articles before nouns. To write "the Seducer" would also be wrong because Giraudoux uses the Russian word without translating it—thus, "Abalstitiel."

Abalstitiel is the music master who seduces his lovely student, and his is the final name Giraudoux finds for the disturbing and seductive presence within Edmée that has led her to forsake husband, son, and home; the presence has been previously referred to variously as demon, demanding master, suborder, kidnapper, Lord, and anonymous God. God as seducer? In this regard the title of Thompson's poem "The Hound of Heaven" comes to mind. In Giraudoux's series of names the religious and mystical overtones are also very clear.

## CHAPTER 10

188
**Fatty Arbuckle (1881–1933)**
Hollywood actor of the period.

## CHAPTER 11

207
**Spontini**
Gaspare Spontini (1774–1851), an Italian composer best known for the opera *La Vestale,* mentioned in the text.

207
**Donizetti**
Gaetano Donizetti (1797–1848), another Italian composer whose *Lucia di Lammermoor* and other operas are still popular today.

211
**Spontini the donkey, Donizetti the ox**
Robichez, editor of the Livre de Poche edition, relates the allusions here to a more famous event in Bethlehem; thus Spontini and Donizetti as donkey and ox humorously echo the attending animals of legend at the birth of the new Edmée.

211
**That quartet *Death and the Maiden* . . . *Guermantes Way***
References are to Schubert's quartet *Death and the Maiden,* Seurat's painting *Circus,* and Proust's *Guermantes Way* from *Remembrance of Things Past.*

223
**Economiques Stéphanois**
Apparently an economy store (compare the old five-and-dime stores).

223
**the Boche**
Slang term for the Germans during World War I (*les Boches*).

224
**Mother . . . Eve and her daughter**
An excursion to the lost paradise is a recurring theme in Giraudoux's work and may also be referred to as a flight, vacation or season outside of time, a return to Eden, and so forth. It seems to reflect the need for a more spiritual side of the self, a sort of spiritual journey, but it is usually followed by a reacceptance of life on earth and the human condition. These themes are often lightened by a humorous touch, as is the case in the cited passage, where, with Edmée and Claudie no doubt in mind, Adam and Eve are replaced by Eve and her daughter!

226
**They were dining slowly . . . a Passion**
Edmée has returned to Pierre and home, and we have come full circle. Pierre is again presiding at the table, with the addition of a fiancée, a son-in-law, and a new baby wailing on the sofa. Life is experience, and each of the original cast has traversed a great deal of life since the birthday dinner that opened the novel. We may come back to the title, *Choice of the Elect:* the elect, Edmée and Claudie, were chosen, and the elect made their choices, in Washington Park and during the vagabond years that followed; those not of the elect, Pierre and Jacques, as befitted their natures, pretty much stayed at home. Some may be the worse for wear, but the

good and the bad are always mixed, and the author as poet seems
to find some sort of human epiphany in it all—is it that the human
is also divine?

232
**Truly, Abalstitiel wasn't wasting any time . . . starting in on
Claudie**
But with the last words we know that the story goes on. Haven't
we been told that the gods are fickle? Abalstitiel may have
dropped Edmée, but he is not through with Claudie.

## ABOUT THE AUTHOR

Jean Giraudoux (1882–1944) combined a career as an avant-garde novelist with work as a diplomat. Known for his Wildean wit—"Only the mediocre are always at their best"—Giraudoux later won an international following as a playwright. His novels include *Les Provinciales* (1909), *Suzanne and the Pacific* (1921), and *My Friend from Limousin* (1922). He died in Paris, perhaps by poisoning.